Confederate Rangers
Book 2 in the Lucky Jack Series
By Griff Hosker

Confederate Ranger

Published by Sword Books Ltd 2013
Copyright © Griff Hosker First Edition

The author has asserted their moral right under the Copyright, Designs and Patents Act, 1988, to be identified as the author of this work.
All Rights reserved. No part of this publication may be reproduced, copied, stored in a retrieval system, or transmitted, in any form or by any means, without the prior written consent of the copyright holder, nor be otherwise circulated in any form of binding or cover other than that in which it is published and without a similar condition being imposed on the subsequent purchaser.

A CIP catalogue record for this title is available from the British Library.

Confederate Ranger

Dedication
To all those men and women in World War Two who made such awesome sacrifices. It means we didn't have to.

Confederate Ranger

Contents

Book 2 in the Lucky Jack Series i
By Griff Hosker i
Chapter 1 2
Chapter 2 18
Chapter 3 34
Chapter 4 52
Chapter 5 69
Chapter 6 82
Interlude.. 102
Chapter 7 105
Chapter 8 124
Chapter 9 139
Chapter 10 155
Chapter 11 174
Chapter 12 189
Chapter 13 203
Chapter 14 215
Chapter 15 234
Chapter 16 248
Chapter 17 266
Epilogue.. 276
The End 279
   Maps 280
Historical note 282
***Griff Hosker August 2013*Other books**........................... 284
by 285
Griff Hosker 285

Confederate Ranger

Chapter 1

Leesburg October 1862

My hands suddenly felt clammy and I didn't know why. It was no hotter than it always was in northern Virginia. In fact, if anything, it was slightly cooler. It was not the first time I had slit someone's throat. I had done it many times. I never enjoyed the experience but I had learned that to delay cost men their lives. I had had to learn to be ruthless. I was a sergeant now and I had the responsibility of leading others who looked to me. I knew I had to do it quickly for Dago and Cecil were waiting for me to do the deed and then they could join me and we could kidnap Colonel Nathan Black, the officer sent by Lincoln to stop the threat of the Partisan Rangers. He was a threat, not only to Boswell's Wildcats, our company but also to the more famous Mosby's Rangers. If he succeeded then one of the most potent forces the Confederate Army had would be nullified. Every second I waited increased the chance of discovery. I suddenly realised what it was; he was little more than a boy. He was barely sixteen. I wondered if I should just hit him with my Army Colt. I knew that was a risk, as sometimes they called out before they blacked out. I felt my knees stiffen and I shifted position. He must have sensed the movement for he gave a half turn and I froze.

Suddenly I heard a mew and a small ginger cat came out of the bushes and walked over to the sentry. It began entwining itself around his legs. His face changed and became a mask of hatred as he slowly reached down to pick it up. He stroked its purring head and then, suddenly, twisted and broke its tiny neck "Damned mangy bag of fleas, good riddance!" And he spat at it.

All thoughts of mercy disappeared and I began to slip along the wall. He whirled around and pointed his rifle and bayonet at me. "Where do you think you are going? This is a restricted area!"

In the Rangers, we learn to think on our feet. I was wearing my deer hide jacket over my shell jacket and, in the dim light could be mistaken for a Union scout. He obviously had not seen me as the rebel I was or he would have shot me out of hand. I had a blank piece of folded paper in my pocket and I pulled it out. "Jeb Hawkins, the Colonel's scout. I have a message for Colonel Black. It is important."

The sentry relaxed and lowered his gun. "A little late for delivering messages ain't it?"

I surreptitiously slipped my nine-inch knife from my sheath and held it behind my back as I covered the five feet to the sentry. I held the paper up to attract and hold his attention. "The thing is this is a list of the names of Mosby's spies in Frederick."

His eyes lit up. "Really? Can I see?"

I furtively looked around and said, "Just a quick look."

As his face came down to read the non-existent names, I despatched him with one lethal strike of the knife. It was an instant and silent kill. More importantly, there was a little mess. It was efficient. I caught his gun in my left hand and lowered his body on to the swing on the porch with my right. He was a slight youth and I was strong. There was little blood to be seen. I covered his face with his kepi and laid his gun next to him. Anyone passing would think him asleep.

I pumped my arm twice and Dago and Cecil raced up. The rest of the company were guarding the two ends of the quiet street and I needed two men I could trust.

Confederate Ranger

"You sure took your time Sarge!"

"Listen, Cecil, it is better to take your time and get the job done rather than rush and fail!"

"Yeah Irish, you listen to the Sarge but watch me eh?"

We had watched the house all day and knew that there were just servants, Colonel Black and his aide, a lieutenant. I thought that three of us should be able to handle them. As soon as we entered the clapboard house we used only hand signals. It was the Ranger way. I gestured for Cecil to get the servants whilst Dago and I headed for the room which had lights on; that was where the two officers would be. Of course, we could be unlucky and one could have made a visit to the outhouse but those things happened. As we approached the door we heard them talking and knew that both of them were within. Lady Luck was still on our side. Dago had his Navy Colt drawn and I took out my Army Colt. They were both excellent weapons but Dago would have had one such as mine if he could. The Army Colt was a more powerful killer.

The door was slightly ajar which made it easier for us to launch ourselves into the room. I nodded to Dago and he pushed the door open while I sprang inside. The colonel and the lieutenant were standing over a desk examining a map. They turned, expecting I think, a servant or the sentry. When they saw the business ends of two Colts they were stunned. The colonel had an expensive-looking cigar in his mouth and it dropped to the floor. Dago dropped to one knee and picked it up with his free hand, never taking his gun off the colonel. "It seems a shame to waste such a fine cigar. I think I will finish that off later on." He nipped the end and put it in his pocket.

I smiled and saluted. "Gentlemen, if you would like to come with me. You are now prisoners of the Confederacy."

Confederate Ranger

The colonel appeared to regain some of his composure. "You boys won't get away with this. There is a company of cavalry bivouacked in this town and there are sentries patrolling. You'll never escape."

"Well colonel, as the cavalry are at the other end of town and your one sentry is taken care of, I guess we'll just have to take our chances."

Dago grinned at the disappointed face of the Yankee Colonel. "I sure would like to play poker with you colonel; you can't bluff worth a damn." The staff lieutenant looked as though he might make a move. Dago cocked the pistol and held it to the young officer's head. "Now son, we need the colonel here but you are just dead weight so any trouble and you get it first."

Cecil popped his head around the door. "I locked them in the cellar and locked the door from the outside."

Dago nodded his approval. "Well done Irish, we'll make a ranger of you yet." He preened at the compliment.

I waved my gun. "Head for the front door. Cecil, get their horses and whistle up the boys. I don't want to outstay our welcome in this fine burg."

Dago went first, walking backwards. As we left the house the colonel glanced down at the sentry. "I'll have him punished! Sleeping on the job."

I shook my head, "Sleeping with the angels more like colonel and a warning to your boy here that we ain't playing at soldiers. We are Rangers and the real deal."

They both paled at those words. "Mosby's men?"

"We'll let our captain tell you that."

I heard a distinctive whistle and then Cecil came round with the two cavalry horses for the officers and a further two in his other hand. He was grinning and when he reached me he said, cheerfully, "It seemed a shame to leave them in the stables. Pity there were no saddles for them."

The hooves announcing the arrival of the rest of our men meant we could allow our prisoners to mount. "Now we could tie your hands but then, if you fell off you would break your necks so how about this? I will have a man behind each of you. You so much as lean the wrong way and you'll lose a leg. My boys can shoot the wings off a horsefly and a knee or two will be no problem. You understand?"

"I understand that you are a bandit and a brigand and not a soldier."

"Well colonel, looks like we just had our first difference of opinion and I had high hopes for some interesting discussions on the way home."

We knew Leesburg very well having raided it on numerous occasions. They had taken to keeping just one company in the town itself while another four were spread out around the outskirts covering the roads. It would have been an effective way of controlling us if we had used roads but we preferred fields and lanes. We also had our base in the Blue Ridge Mountains which we now knew like the back of our hands. Our leader, Captain James Boswell had been a native of the area and we had soon picked up much of his knowledge. One trick we had learned was to behave as though we were not the enemy. We found that if we rode through a town, especially at night, then a cheery wave from us would make the locals think that we were union cavalry. Of course, when that went wrong we would ride as hard and fast as we could. It helped to have the finest grain-fed mounts in Virginia.

Davy brought the rest of the men and they formed a screen around our two prisoners. There were two men to each horse. We still had six men who could shoot if it came to a gunfight but we hoped it would not. "A patrol left the barracks ten minutes ago and headed south."

"Good." That suited us for we would head west and then cut through Mulligan's farm. He was a secret Confederate supporter but we only used his land to pass through knowing that his silence was guaranteed. We rode through the quiet street at a leisurely pace. Dago was behind the two Union officers. "Now if you gentlemen were thinking of shouting for help then a powerful number of people would die, you two, being the first. Let's just get back to our camp. That way you two will still be alive."

I smiled to myself knowing how much it must have galled them but they were being led by some of the most terrifying enemies that there were. We were the Rangers and Yankee mothers frightened their children with tales of us coming in the night to take them away if they were bad. I saw a knot of men on a street corner. I said, quietly, "Give them a wave Colonel, and smile."

The wave brought a cheery response from the men and secured our exit from the town. As we reached the crossroads we kicked on a little and disappeared from sight. Of course, the hardest part was yet to come. There would be night patrols and vedettes on the roads ahead. We had scouted and we estimated that they would not be patrolling where we would leave the road. We had learned by our own ingenuity not to ignore that trait in others. They could learn to be as cunning as us. So far none had shown those skills but the Yankees were getting better. "Davy and Jimmy, you two, ride ahead to the trail and make sure it is clear."

The wall which ran along the turnpike had a gap about a mile and a half from where we were. It made an easy way to enter the land close to Mulligan's fields. Suddenly there was the sound of rapidly approaching horses and Davy and Jimmy reined in. "Union Cavalry, about thirty of them up ahead."

"Dago, you take the Union officers with John and Bill here. We'll lead them away. See you back at the rendezvous on the other side of the farm."

Dago grinned. "Right Yankees, let's see if you can jump this wall without falling off!"

"The rest of you, over the wall and pull both your Colts!"

I could now hear the thunder of hooves as the Union cavalry raced down the turnpike. The wall was no obstacle to us and I sighed with relief when I saw Dago wave as he led his prisoners towards the trees. There were just five of us but I was counting on surprise. The cavalry had only seen Davy and Jimmy in the distance and had no way of knowing where they had gone. They must have thought that they would hightail it down the road to the crossroads. They were in for a shock. I waited until the first of the riders was level with Cecil and then shouted, "Fire!" Ten lead balls at four yards distance can do terrible damage to both man and beast. The officer and sergeant were leading and they both fell to the ground as did the bugler. "Keep firing!" The cavalry had not bothered to draw their weapons and we fired another two rounds before they could fire back. By then they were demoralised. Two put their hands up to surrender while the rest carried on towards Leesburg. I daresay our numbers would be exaggerated. Our tiny group was often referred to as, hundreds of cavalrymen. There had never been more than forty of us.

We had little time to waste. "Jimmy, disarm and secure the prisoners. Tie their hands around the pommels of their saddles. These boys are cavalry they should be able to manage. Cecil and Davy get the horses. You two collect any weapons and make it quick." Every man did his job efficiently and quickly. As soon as we had cleared the road of the encounter we headed along the turnpike to take the turn off we had originally intended. Dago and his charges would have a longer route to get to the rendezvous point and we might just beat them.

The place we were going to meet was a small track leading over the Blue Ridge. It looked as though it went north but in fact, after a mile or so it looped back on itself. We had found a perfect place to keep a sentry who could watch anyone following the trail and be in the camp warning the rest before an intruder could get close. We reined in and I loosened the ropes on the two prisoners. "Boys, you better have a drink."

They took out their canteens and drank. "Are you Mosby's Ghosts?"

Cecil snorted his derision, "Dumb ass! We are Boswell's Wildcats! We make Mosby's boys look like pussycats." I shook my head; Cecil had embraced the Rangers there was no doubt about that.

"Riders coming."

When we heard Jimmy's warning we all drew and cocked our weapons. We realised that it would probably be Dago but we didn't like to take chances. As soon as we recognised him we lowered our guns. "Colonel, you better have a drink. You won't be getting another for quite a while." After they had drunk I nodded to the men. "Cover their eyes. Sorry gentlemen but we ain't gonna show you the way into our palatial little home. You will be blindfolded and one of my boys will lead you. Best keep your hands on the reins as the track is a mite steep in places."

None of the four were happy but with our guns aimed at their chests, they had little choice. I sent Dago and the prisoners up first and then I followed with the horses and the rest of the boys. It would be dawn before we reached the rest of our company. The sentry did not speak as we passed him half an hour later. He saw the prisoners and knew he had to remain silent. I just waved to let him know that I was the last man in the line.

We could smell the meat cooking on the open fire as we entered the clearing. The tents were all hidden in the trees as were the horses. It was a basic camp but it served its purpose for we were almost invisible. We had stumbled upon it and that was the only way we would be discovered.

Captain Boswell and Lieutenant Murphy stood and began to walk over to us as we entered the camp proper. I could see the relief on their faces. When they had briefed me they had not been certain that we could carry out such an audacious raid. Captain Boswell was the disgraced son of a rich landowner who had had to make his money selling slaves. When the war broke out he had enrolled us, his men, as a group of Partisan Rangers. His family had influence and had ensured that he could not get a commission in the Confederacy. We thought that it was a shame as he was a natural leader but our independence meant that we had all accumulated money from the proceeds of our raids. The horses we had just captured would bring us $100 for each one. As we had eight of such horse that was $800 for my men to share. Then there was the money for the weapons. The Quartermaster would buy all that we captured for the Union weapons and horses were of good quality.

"I see you brought a little extra back eh Jack?"

"Yes, captain. The Yankees tried an ambush but they forgot to take out their weapons." I pointed at the colonel. "There is the man you wanted, Colonel Black. The lieutenant was a little feisty until the colonel had a word with him."

"Leave them with me, Jackie boy. You get your men fed and then get some sleep. The captain and I can take it from here."

Confederate Ranger

Daniel Murphy's family came from the same part of Ireland as I did and was a reassuring presence for me. "You heard the lieutenant boys. Rub down your horses then we eat. And it had better be good for I am starving."

Dago nodded at the fire in the middle. "It will be. It is Jed who was cook today." Jed was not only a good hunter but skilled around the campfire and it would be a fine meal we ate that morning.

When I awoke the camp was almost deserted. Captain Boswell had left two of his men on guard while my men slept. He had taken the rest of the troopers to Front Royal to deliver our prisoners and our horses. Cecil was already at the fire brewing up some coffee. The rest of the men called him Irish as he got into a fight if they pronounced his name incorrectly. I was the only one who used his real name correctly and, for some reason, he seemed to attach special attention to me. The others had been reluctant to accept him into the company because of his temper and his relatively poor skills as a horseman. He had become a better horseman and had learned to keep his temper. One unforeseen bonus was his amazing skill with anything mechanical. He could repair a gun better than a gunsmith and he could make anything from iron if we had a forge close by. Every time we were with the army he took advantage to fabricate or improve something we owned. I watched him from my tent as he sat close to the coffee to watch it while he repaired an Army Colt. I could tell what weapon it was from its size. He was a loner but he was as vital to the company as any of us, including me, Lucky Jack Hogan.

They called me Lucky Jack because of the number of times I emerged from a gunfight with neither wounds nor injuries. Everyone else who had served with the captain since the early days now sported a wound of some description; but not Lucky Jack.

Confederate Ranger

They also knew my story; how my parents had been murdered by a blaggard of a landowner, Arthur Beauregard and how my sister and I had had to live on the streets of Cork. They called me Lucky Jack because when I escaped from that dire existence it was to join a slaver where Captain Boswell rescued me. I still did not know where my sister was. I was determined to find her once this war was over. I would be a relatively rich man by then. The captain invested our money in European banks. While we had little money in our pockets we had a great deal safely stored out of the country.

I washed myself in the bucket and wandered over to the fire. Cecil saw me and poured me a cup of strong black coffee. He went back to his gun. In the Wildcats, we didn't go in for filling the silences. If we had nothing of importance to say, we kept quiet. I noticed the gun was in bits.

"Is that worth repairing? It looks to be beyond repair."

"Nah sergeant. This is a Colt. They are solid guns. The Yankee who had this just didn't look after it. It jammed last night when he tried to fire it. He was aiming at you. It won't take me long to repair and then I will have an Army Colt just like you."

If the story was circulating then the jammed gun would add to the mystique of Lucky Jack. "I'll get you some ammo. I always make sure I collect that before anything else. A gun is only useful if it has lead to fire!"

Captain Boswell had equipped us with Navy Colts. The Navy Colt is a good weapon but the Army Colt has more stopping power. I had managed to get two early in the war and the rest of the company had all been trying to get the same weapon. Inevitably Cecil and the younger recruits had still to get one.

He put it together and cocked it. The action sounded right."There, it is finished and ready to use." He looked up as though he had just noticed me. "Captain Boswell took the boys to

Confederate Ranger

Front Royal. He said they would be back in the morning and you were to be in charge until then."

"Then I guess Dago and me'll go hunting. Want to come?"

He looked down at the ground. "I don't think Dago likes me very much and I'm not very good at hunting anyway."

"Forget what others think and, as for hunting, the more you do it, the better you get." I hesitated. "I would like you to come." My ma had always said that simple acts of kindness are the best. I think it is true. Cecil's face lit up like a new dawn and he nodded.

Dago just shrugged when I suggested hunting with Cecil. "Just so long as you don't get your skinny ass in my sights; I might just think you are a squirrel."

"Don't pay him no mind Cecil. You'll do just fine and he couldn't hit a squirrel unless it jumped in front of his sights and surrendered!"

We took our Henry carbines. They did not have the long range of a rifle but in the trees of the forest, they were better. They had a much shorter barrel. We headed downstream with the wind in our faces. I led with Dago to my right and Cecil to my left. It was late autumn and almost winter. There was still a cool feel to the air in the mountains but the land still had islands of green growth from the summer. I soon saw the tracks of the deer. There looked to be a small herd and I held my hand up to go a little slower. Just ahead I noticed some berries. They looked nothing like the berries we had in Ireland but something had been nibbling them. I assumed deer and I slowed down even more. There was juice dripping from some of them. There was a powerfully pungent smell, and it wasn't deer. Suddenly a brown bear with two cubs rose up in front of me. In an instant, I knew that the berries had been the fodder of bears and not deer and the bears had come upstream while the deer went down. None of that helped me as she sprang towards me. I half turned and fired at her. The bullet hit her chest but she kept coming. I loaded another shell and then I heard Cecil's Henry from behind me. He fired four well-placed shots and they all struck her head. Even though she was dead, she still managed to collapse on top of me, her blood pouring over my face and her weight crushing me.

"Get this damn bear off of me!"

I heard Dago's laconic voice as the two of them joined with me to push off the beast. "You're still alive then eh, Lucky Jack."

As it was heaved from me I said, "Yeah. Thanks to Cecil. I owe you my life, Cecil."

He was so embarrassed that he looked to the ground and shuffled from side to side. "Yeah Irish! They were four damn fine shots. You'll do!"

Cecil suddenly seemed to grow about six inches at that praise. The two cubs had raced off into the brush. Their size led me to believe that they would survive. There were plenty of berries and fish for the cubs. The bear would provide us with some good eating and a bearskin for the winter. We had discovered just how cold it could get in the Blue Ridge in December and January.

The beast was skinned, butchered and cooked by the time the rest of the company had returned. Jed looked unhappy that he had neither shot nor cooked the bear but everyone was surprised that it had been Irish who had saved the day. From that day on he was accepted, despite his occasional temper tantrums.

"We can sort of celebrating tonight. General Stuart was real pleased with our prisoner. I don't think they will learn anything from him but it must have upset them that the man they sent to capture us was captured by us. He said to thank the boys who did it. When I told him your names, Dago and Jack, he didn't seem surprised. He just said that he was in your debt again."

Confederate Ranger

Dago added dryly, "I can't see when the hell he is gonna pay the debt seeing as how he is always on the other side of the state."

"You never know Dago; one day he might be able to do something for you." He shook his head as though to clear it. "Anyway the other reason for the celebration is that we are heading north of the Potomac!" We all cheered. North of the Potomac was Yankee country. "It seems John Mosby has this area nailed!" We all jeered. There was, what one might call, sibling rivalry between us. He waved his arms to calm us down. "The thing of it is, I don't mind. We know the land north of the river. They won't have any patrols looking for us and we have more freedom to do what we want. We can really hurt the Yankees."

I wasn't certain. We would not be able to get any loot to the quartermaster and there would be no Mulligans or other patriots to shelter us. But he was our captain and we followed him wherever he led. Lieutenant Murphy, Danny, was standing close to me. "Don't you worry Jack. We could all end up being shot by a firing squad but Lucky Jack will fall in a shithole and come up smelling of roses."

I shook my head, "Don't you start, Danny. It's bad enough the rest but you know there is no luck of the Irish."

"Don't give me that! A gun misfires when the Yank has you dead to rights. A bear stands up in front of you and the worst shot in the company saves your life. You are lucky and then some!"

The following day was spent in preserving as much meat as we could and packing away the tents. We left in the afternoon so that we could travel at dusk. We weren't far from the river but we wanted no witnesses to our crossing. We headed towards Leesburg; we all knew that it was dangerous but we counted on the fact that we would be travelling to the north and over the wooded ridge which ran parallel to the Blue Ridge. We were heading for

Confederate Ranger

Balls Bluff. We had crossed the ford over the Potomac there before. There was an island in the middle and the swim was not that bad. At this time of year, we hoped that it would not be too cold but we had done it enough times to know that it would not last long.

I rode next to Danny as we headed north of the Potomac. We used White's Ford. We had crossed easily enough and avoided any of the enemy patrols that were in the area. Yankee cavalry were very predictable and they liked to keep together in larger groups than we did. It made our job much easier. Captain Boswell said the reason they used large companies was that they feared us. That may have been true. Every prisoner we took seemed in awe of us. We steered clear of the houses and then crossed the Potomac, swimming the last part. We had time to stop and check cinches and girths. "You know, Danny, I have travelled these roads before. Apart from the mountain ridge which runs to the west of Gettysburg and Frederick, there isn't a great deal of cover. Where are we going to operate and what is our target?"

"I think the captain would like to disrupt the supplies up here. Do something with the Baltimore and Ohio Railroad. After Antietam, the generals thought that it would be possible to invade the north." He shrugged. "I'm with you on this. The last place we want to get caught is north of the river." We remounted. "You say there is a mountain area to the west?"

"Yeah, Dago and I hid there when we rescued Stuart's nephew."

"I'll see if the captain will base us there. We would have further to go each day but at least we would have somewhere to hide if they decided to come looking for us."

The forty man company twisted and turned along small trails as we headed north. Every step took us further from friends and closer to foes. What made it worse was that Lee and the Army of Northern Virginia had retreated south of the Potomac. I felt very uneasy about this patrol.

Chapter 2

We reached the outskirts of Frederick well before dawn. Captain Boswell waved me and Dago forward. "You guys know this area?"

"Yeah. We even ate with a Yankee officer in the town." I looked at the captain and spoke slowly so that he would not misinterpret my words. "It is full of Yankees sir. They have checkpoints at either end of town and here is where they base the guys trying to catch us."

He grinned at me. "I get it, Jack. Danny told me about your worries. I do not intend to get us killed. You and Dago take us around this burg and find that mountain you were talking about."

"Yes, sir!"

We followed the main road until it turned north towards Frederick and then Gettysburg. When we reached the railway track I knew exactly where we were. The captain made us halt at the tracks and it did not take a mind reader to work out that he was reconnoitring for an ambush. We shadowed the Boonsboro road for a while and then, as the sun broke behind us, I pointed at the mountain range rising ahead of us. "There we are, sir."

"Well done, Jack. Find us a camp hidden from the trails and I'll be a happy man."

Dago pointed towards the south-west. "Didn't we camp over there? There was a nice spring as I recall."

"You are right. Let's head there."

As soon as we saw it we remembered it. We had chanced upon it the first time but had we searched for weeks we could not have found a better hide out. There was a small dell with trees for cover. The ridge above us was dotted with rock and small bushes from which sentries could observe the land for miles around. Most importantly, the camp was a number of miles from any track and any habitation. No one would stumble upon us accidentally; if they found us then they were searching for us.

We erected our tents in the four sections we used. There were ten of us in each section. Dago and Jed, as the two corporals were used when we needed to divide one of the sections further. I had two of the new men in my sections, Jacob and Wilkie. I had been disappointed when Colm and Geraghty, the two new Irish lads had been placed in Danny's section. The captain had said, jokingly, "We can't have all the Irish in once section, now can we? We have to spread the luck around."

I knew he was right but it was galling as both the Irish lads showed greater competence and skills than the other recruits. And I had remembered how long it had taken me to make a soldier out of Cecil. It took Danny less than a week and then they looked like veterans. Still, it meant we had good *craich* around the fire at night. As we were finishing putting the tents up the two of them wandered over. They had joined with Jacob and appeared to be friends. "So the lieutenant was telling us that you and Dago were hiding out here last year?"

"Aye. We had freed a prisoner from Gettysburg and the Yankees were hot on our trail. It's a nice quiet place and that spring is as sweet a taste of water as you could wish."

"Will we be working around Gettysburg then?"

"I don't know Geraghty. The captain sort of makes his mind up as we leave the camp. It makes for an exciting life. I dare say we will go on four patrols and see what we can find. We will only be here for a month at the most. Any more than that and the Yankees will spot our new trails."

"Where will we go then?"

Confederate Ranger

"I told you, it depends on the captain's mood, the weather, who knows? In the Wildcats you have to learn to think on your feet."

The next morning I was proved correct as the captain sent us north, south, east and west to reconnoitre and scout the land around our new camp. Our mission was simple: don't get seen and find juicy targets. As I said to Wilkie as we rode east, "That's easier said than done."

I liked to ride with the new men to get to know them. As I had discovered with Cecil, there were many stories behind their enlistment. Wilkie's was much like mine. He had been orphaned during an outbreak of fever and had had to live on his wits in Baltimore. The authorities and the police in that town had made life hard for the boy without a home and without money. He had had to resort to stealing and then fled south when he was almost caught. He had joined the Confederacy out of expediency rather than a belief in the cause. I, too, was there because of reasons other than political ones but all of us fought just as hard as the patriots like Captain Boswell.

We headed south towards Brunswick. I felt lucky in that I knew the area well but I was taking no chances. Dago was with the captain and I had to rely on my relatively inexperienced section. I gave Cecil his chance and hoped that his recent successes would give him more confidence. "Cecil, you ride half a mile ahead. Wave your hat if you see trouble." We were wearing a collection of slouch hats to make us look less obviously Confederates. A single rider had more chance of escaping notice but the rest of us riding together would identify us clearly as Confederates.

I turned to my most experienced men, "Jimmy and Davy, you ride half a mile to the rear." They knew what was expected of them. When we rode through open ground or trees they made sure that the trail was as little disturbed as possible. When we rode on the pikes and roads they would stop frequently to listen for the sounds of others using the roads.

 Cecil halted us close by a stand of trees overlooking Brunswick just after we had crossed the Burkittsville Road. The heights above the town gave us the opportunity to dismount and look at the Union town in relative comfort and safety. "Feed your horses and give them some water. Jacob and Wilkie, keep watch for anyone coming up to the trees." When Davy and Jimmy reported that our rear was safe I could relax a little. I chewed on some dried bear meat as I slithered towards the rocks just below the tree line. I took off my hat and took out the pencil and paper I carried. Dago had told me that when the mapmaker Jedediah Hotchkiss travelled making maps he always had a pencil and paper to draw quick sketches of what he saw. I found it a useful practice and helped me to make better reports to the captain.

 There were a pair of guns on the bridge which led to the Berlin Pike and they looked to be manned by about forty men. The guns were Parrot Rifles. I could see no sign of stables, which was a good thing, as it meant that there were only infantry there. There were some large warehouses close to the river. I would suggest a night visit to investigate them when I returned to the captain. I slid down to the men. "Mount up. Bert, you take the point. We will head down towards the river. Ride east but be careful. There are Yankees down there."

 The bluffs rose to about four hundred feet above the river and we rode halfway up to avoid being seen against the skyline. The trees were both a help and a hindrance. They hid us but they made it difficult to see long distances. Suddenly Bert rode in waving his hat.

Confederate Ranger

"Sarge! There's a railway line at the bottom of the bluff. Real close to the river."

"That will be the Baltimore and Ohio sarge."

"Yeah, I remember Jimmy. Let's go and have a look eh?"

We left the trail and began to work our way down the hillside. It was not too steep and we weren't trying to keep order so that we negotiated the many twists, turns and falls easily. I smiled at the grim determination on Cecil's face as he clung on to the reins and leaned back as I had taught him. He would never be a confident rider but he was getting better.

Once we were in sight of the line I had the men dismount and left the horses with the two new men; much to their disappointment. "Half of you go with Jimmy and Davy. Head west. You are looking for any toolboxes, points or workmen's huts." I looked at Davy, "You know how far we need to check." He nodded and led his half off. "You three come with me."

This was the nerve-wracking part. If a train came we would have to run for shelter and there was always a chance we could be seen. There could also be men repairing and inspecting the track. They would be equally dangerous. "Cecil and Bert, take the riverside of the track."

I noticed that it was just a single track at this point. I could see that it was probably too narrow for two sets of rails but that suited us. Any damage would close the line in both directions. As soon as I found the trackside toolbox I halted. It had a lock on it but we could smash that off. It looked to be an oiled and well-used lock which suggested regular visits by the crews who maintained the line.

"Bert and Cecil; go back and bring the horses and the rest of the section. Take the horses into the trees." I pointed to a clump of scrubby bushes. "We'll be there." As they trotted down the track I checked to make sure we hadn't left any obvious tracks. The stones around the box showed our boot prints. "We'll tidy this little lot up." I knelt down next to Johnny and we hand smoothed the stones so that they showed no sign of being disturbed. There was a line of scrubby weeds next to the line. "Follow me and jump over so that we don't leave a sign that we were here." I quickly checked to see that there was not a huge drop on the other side and leapt. It was just long grass and I rolled clear. When we had both managed to move a couple of yards away I looked back. The grass was already rising; there would be no sign that we had ever been there.

 We raced up to the bushes and crouched behind a couple of the larger ones. We had all managed to acquire watches during our raids and robberies. I took mine out to check the time. It was twelve twenty-five. I figured it was a three-hour ride back to camp and so we would wait until three to see if any track inspectors or trains came along. I heard a noise to my right and cocked my Colt. "It's us sarge."

 Davy's voice made me holster my gun. "Did you see anything that way?"

 "No. I see you found a box."

 "Yup. It looks well used. We'll just watch it for a while and see if anything turns up."

 Wilkie gave me a curious look. "What for sarge?"

 Cecil clucked his tongue as though Wilkie had said something stupid. I smiled for that would have been the Irishman three months ago. "If we know what time a train comes through then we can plan when to ambush or derail it. At the same time, we need to know when the track crews come by and how many men are in them. We may not find any of that today but it is worth a three-hour wait eh?"

 He grinned sheepishly, "Yes sarge."

Confederate Ranger

"The Wildcats aren't all about shooting and fighting. Sometimes we are just plain sneaky."

I allowed the men to pair up to share the watches. I would watch the whole time. I didn't like letting Captain Boswell down. I was a sergeant now and I took my responsibilities seriously. We had only been watching for a matter of thirty minutes when we heard the sound of squeaking and wheels trundling along the line. It was coming from the east. I held up my hand and we all lay flat on the ground. A trolley, with five men on board, creaked to a noisy halt beside the track. One of the men went to the line box and opened it. He was obviously the leader as he handed the tools to the men and, while they walked along the track tapping the rails, he sat on the trolley and smoked his short, stubby pipe. The smell drifted up to us. It smelled like a European mix, probably Dutch. We had noticed that the European tobaccos each had a distinctive smell. It was all useful information. After they had walked up and down checking the rails they all gathered for a meal. The leader had not moved and he had smoked a second pipe after his meal. He tapped out his pipe and blew on a whistle. A few minutes later they returned and the tools were locked in the locker and the trolley squeaked and squealed its way towards the west and Brunswick.

It was silent and Jacob began to speak. I held up my hand and Davy put his finger to his lips. I waited five minutes before I spoke. "Don't talk until you are sure there is no-one around. Now, what were you going to ask?"

"Do we go now?"

I took my watch out and opened it. "It isn't even three o'clock yet. You got a date tonight?"

The others laughed and the young recruit blushed. "No, but I thought that there wouldn't be a train if there was a trolley on the track."

"They'll just lift the trolley off the track when they hear the train whistle."

"Ah!"

It was two-thirty when we heard the train whistle sound three times in the distance. We became alert. Ten minutes later and it sounded three times again but closer. Then we heard the clank of its wheels and the hiss of its engine as it lumbered along the track. It was not travelling quickly and we saw why; it was carrying cannons on open-top cars and the boxcars had guards upon them. I made a guess that it was ammunition and cannons to reinforce McClellan's army and to make good the losses from Antietam. It seemed to take an age to pass by but once it had I circled my hand above my head and we headed back to the horses.

"Nice train sarge. Pity we didn't derail it."

"No Davy, that would be the dumb way of doing it. That train was going so slowly that derailing would not have done as much damage as the last one we destroyed. Hell, they would probably just bring another engine and push the train to Brunswick. That's why we report back to Captain Boswell and let him come up with a plan. You never know they may have a better target anyway."

However, when we returned to the camp, we discovered that it was the best target. "Well done, Jack. We found the railroad as well but you found it close to the river with an exit for us. We found it close to warehouses and buildings. What about you Danny?"

"There is a munitions warehouse at Hagerstown but it looks like it has a regiment guarding it."

Jed too had found only difficult targets and so we decided to hit the railroad first. "When we have done that one, we will see if we can do a little explosive work in Hagerstown. It is far enough away from the river to make them think we have gone home again."

The captain decided that we would take down the tents and hide them. He and his section would leave first with Davy and they would watch the trains from noon. We would hide all traces of the camp and join them about mid-afternoon. The captain reasoned that we would then have the hours of darkness to do a good job of destroying the railroad. We would hide up during the next day and then be on hand should anything go wrong.

The younger men, the likes of Colm, Jacob and Geraghty couldn't wait to get going and they were racing around the camp like nettled hens. "Will you lads calm down? We don't want you wetting yourselves before we get to the ambush."

"It's alright for you and the sergeant, you have done this before. We can't wait to do something for the Confederacy!"

Danny relented and gave a smile, "Sure and I understand your enthusiasm but it won't make it come any quicker. We have a way of doing things. Now make sure there are no signs that we camped here."

Despite Danny's words, the older hands knew that we could never eradicate all signs of our presence. The blackened area around the fire, even though we had cut the turf and replaced it on the burnt soil, was a clear sign that someone had been there. All we could do was disguise the number of men who had been there. We all rode in different directions and then met up a mile south of the camp. It would take a good tracker to follow us.

When we reached the ambush site the captain had made a corral in a small clearing in the forest. It looked to me as though someone had taken the trees for some lumber but it aided us. He summoned Danny, Jed and me. "Two trains went by. Did one go by at around two-thirty yesterday, Jack."

Confederate Ranger

"About that time sir. It was a very slow train with lots of cannons on board."

He nodded. "Another one came by today filled with horses, looked like a couple of companies and that was a fast train."

"Any track workers?"

"Not today. It may be that they won't be back this way for a few days."

"Did the train sound its whistle?"

"No Jack, why?"

"Yesterday it kept blowing its whistle to warn the workers. So I am guessing no whistle means no track workers."

"Tell your men to get some rest. Harry, have your boys take the first watch, Jack, you have the second watch, Danny the third and my boys will do the last one. Just make a note of the trains and their make up."

When I relieved Jed he said, "No trains heading west but two headed east."

I lay down resting my head upon my hands watching and listening. I glanced to my right and saw that Cecil was copying me exactly. Beyond him Davy caught my eye and shook his head. Poor Irish certainly had a bad case of hero worship. I heard the engine coming from the west. I didn't need to tell the boys to lie down; they all just did it without thinking. The train was moving quite quickly and appeared to be empty. Soon I found it time to wake Danny. We had all learned to sleep when we could. We operated a great deal at night. I put my head on my saddle and the next thing I knew Harry was shaking my shoulder. "Come on Jackie boy. Time for work."

Harry and I were the two sergeants in the company and we were good friends. He was from the north of England and had a bluff humour which I liked. He was more dependable than anyone else and that included the two officers. If you had Harry at your back then you were safe.

The captain waved us over. "It looks like they send full trains east to west in the morning and then empty ones west to east in the afternoon. That means that we can choose a good target. We will attack a westbound train. We will take out sixty feet of rail, bend them and then throw them in the river." One of the engineers at Front Royal had told us that if you could bend a rail, however slightly, then it was almost impossible to straighten it. Of course, he had recommended heating the rail first but we couldn't risk a fire. I knew that Danny would have an idea about that. "Then I want Jack and Harry to take their sections to the east. Go beyond where we have taken out the rails. If we get the chance we will take whatever we can from the train. You two will need to take care of any guards. Danny and I will deal with the engine."

Danny pointed to two huge rocks just visible in the river. "When you have lifted your rail then use the rocks to bend them. We won't have far to throw them. Put one end between them and then have all your men bend them. It doesn't have to be a big bend; even a small one will weaken the metal."

We worked just like the team building the railroad but in reverse. With the tools taken from the locker, one section loosened the bolts. A second section lifted the bolts and then the other two sections bent and disposed of the rails. Even the captain and the lieutenant joined in and by dawn, there was a gap of sixty feet. We still had time before dawn and the captain said, "Now throw the sleepers into the river and then get rid of the gravel. They will have a really big job to get this railroad going again."

We were exhausted by dawn but I led my weary section to the east along with Harry. We were not finished yet. We saddled our horses first and then took our carbines. Harry had the idea of taking half a dozen sleepers and making a breastwork behind which we could shelter. Once we had done that we had our own little fort. We had no idea what would be on the train that we would derail. It was a lottery. If it was filled with infantry then we might have a problem. Jimmy spotted the smoke in the distance. "Sarge! Smoke!"

"Davy, run and tell the captain. The rest of you check your carbines and your Colts. This will be your last chance."

Harry growled, "And if any of you dozy buggers fires before we say I'll have your bollocks for breakfast."

Davy had returned by the time we began to hear it as it hurtled along the rails. "This one is certainly shifting, sarge."

"It sounds like it is." I was disappointed. I had hoped for cannon or ammunition but this seemed almost empty. I could see, even at a distance of a mile that there were blue uniforms on the train. "Looks like it is guarded then, Harry."

"You didn't think this would be easy did you?" He raised himself on one arm. "As soon as I give the word shoot anything in blue and keep shooting until I say otherwise. There are soldier boys on this train. Don't miss!"

The first missing rail was just beyond the bend to our right. The engineer would brake as soon as he saw that the track had been damaged but by then it would be too late to stop the metal behemoth. As soon as we heard the brakes then we would fire. I saw the engineer and the fireman as they laboured to keep up the speed. I noted that there were two guards on the footplate too and a flatcar just behind the tender with men and sandbags. There were just two wagons and the rest had men on flatcars behind sandbags. Whatever was in the wagons was valuable. We heard the squeal of the brakes and then Harry shouted, "Fire!"

Confederate Ranger

Twenty Henry carbines provide a huge amount of firepower. The men on the flatcars were assaulted on two fronts; they had to face us and then try to keep their balance as the cars and the wagons began to tip over. We lost sight of them all as our guns spewed smoke but we kept firing anyway. A sporadic shot or two came back at us but as I heard the branches above us cracking as they were struck, I knew that they were firing blind. After a few moments, there were no more bullets coming in our direction and I held my hand, "Cease fire! Reload." I nodded at Harry. We reloaded and rose to our feet.

Harry said, "Right lads, take it easy and keep your eyes open."

As the smoke cleared we could see the whole train had derailed and was on its side. I looked east and saw the half-submerged loco and heard the hiss of steam from its cooling boiler. There were some wounded amongst the Union soldiers but most of them were dead. Some had died in the impact while our fusillade had finished the rest. I headed for the wagons. "My section, cover me. Davy! On my right."

The wagon was lying half on its side but the doors had held and it was still locked. "Cecil, bring me the crowbar we used on the rails."

With two of us leaning on the long crowbar used to lift the rails we prised the latch from the door. It groaned and cracked as it broke. We had to drop down from the door to slide it open. As we were doing so Davy shouted, "Sarge! It says paymaster on the wagon!"

Cecil and I slid the door open. It was not easy as the door was at an acute angle. Once it opened we saw the boxes lying in disorganised heaps, all of them imprinted with U.S. Paymaster. Cecil and I hauled ourselves into the car. I still had the crowbar and I picked up one box. It did not feel heavy. I prised open the lock and saw that it was filled with U.S. dollar bills. "Here Cecil get some of the guys to start unloading this. We'll see what the captain wants us to do with it." He hefted the box and manhandled it from the car. I picked up another box and this one felt heavier. When I opened this one I saw that it was filled with U.S. silver dollars. This was a better find. I laid it to one side and began to search through the car. By the time Cecil and the rest of the section returned I had worked out which boxes contained paper. I pointed to the boxes containing coins. "Two men to a box. Take these off the car. They are coins."

I heard the captain outside and I went to join him. "Looks like we hit the jackpot sir. That box is filled with paper money. There are more inside." Cecil and Jimmy were just emerging with the second box. "This one has coins. Silver dollars. I have the boys bringing them out. The coins are bagged inside."

"Well done boys. Put the paper money back in and open the boxes. We'll burn it. Harry, get your boys to check the second wagon." He strode over and opened the box. He began to empty it. "It looks like there are twenty bags in each one." He weighed one in his hand. "I reckon one man can carry about six of these in his saddlebags."

I grinned, "I reckon." I turned to Jacob. "When the boxes come out, you open them."

Harry and his boys had collected the weapons already and I wondered at how we would carry the extra weight back to our camp. He took the crowbar from me and opened the second car. I heard a rebel yell from one of his men and then saw Harry's grinning face. "Ammunition sir. Forty-four calibre!"

That was good news for it would fit both the Henry and the Army Colts I used. The captain shouted over. "Divide it between the men. I want us out of here in fifteen minutes and I want the train ready to burn. Jed, take Colm and Geraghty and get some kindling. The paper money should burn real well."

Just then we heard the sound of horses as Danny and his section led our mounts from the trees. I turned to my men. "Get the coins and the ammunition distributed amongst all of the horses. Make sure you balance the weight. I don't want to lose any on the way back."

We were all mounted, waiting for Jed and the other two to set the fire. I could hear another train, although it was way off in the distance. The captain heard it too. "Come on boys. Get a move on."

I watched as Jed fired into the paper. There was a pause and then it whooshed into life. The three of them raced over to us and leapt on their horses. "Come on boys. Head for the ridge. When that fire gets to the ammunition there will be a fourth of July to end all."

Colm suddenly shouted, "Sir I dropped my Colt by the track box."

Danny shouted, "Leave it Colm, we'll get you another."

He grinned, "Sure and I'll be but a minute." He turned and galloped along the track.

Danny shook his head, "He's a mad bugger but a good man in a fight. He shot two of the guards on the engine who were about to plug the captain. He is really fast with the Colt. I can see why he doesn't want to lose it."

"Is it worth getting blown to kingdom come for?"

Danny laughed, "I think Colm is going to be as lucky as you Jack and that is going some."

We were in the tree line when there was an almighty crump as the ammunition wagon exploded. We began to be showered with small pieces of wood which cascaded down from the skies. We all turned in our saddles although all that we could see was the plume of smoke rising above the trees.

    Then we saw Colm grinning and galloping towards us. "Well, boys that was as close as I want to get to an explosion. Damned near lost my eyebrows!" Even the captain laughed. Colm was an easy man to like.

Chapter 3

We made it back safely to our camp. The first thing that we did was to check that it had not been disturbed and we were relieved to find it had not. There were no signs of even an occasional wild animal paying us a visit. We put the tents up and then each section cleared the turf from the fires and began to cook our meal. The captain called the corporals and sergeants together at his tent. He took out a bottle of whiskey. It was Irish. "It seems the engineer was a drinking man and, miraculously, this didn't break. I thought that we could celebrate." Even in a tin mug, the whisky tasted fine. "Here's to the Wildcats."

"Cheers!"

"Even after just one raid we have achieved more than Mosby has in a month!" Captain Boswell was always a little jealous of John Mosby. I don't know why for we all were working towards the same end. "Jack, bring one of the bags of dollars from my saddlebags, let's see how much we have."

I got one and emptied it out. We began to count. "It looks like fifty dollars to a bag."

"How many bags?"

I shrugged, "I didn't count but I told Cecil to give all of the men equal numbers and I have five so that would be forty times two hundred and fifty." I wasn't good at arithmetic but Harry was and he said, "I reckon that is around ten thousand dollars."

Danny had a sly smile upon his face, "And does this go to the quartermaster sir?"

I could see the dilemma on the captain's face. He didn't need the money but he knew that we did and that we were not paid like regulars. "I suppose that can wait until we get back."

Confederate Ranger

Dago ventured, "The lads need something, sir. I mean it isn't as though we are going to have much to take back to the quartermaster to exchange for money is it?"

The argument swayed the captain. The fact that we would have nothing to exchange settled it. "Very well then. We'll tell them when we have eaten." And that was how we got the reputation as train robbers and thieves. What our detractors forgot was that we were fighting for the Confederacy and the money we burned would have been used to pay the Union army. The demoralising effect of the robbery would have an effect on their soldiers over the next few months. "And now we need to plan Hagerstown. I want to leave tomorrow night and scout out the warehouse, ready to attack the following night. Danny, you found it. What can you tell us?"

"They have a small barracks close by. I think they were ordnance troops rather than fighting men but there looked to be forty or so of them. There is also a company of cavalry at the southern end of the town."

"Where is the warehouse?"

"At the northern end, Harry, so we can avoid the cavalry easily. There is another range of hills on the other side of the valley. We have two escape routes. We can come back here or we can head west and head for the valley that way."

Captain Boswell shook his head. "This is too good an area to leave. I can see us operating here for some time to come. What we will do is to divide into two groups. The sergeants and the corporals can form a perimeter around the warehouse and the barracks with their men in case anyone gets inquisitive. Danny you and I will deal with the men in the barracks and blow it up. Then we just head back here."

Confederate Ranger

I looked at Harry who looked as bemused as I did. "Sir, you will be outnumbered by two to one."

"Don't forget Jack, we will be reconnoitring first. If I think we can't do it that way then we can change it but I am sure that our lads can deal with twenty ordnance troops who wouldn't know one end of a pistol from the other. Now go and eat and tell your men about the money!" Confidence exuded from every pore of the captain's body. We had never failed against the best the Union had to send against us; he thought that troops not used to combat would be easy to defeat. I was not so sure.

Jacob and Wilkie moaned about hiding the tents as we left the next afternoon. "No one came when we were away sarge. It is a waste of time putting them up just to take them down again."

"That's the way it is Wilkie, and I would rather do that than be ambushed when we got back here. Don't forget we all have extra weight now and we can't run as fast as we would like." They all grinned and looked at their bulging saddlebags. What I hadn't told them was that I had buried most of my coins and most of my ammunition underneath the fire. I would risk losing the money rather than struggling to escape. I had just fifty dollars with me and I knew that my mount would appreciate the lighter load. I knew that Harry, Dago and Jed had done the same. We had survived as long as we had because of our caution.

The town of Hagerstown was just ten miles from our camp. We left the hidden dell as the sun was setting in the west. We negotiated the steep part of the journey whilst there was still some light to see any obstacles on the track. We reached the road leading from Hagerstown to Waynesboro just after dark. We could see the glowing lights of our destination to the south and we rode along the road warily. I am sure that any who saw us would have taken us for Union cavalry. Many of our horses had been stolen from the

Union cavalry we had bested and our slouch hats were similar to those worn by some of the western cavalry regiments. Confidence was all. We rode towards Hagerstown from the north knowing that the Union troops were to the south of the town.

Danny halted us some way from the warehouse. Captain Boswell summoned Harry, Jed, Dago and me. "You take your men and block the main road north. We will just scout and I will send a man to tell you when to go."

The twenty men headed east. "How do you want to work this Jack?"

Harry and I understood each other. We obeyed orders but we tended to make them suit us. "I don't like the idea of twenty of us sitting in the middle of the road. We'll attract too much attention."

"I agree. What say we give Dago half of your men and I'll give Jed half of my boys? I'll watch the main road. Jack, you ride further into the town and watch there. Jed, take the western road and Dago the east. I'll send one of my boys when the captain sends for us. With fewer men, we can spread out more and look a little more casual."

I took Cecil and the new boys Wilkie and Jacob. I could keep an eye on them. They were both nervous, I could see that by watching the way they played with their reins and their guns. "Look, boys, me and Cecil have done this before. Just ride as though you are the Seventh Michigan. We are on our way south to join McClellan. If you see anyone smile at them and wave. They won't notice the grey; it's too murky to distinguish colours. We'll stop and just take some stones from my horse's hoof. Right?"

"What if someone speaks to us?"

Cecil snorted with derision, "You answer them. Didn't you hear the sergeant? We pretend we are Yanks."

Confederate Ranger

"It's going to be fine. Irish and me have the advantage of an Irish accent which means they will assume we are from the north anyway but just smile and pretend we have every right to be here."

There were not many people on the street as it was a chilly evening. When we were in the middle of the town I halted and climbed from my horse. I took one of Copper's hooves in my hand and pretended to examine it. Copper would happily play along. She was a Ranger. In reality, I was watching for any danger. I could see none. Suddenly all hell broke loose. From the north, we heard a firefight. There were carbines and handguns popping off. I swung on to the back of my horse. "Ready your weapons."

"Aren't we riding to the guns?"

"Our job is to stop anyone attacking from this direction."

"But there are just four of us!"

"And we can all fire six balls in the direction of whoever comes up this road. We will be still and they will be riding. Even a poor shot should hit a couple of men and they will be lucky to hit the side of a barn if they are riding. Just do as I say and I will get you out of this."

"Listen to him, boys. He isn't called Lucky Jack for nothing."

Just then I heard hooves behind me and Dago and the rest of my section rode up. "Thought you might need some help here. There was jack shit down that road and we know there are cavalry down the other end of town."

The hairs on my neck started to prickle. "Then why aren't they galloping up to see what the commotion is all about? You reached here after hearing the firing. I would have expected someone from the south by now."

Dago too looked puzzled. "You are right but if the cavalry aren't there…"

Confederate Ranger

"It was an ambush. Davy, ride to the sergeant and tell him I think it is an ambush. I am going to help the captain."

I headed east towards the sounds of the guns which were still firing. As we closed the sounds grew in volume. Dago turned in his saddle. "You boys make sure you can get to your other guns real quick!"

I slowed us down to a walk as we rode down a small side street. I could hear the gunfire to the north of us. There were flashes of light in the street ahead. "Dago. Take three men and go up this alley. I will take the others up the next one." I turned to Cecil. "You ride next to me." I looped my reins around my pommel and took out my second Colt. I would be ready no matter what I saw. The smoke from the gunfire drifted towards us and afforded us some protection. We emerged from the alley and I saw about a hundred Union cavalrymen firing at Danny and the captain who were sheltering behind some wagons. I saw, in an instant, the dead lying before them. I glanced to my left and saw Dago and his men. "Fire!" I unloaded both guns as fast as I could fire. I replaced one and drew my last Colt and fired again. I yelled, "Yee-haw! Wildcats!"

I heard the reply and knew that they would try to break out in my direction. My pistols were empty and I holstered them and drew my Henry. "Aim to the left and the right and watch out for our men."

I saw a Union sergeant aiming his gun at me and I swung my Henry and took a snapshot. His bullet smacked into the building behind me but he was thrown backwards by the force of my shot and he crashed into their wooden barrier. I saw the captain. "Cecil, make a gap!" I pulled my horse to the left as Cecil moved to the right and then the remnants of our men galloped through us.

Danny, bleeding from his left arm was the last through. "That's it, Jackie! The rest are dead!"

"Dago! Retreat!" I fired one last shot and then turned, with Cecil to follow Danny.

The captain, who was also wounded, was waiting for us on the main street. He looked to be wounded but more than that, he was in a state of shock. "Captain let's head back this way and meet Harry. I think the road to the south is free. It will take them some time to mount and pursue us."

"Lead the way, Jack." His voice sounded distant and he kept looking back to the bodies lying in the street.

Dago emerged from his alley and rode next to me. "That was a cock-up."

"And then some." I saw Davy. "Davy, tell Harry we are heading towards him and then we will go south! Tell him we have wounded. He will know what to do."

He wheeled his horse around. I felt happier knowing that Harry would be watching our back. People were emerging from their houses and the bars to see what the noise was. As they saw us galloping by they ran back in to shelter. However, some of them went to get shotguns and handguns and soon they were on the streets peppering away.

"Someone could get hurt. Should we fire back, Jack?"

"No Dago. They are civilians. The last thing we need is to be accused of murdering innocent citizens. Everybody ride fast and keep your heads down." When we reached the main road I saw Harry and his men readying a skirmish line. If the enemy were close behind us they would be in for a shock. As we wheeled south I waved and Harry gave a laconic nod. I noticed that many of the horses which had lost their riders had followed us. That could prove useful later on. He shouted to us as rode by, "Get ready with your pistols. There are guards at the crossroads."

I heard Jacob moan, "I am out of ammunition!"

And I heard Dago growl, "Then use your sword! You soft little bugger!"

I drew my Henry and leaned over my saddle. I fired at the sergeant who was trying to organise his surprised men. The motion of the horse meant that I had no accuracy but I managed to hit him in the knee and he crumpled to the ground. The others opened up with a barrage of balls and the road cleared. It is hard to face horses and men who are firing at you. These men had places they could hide and hide they did. Suddenly we emerged from the crossroads. We were through the town and into the dark again.

A mile from Hagerstown I slowed down. "Wilkie, Cecil, collect the strays. Jacob, check the wounded." I could see the main east-west road a mile south. I did not want to take it. If we did we would be easy to find but I did not know what the captain intended.

I turned as they reined in next to me. The captain appeared to have regained some of his normal composure. "Thanks, Jack. If you and Dago hadn't arrived when you did then we were a-gonna."

As much as I wanted to know what had gone wrong I needed us to get to safety as soon as possible. "Sir, I think that we need to head back to our camp." I saw the puzzled look on his face. "They won't expect it. With respect sir, they had whipped us good and they think they will be chasing us all the way back to Virginia. They won't expect us to go north and we can rest and then head back to Leesburg if you have a mind."

Danny nodded his assent. "He's right sir and it will allow us to check on the wounded."

His shoulders sagged and he said, "Very well. Lead on Macduff!"

Confederate Ranger

I had no idea what he was talking about but I saluted and said, "Yes sir." I sought the Rangers I could really rely on. "Dago, take Colm and scout the road to the camp."

"Aren't we heading south sarge?"

Dago snorted, "Colm, wash your ears out. You heard Jack, now move it!"

I knew that we had to concentrate on escaping this cleverly worked trap or Boswell's Wildcats would perish north of the Potomac. I had no idea just how many of Danny and the captain's men had survived the ambush. I knew that I still had ten men and I think that Harry had the same but, as we rode along the road east, I could see empty saddles. Colm was waiting for us at a gap in the bushes. He looked a little shamefaced. "The corporal says this is the shortest route back."

"Good lad. You lead the rest along. I will see how Harry is doing." I watched the men ride through. I was relieved to see David, our only medical expert, tending to Danny as they passed me. "Keep going sir, Dago has found a short cut to the camp and Colm is waiting for you."

I rode slowly back down the road and met Jed and the rest of Harry's men. Jed spat. "We lost two back there."

"At least we got out of it alive."

Harry reined in. "What an absolute cock-up! Did you lose any of your men, Jack?"

"No I was lucky but there aren't many from Danny and the captain's sections."

"Jed, take the men along Jack and I will wait here and make sure we aren't followed." After Jed had led the men away Harry said, "We were betrayed."

The gut feeling I had returned and I knew that Harry was right. "I think you are right but what makes you think so?"

"They were waiting for us."

"I know. When no-one came from the cavalry camp I knew. But who betrayed us? We have fought alongside these men for a long time."

"I know but they were waiting for us."

"You are right there. I saw at least a hundred cavalry and there were foot soldiers too."

"It is a hard pill to swallow Jack but we have a traitor and a spy in the ranks. We'll need to keep our wits about us."

"Come on Harry. There's no-one following." As we left the road I stopped. I could see something jammed in the wall. It was yellow.

"What's up Jack?"

I pointed to the yellow bandana. "That bandana, it wasn't there when I left. I was at the head of the column and I remember checking that the road was clear. I would have seen it." I leaned down and picked up the bandana. As I did so a silver dollar dropped from it.

Harry spat, "Well that confirms it. Someone left that for the Yanks to follow."

"We will have to make sure that we are the last ones to leave the camp and we will have to check that no-one has left a message."

"Do we tell Danny and the captain?"

"We'll have to. I trust Dago and Jed, but as for the rest…"

"You are right. I still can't believe that someone has betrayed us."

"It could be more than one person. We will have to tread very carefully."

We kept our eyes peeled as we followed the trail to the camp. We found a discarded kepi where the trail suddenly turned left.

Confederate Ranger

"Look, Harry. Another sign left by our spy or spies!" I picked it up and another freshly minted silver dollar fell out. "It is every place where the rest turned off. Someone is leading them to our camp."

"I suppose we just look for someone missing a reb kepi now eh Jack?"

I shook my head, "There will be no point. If they are clever enough to stay hidden then they will have used someone else's. It will be the same with the bandana. If they left it, they have a spare. In fact, my guess is that anyone missing a kepi or a bandana is innocent but until we get proof, I trust no one."

The sun was just breaking in the east, over Frederick, as Harry and I rode into the camp. Jed and Dago had organised the tents and I saw that Cecil was getting a fire going. He had come on in the past few months and had so much more confidence now. We rode directly to where David was looking at the wounds suffered by Danny and the captain. The other wounds were superficial but Danny looked to have one deep one. I reached into the captain's saddlebag and took out the last of the whisky. I poured some on the wound and then said to Danny, "Here you go sir, take a deep swallow. I guess David will have to stitch."

I saw David's grateful nod as Danny swallowed off a quarter of the bottle. Before the liquor could take effect he grabbed my arm. "You and Harry look after the lads eh Jack?"

I grinned, "Of course!" I nodded to Dago. As he came close I murmured, "Bring Jed to me and Harry. We have something to tell you."

Harry and I ensured that all the horses and men were taken care of and then wandered over to the rock which overlooked the camp. It would not look unusual or out of place for us to meet and talk there.

"There is a traitor amongst the lads." Neither Dago nor Jed looked surprised.

"After the cock up tonight I can believe it but I suppose you have some evidence?"

I took out the kepi and the bandana. "Both were left to lead them here." I let them examine them but they could have been anyone's. "You two, Danny and the captain; we are the only ones, not suspects. We need to watch for little tricks like this."

"Does the captain know?"

"Not yet. Let David make them whole again and we can tell them. From now on one of us is on duty at all times. Don't let anyone know we are suspicious. We will just pretend that the ambush was unfortunate. We need to watch for anyone trying to leave the camp or wandering off and leaving little clues."

"Do we go south when they are healed?"

Harry growled, "It would seem the best. I did a quick count. The captain and Danny have three men left between them. And I lost two. That makes just twenty-three men who can fight and our two officers are wounded. Yes, I think we go south and Jack and I will persuade the captain it is for the best."

David strode over to us. "How are they?"

The young man who had such an aptitude for healing smiled. "I think they are just annoyed that they were wounded at all. They can ride in the next day or two."

Harry and I wandered over to the two officers. Danny was looking a little pale, having lost a lot of blood but the captain looked hale and hearty. Harry looked at me and I nodded. "We think we should head back to Virginia in the next couple of days captain."

I saw Danny give an affirmative smile. "Why? It was just one little setback boys."

"Captain, you were ambushed."

"We were just unlucky and it could have been worse if those new boys Colm and Geraghty hadn't seen the Yanks early and yelled out. We had a little warning; otherwise, they would have had us cold."

"Exactly and that makes my point. Besides… go on Jack tell them."

"Someone was leaving signs for the cavalry to help them find us here." I brought the evidence out from my jacket. "I found these left where we turned off and there was a Yankee silver dollar in each one. Just like the ones we took from the train. I was riding at the rear and so I was able to take the kepi and the bandana. We covered our tracks but it won't take them long to find us." I took a deep breath. "There is a traitor amongst us and if we can't trust our men then we will die."

The captain looked incredulous, "A traitor? Could it have been one of the men who were killed in the ambush?"

The captain was clutching at straws because he believed and trusted in these men."If it was he has an accomplice because the clues were left after the ambush."

Danny tried to struggle to his good elbow. "Won't it be more dangerous taking them back to our lines?"

"We hope that we can discover the identity of the spy or spies by then. We told Dago and Jed but everyone else is suspect."

"Even David? Colm?"

"Everyone captain. We have six of us able to watch and they will make a mistake. They don't know that we are on to them. We thought that, until you two are well again, Harry would take your men to replace his losses and David can care for the two of you. We will organise the watches. That way we have eyes on all of the suspects. We need to eliminate suspects and make our task easier.

Confederate Ranger

At least we have some spare horses now and the coins and the ammunition will be easier to carry if we have to leave in a hurry."

The captain lay back with a resigned look on his face. "It looks like you two had better make all the decisions until we are south of the Potomac again."

Danny put his hand on the captain's shoulder. "Don't take it to heart captain. There were thirty-nine loyal men and just one bad apple."

As I walked to the horse lines I wondered about that. I would not assume that there was only one traitor. Until I had the proof then all of the men were potential traitors. It was uncomfortable looking at men I had fought alongside with new eyes. I could not believe that Cecil, the young man who had saved my life on two occasions, could be a traitor. Davy, who was as loyal and brave a man as you could wish- could he be a spy? I suppose if I were a traitor then I would do that to allay suspicion. The same was true of David who had saved many limbs and lives since he had joined us. And what of the new boys Colm and Geraghty? Had they not been alert then our officers would also be dead along with the brave men they had lost. There was little point in speculating; I needed evidence and information.

By the time we packed the horses to head south, none of us had any more information. We had seen no suspicious behaviour. No-one had attempted to leave the camp and no-one was looking anxiously for friends coming to rescue them. We decided that Dago and Jed would ride half a mile behind us to look for any messages sent or dropped by the spy. We had been evasive about our destination just telling the men that we were heading south of the Potomac. None showed any curiosity and we left the camp just before dusk. We headed towards the ford we had crossed near Leesburg. Although it meant we would have to skirt that nest of cavalry who patrolled that area, we were familiar with the land and could easily get back to the Blue Ridge. Our final destination would have to be the Shenandoah Valley. Our spies had to have the opportunity to give themselves away and that was more likely in a busy military area rather than an isolated camp in the mountains. We hoped that they would show their hand before we reached our camp.

I led the column while Harry had the rearguard. Cecil rode next to me. "You've been kinda quiet for a couple of days, sarge. What's up?"

Why was it that I was now suspicious of such an innocuous question? I bit back my retort and gave him a reassuring smile. "Best keep silent, Cecil. Noise travels a long way at night. Wait until we cross the Potomac eh?"

He smiled, "Yes sarge. I just didn't want to have annoyed you. That's all."

I felt relieved as we reached the heights above the river. It meant that we were almost out of Union territory. I wondered if they had repaired the railroad yet. There was a danger that they would be watching along the line for a repeat of our raid. I made the signal for single file and silence. Cecil dropped in behind me and I took out my Colt. Copper was very sure-footed and I had the luxury of being able to scan the track of the railroad as we approached it. I could see no signs of waiting men. I signalled for the rest to wait and then I edged slowly forward. It was always a nervous time as you awaited the crack of a pistol. I reached the track and glanced down in both directions. It appeared to be clear and, as I listened, I could hear neither engine nor the sound of metal clanging. There were no railroad men out that night. I waved them forwards as I dropped down the steep slope to the river.

Confederate Ranger

There were a number of fords we could use. White's Ford was a good one but there were others that riders with good horses could cross. The river was cold at this time of year but, as yet, there was no ice. As I rode along the river bank I felt that prickling around my scalp. I halted and held up my hand. Soon the only sound I could hear was the sound of the river as it headed towards the sea. The company knew how to sit silently and all of us trusted the rider on point. Then I heard it again. It was the sound of creaking leather and the jingle of reins on bits. There were cavalry ahead! I looked across the river. It was fordable, but only just. I turned in the saddle and gave the signal for danger and then plunged into the river. I heard the rest join me as we began to cross the Potomac. I kept glancing to my left where I had heard the sound of horses. Perhaps I had been mistaken. I stepped out of the water onto one of the flat rocks in the middle of the river. I looked behind me and saw that the whole company, except for Dago and Jed were in the river.

I was about to carry on when a sudden movement to my left caught my eye. It was a company of cavalry and they were racing along the river. I drew my Henry. "Cecil, lead them across and then form a skirmish line on the other side."

"But…"

"Just do it!"

I heard him splash into the water and call out. "Follow me!" I made sure the Henry was cocked. There was little point in wasting ammunition. They were too far away and my only intention was to give Dago and Jed a chance to reach the middle of the river before they were seen.

Danny said, "Well spotted," as he and the captain trotted across the rock.

Confederate Ranger

"It was my ears, sir. I told Cecil to form a skirmish line." I never took my eyes from the cavalry who were now beginning to ford the river themselves. I sighted the gun on the leading rider. He was an officer and appeared to be giving orders. When I saw the sabre in his hand I knew the type. He was a glory hunter. The graveyards were filled with them. Harry reined in next to me. "Ritchie, take the boys across. I'll wait here with Lucky Jack." The quiet, gangly trooper nodded and led the rest of the men over the river. Harry, too, took out his Henry. "You got the officer?"

"Yup!"

"I'll take the one with the guidon."

Although it was dark there was enough light from the moon to enable us to see our targets clearly. I hoped that Dago and Jed were close but I knew that they could handle themselves. The officer was about a hundred yards away and I squeezed the trigger. His horse was unfortunate enough to raise its head at the wrong time and the bullet smacked into it. The horse died and the officer plunged into the water. Harry's gun sounded a heartbeat later and he was luckier. The bugler was thrown from his horse. It bought us time as they tried to help the officer to his feet. I fired a second shot as did Harry. There was so much movement amongst the cavalry that it was difficult to see if we had hit anyone or they had just dismounted. A couple of the troopers tried to fire as they swam the river but their shots were wasted. I risked a look across to our two corporals and saw that they were just forty yards from us.

"One more, eh Jack?"

"One more, Harry."

I aimed at the officer again as he began to mount the bugler's horse. I saw him clutch at his shoulder as he fell back into the water. Harry's shot struck another trooper who plunged into the river. Our job done we turned and joined Dago and Jed as we headed towards the rest of the Wildcats. South of the Potomac, we were confident that no-one would catch us and we headed to the Valley just as quickly as we could. The camp in the Blue Ridge would have to remain unoccupied until we had discovered who the spy was. The camp would be a bad place for us to be trapped and our spy knew the way in and the way out. It had to be the Valley and we would need to be clever to catch our traitor.

Chapter 4

The army had left Front Royal by the time we reached our old stomping ground. The generals had moved everyone north to Winchester. General Lee was busily preparing his army to repulse an attack on Richmond. We reached Front Royal about noon and the last thing David wanted was more travelling. He had worries about his patients. The journey had not helped their recovery. Danny's wound had burst and, although there would be a surgeon with the army, we thought it best to stay in the town. As events turned out we saved ourselves a wasted journey for the next day J.E.B. Stuart and his cavalry corps rode through the town on their way down the valley. The captain was well enough to speak with the general. He was keen to explain why we were no longer north of the Potomac. When he returned to us he was in a much better humour.

"It seems that we are no longer needed north of the river. Our little train wreck made the Union soldier boys move more cavalry north of the river to stop us. Those cavalry are no longer facing Lee. And they have replaced the general in charge of the Yankees. It is now Burnside. I don't think we made them do that but it would be nice to think we helped. Stuart and Jackson are heading east towards the Rappahannock River."

We can have a couple of days to recover here and then head towards Manassas Junction. It is an important route for the army's supplies and we can hurt them there. The generals like our work on railroads."

"Did the general say anything about the money sir?"

"No Jed and, you know, it never came up in the conversation." He nodded towards the door and I got up to make sure that no-one was listening. We had rented a house for the captain and he was appreciating the comfort.

I shook my head. "All clear sir."

"Now are we any closer to finding out who the traitor is?" We all sat in silence. It was eloquent. "Then we have a problem, don't we? How do we uncover him?"

"Or them."

The captain looked horrified. "Them, Jack? It is bad enough to have one bad apple but to have more does not bear thinking about."

"I am just saying, sir, that until we know, let's not make any assumptions."

"We could try a trap?"

"A trap, Danny?"

"Aye, sir. I have had time to think while I rested my wounded wing. If we give the lads some information and the information is a lie then if the enemy reacts to it we know where it came from."

I had thought of that but there was something in what Danny said. "That doesn't help us, sir. We would still need to know who to watch. But what we could do is give some information to some of the boys. If nothing comes of it then they might be innocent and we try some others."

"You mean eliminate the ones who aren't traitors?"

"Yes, sir. It whittles down the possibilities. It might take time but it would be safe."

We spent the next hour working out our strategy. We had two days to set it up. One problem Harry mentioned was that it might tip the hand of the spies if the information was found to be totally erroneous and so we baited the trap; with me. Actually, to be fair, it was with Dago, Jed and me. We decided that as we had done missions like this before, it would not look unusual if Dago and I were sent to Berryville to see if there were any senior officers billeted there as there had been the previous year. We took just Cecil, Wilkie and Jacob. They were my choice. I was convinced that they were all innocent and this would prove it and eliminate three suspects. Once we were on the road Dago and I would let slip some information about a raid on Leesburg. Jed would hide close to Leesburg and see if any troops came to reinforce it. He would be away for a few days but we thought it was worth it. There were two chances for our three suspects to betray us. I didn't think they would and the bonus would be that we would gather intelligence on two important targets.

We left in the afternoon and I rode next to Dago. He was a born actor and played his part well. "Well, I don't know why Jed was chosen to be the one for the top-secret mission to Leesburg. Why couldn't it be me?"

I lowered my voice but still kept it loud enough for the others to hear. "And I told you before, Jed knows the spy in the Union headquarters. He is a cousin of his or something like that. The spy trusts no-one else. Besides, it is a secret. It will be dangerous for him if anyone finds out he is there alone."

The trap was baited. We would, of course, be scouting Berryville but we were fairly certain that the Union army would have their senior officers further east. We found the place strangely quiet as we rode around the familiar streets. There was no sign of cavalry horses or armed guards. We had frightened them away. We returned to Front Royal just after midnight.

"Sorry, that was a wasted journey, boys. Get some sleep. We won't be needing you until again noon."

Dago and I were now set to watch the three of them. Dago had the first shift and I would have the second. Jed had already left on his alleged reconnoitre. I hoped that the trap would not be sprung but was also disappointed that if it were not sprung then it would all have been a wasted effort.

I felt like I had only been in bed for five minutes when Dago awoke me. "Quiet as the grave. The three of them are still in their tent."

I waited and watched from the large tree close to the tent line. I knew that I could not be seen so long as I remained still. Four hours can seem a long time to be alone with your thoughts. A short time ago our world had been perfect. We had destroyed a train and become rich men. Within two days it had turned into an unmitigated disaster. As I mulled over the events something jarred in my mind. I couldn't quite place it. It was like the piece of meat hidden between teeth that no amount of poking and picking will remove. It was just before dawn. I was as cold as I had been at home in Ireland when the flap of the tent I was watching twitched. A figure emerged and I became alert. It was Wilkie. He looked left and right. I could not work out if it was furtive or just naturally careful. Then he walked to the line of bushes and after a moment or two began to pee. I had just started to relax when the flap of the next tent inline opened and Geraghty stepped out. He looked from left to right and then joined Wilkie to relieve himself.

"You boys got in late last night."

"Yes. It was a wasted journey. We found nothing."

"Colm and I wondered if Jed had met you. He lit out soon after you guys."

I tensed. Would Wilkie reveal the information? If he did then that might not make him a spy but it would mark him as a blather mouth.

"Nah. We just had the sarge and the corporal with us. Anyway, we get a lie-in tomorrow. We won't be needed until after noon."

Confederate Ranger

When he returned to his tent Geraghty waited a while and then went to the horse lines. I didn't need to move from my position to see him. He walked down the line and stopped at my horse and Dago's. He stroked them both and then returned to his tent. It was a strange thing to do and nagged at me right through until dawn.

I reported to the captain and told him what had transpired. "I am pretty certain that Jed will have nothing to report when he returns tomorrow but Harry can watch the three of them today. My money is on their innocence. And that means we have eliminated three suspects."

"Well I am feeling better already and as soon as Danny is up and about we will head for Manassas. I hope by then that we have some clue as to the traitor's identity."

I started to leave and then I paused. "There is something about the train wreck and the ambush that is lurking in the back of my mind. I am sure there is something there. I just can't see it."

"Listen, Jack, you have already saved the Wildcats. If you hadn't spotted the bandana and the kepi then we would all be dead or prisoners. You have given us a chance. We will find whoever it is; believe me."

When Jed returned he did have news. It just wasn't the news we had expected. "Well there was no one waiting to ambush me but I did see four regiments of cavalry heading south-east. There were plenty of cannons on the road too. This Burnside is moving."

Captain Boswell thought so too. "Jack, you go with Jed and find Stuart and tell him what we have learned. We will meet you in Manassas. We'll camp close to the railroad, south of the town."

I hesitated as I was leaving. I looked at Danny and then the captain, "Sir. Don't forget, don't tell the boys until we are on the road and…"

Confederate Ranger

Danny laughed, "If you could tell me again how to suck eggs! I know what you are going to say. Keep Dago at the back of the patrol to watch for our spy leaving his trail of breadcrumbs."

"Sorry, Danny! You must be getting better eh?"

This was the first time Jed and I had been on a solo patrol for a while. It was different from one with Dago. With Dago, I almost knew what he was thinking. Jed was good but he was deeper than his friend. We had been riding for an hour when he asked. "Who do you think it is?"

"The traitor?" He nodded. "I think it must be one of the last batches of men we got. There are seven of them. The others I can't prove are loyal but something," I patted my heart, "here, tells me it isn't one of those. As I think we have eliminated Wilkie and Jacob then there are just five new boys. I would have mentioned it to the captain but it seems to go against what I outlined to you all."

"For what it is worth I agree with you. There's nothing I can put my finger on but the other guys, well we have been through too much with them. But you are right. We need to be fair and let the innocent ones prove their innocence."

We headed for the Rappahannock River. We knew that the army would not be north of it and it shortened our ride. At the end of a long day, we saw the mass of men which told us it was Stonewall Jackson and his foot cavalry. They were filling the road heading east and we took to the fields to get ahead of them and find General Stuart. We were close to Chancellorsville when we found the corps of cavalry. We never received a warm greeting from the officers or the regular cavalry. They thought that we had too much freedom. However, they all knew that Stuart liked us. That overcame their antipathy and we were pointed in the right direction. When we reached the town we headed for the biggest hotel we could find. Stuart liked his comfort and he liked his drink. We found him straight away.

I was lucky in more ways than one. Stuart liked me. I had rescued his nephew and been involved in the capture of an intelligence officer and I received a warm welcome. "Sir, the corporal has news of the Union cavalry."

All of the officers became alert as Jed recounted what he had seen. "Well done boys. That confirms what we thought. The Yankees are planning something around here." He leaned forward to speak conspiratorially, "My money is on Fredericksburg so if you boys could cause a little mayhem up north I sure would appreciate it." He grabbed my arm after I had saluted and turned to leave. "Sergeant Hogan, should you ever leave the Wildcats I can give you a commission in a good cavalry regiment you know."

"Thank you for the offer sir but I am still Captain Boswell's man. We all are."

"And he is damned lucky to have such loyalty."

As we headed to the street I wondered about that. I would have agreed with him before I had found the bandana. Not all of the Wildcats were loyal; that much was obvious. "Well, Jack, what say we find a room? These Yankee dollars are burning a hole in my saddlebags and I have a hankering for a bath and some good food."

It suddenly seemed like a good idea to me too. "Why not?" We turned around, much to the surprise of the sentry on the door and headed for the desk. "We need rooms."

The clerk looked at us both with disdain written all over his face. We looked dirty and dishevelled. We were not officers and we looked too young to have enough money for this expensive hotel. We looked as though we didn't have ten cents between us. "I am sorry gentlemen but I think our prices are too high for you.

Confederate Ranger

There is a boarding-house down the road a ways." He tried to make it less offensive by smiling effusively.

I looked at Jed who winked. He said, "You tell me the price of your most expensive room and I will tell you if we can afford it."

The clerk was taken aback. "We have the Presidential Suite."

I shook my head, "And I bet you five dollars that no President has ever come within fifty miles of it."

The clerk had the good grace to blush. "That is ten dollars a night." He said it as though we had never even seen ten dollars, let alone possess it.

Jed had already seen the price list on the desk and he slapped down ten dollars. "We'll take it and I assume that for that kind of money we get a bath thrown in."

"Well a bath is normally fifty cents…" he saw Jed's hand slide down to his holster, "but it is free with the Presidential. I'll have one of the boys run you gentleman a bath each."

"Good and then we'll try your dining room too! Have the horses taken to the stables and make sure they get a rub down and some grain."

The bath was hot. The towels were soft and they even put the bubbly stuff in that made you smell like a French whore. It didn't make us smell any sweeter but we were a little less gamey when we went to dinner. The dining room was almost full. General Stuart waved at us as we sat down. The menu was vast and both of us looked forward to a wonderful meal. The waiter who served us looked at us a little askance at first. Jed slipped him five Yankee dollar bills. My eyes opened in surprise, I had thought that we had burned them all. Jed winked at me. "Now my friend and I would like some really good service. There are ten of these," he snapped one open, "if we are really satisfied."

Confederate Ranger

"Yes, sir. If I might suggest some things from the menu?"

"Go ahead." I had not heard of half of them and I don't think Jed had but we were paying with stolen money so it didn't really matter.

When he had gone I leaned over the table. "I thought we had burned them all?"

"Well, I just kept a handful. I thought they might come in handy if we had to start a fire… or get some good service. Just enjoy it, sergeant. You can be damned sure that nights like this will be few and far between."

He was right and we did both enjoy the service, the food and the drink. General Stuart finished before we did and he called at our table on his way out. He held out two cigars for us. "Seeing as you boys are pushing the boat out I thought you might enjoy these. They came courtesy of Colonel Black."

"Thank you, General Stuart."

"Say boys where did you get the money for this place? It is a little pricey. You intending on washing the dishes?"

Jed leaned back, "Well you see General Stuart. Some of these Yankee boys we capture have more than cigars in their pockets and as we don't get paid we take our money wherever we can get it. This dinner is courtesy of some Michigan boys!"

The general laughed, "Then enjoy it." He turned to his aide. "I tell you Melville, this free enterprise in war does work. Look at these two boys, living it up like Old Jeff Davis himself."

We left a healthy tip and wandered back to that rare luxury, a bed with clean sheets. Inevitably we both woke up early. Apart from nature's demands both of us were used to rising at dawn's early light. We were the first in the dining room and as we had tipped so well the night before the waiters were all over us. I had so much ham and so many eggs that I could only manage a dozen pancakes.

The horses looked as pleased as we did when we finally left the hotel. "I suppose it is back to the war for us now Jed."

"Yes, but it was worth it."

I looked at the map we had been given. "It seems to me that the quick way to Manassas Junction is through Falmouth or Fredericksburg."

"I heard them talking at the general's table last night and it is highly likely that Fredericksburg is where Stuart and Jackson are heading. "

"I can see a ford at Falmouth. Let's take it steady until nightfall and slip over during darkness. We might be able to get some intelligence for the captain." It was just about fourteen miles to the ford and we found ourselves amongst the cavalry scouts of Stuart's Corps. As night drew closer they thinned out to return to their camp. We reached the river bank just after dusk. As far as we could see we were totally alone. We could see the lights of Falmouth and, down the river in the distance, Fredericksburg. We halted at the bank and checked for any Union vedettes but there were none. The water was icy as we slipped into it and we had to swim our horses for part of the way but, the island in the middle was quite large and the last swim didn't seem as bad.

"I don't know about you Jed but I am happy to push on through the dark and rest up in the morning."

"Me too. I can still taste that breakfast."

It was flatter land than we were used to and the hills were little more than rises. The roads were not pikes and we made good progress. I hoped that two men travelling alone would not attract too much attention. I had my deer hide jacket over my grey jacket so that any curious eyes might take us for travellers. We found a copse just after dawn and we were both ready for a rest. It was on a slight rise which gave a good view for a mile or so around and we could see the main road. While Jed found water I fed the horses and laid some tripwires around the perimeter. When Jed returned we hobbled the horses and fell asleep.

I was suddenly awake. Something had disturbed me. A moment later and Jed jerked upright. I took my Henry and cocked it. We didn't need words. Firstly we listened. Hearing nothing close by, we both stood and walked to the edge of the copse. Then we saw what had disturbed us. It was Union troops; a large number of Union soldiers with both cavalry and artillery as well as the inevitable infantry. We lay down to examine them. There was no chance they would head in our direction. I took out my paper and pencil and wrote down what we could see. "It looks like a whole Grand Division. It's mainly infantry and artillery. Can you see any horses?"

Jed clambered up to the lower branches of one of the trees. "It looks like just one regiment, that's all."

"In that case, we can sit tight until they have passed. Put on a pot of coffee and I will get some ham going. We might as well wait until dark."

By the time we left our hiding place, the Grand Division was long gone and we had the road to ourselves. We had to push on as the captain would be worrying about us. We were both known for our punctuality. I began to regret our overnight stop in the hotel. We had, however, discovered valuable intelligence so it balanced out. We were aided in finding our comrades by the sound of the train hurtling along the railroad. It showed me that we were close to the line and that meant close to the company. We both drew our Colts. We knew we were deep in Yankee territory and they would be sure to guard their railroads well.

Confederate Ranger

We found the track and crossed over. Dawn was breaking and we were both warily watching for a sign that our men were close by. I spied a track box similar to the one on the Baltimore and Ohio. "Hold up Jed. This may be useful."

I dismounted to examine the lock in case it was not well used. Suddenly I froze. Jed saw my reaction. "What's up Jack? Seen a snake?"

"Something like that. Come and take a look." When he came around the box he whistled his reaction. There was a bandana. Suddenly everything clicked into place and I knew who the traitors were. I had no proof yet but I knew. Until I had the proof then I would keep the information to myself.

Jed picked it up and, as he did so, something fell from it. It was a piece of paper. I unfolded it. Scrawled in capitals it said, *"TOMORROW NOON*

"Well if don't that beat all?"

I folded the paper up and balled the bandana. "We'll show this to the captain. At least this shows us the camp must be close by here. Have a look around and see if you can see any tracks."

Disappointingly there were too many tracks. The company had been here and our traitor had managed to return and leave his message. Two stars was obviously his code name.

"We keep this to ourselves. I'll see the captain when we get back. I have a little trap in mind. I'll tell you about it this afternoon when I have spoken with the captain."

We used the tracks of the company to reach the camp. Jacob was the sentry and I heard his whistle to warn the rest of visitors. When he saw it was me he grinned. "We thought you was lost. Harry said you had found a whorehouse."

Jed laughed, "We're real men we don't need whores. The women just throw themselves at us."

Confederate Ranger

The captain and Danny were sat in his tent along with Harry and they were poring over the map. There was a slight look of irritation on the captain's face which he managed to mask. "What kept you?"

"General Stuart. They are attacking in the south. Harry, watch the tent flap."

"What's up Jack?" I could see that Danny was back to his old self and didn't miss a trick.

In answer, I took out the bandana and placed it on the map. Harry said, "So the spy is still with us then."

"And in it was this." I dropped the note on the table.

"Dammit. We were going to destroy the tracks today at noon. We were just waiting for you."

"Well we can go ahead with it, can't we? The note wasn't delivered."

The captain looked at Danny who ruefully shook his head. "The captain hoped you were wrong Jackie boy."

"I wish I was sir but I'm not. I do have an idea who they might be."

"Well out with it! Tell us!"

"I have no proof yet sir and it is unfair to accuse someone unjustly. I think I can prove it but that will have to wait until after we have wrecked the train tracks."

"I don't like it but I can understand and respect your reasons. Come on let's get this over with and then we might find out just who this canker is."

"If you don't mind sir. I'll hang around at the back and that way I can keep an eye on the men I suspect."

"It's your play, Jack. I just hope you know what you are doing."

Confederate Ranger

So did I; if the two men did as I expected they would hang back so as not to be caught in the first shots of the ambush. We rode in single file which made it easier for me to watch them. I noticed that they allowed a gap to open up between them and Cecil who was just in front. Jed had pulled to one side and was waiting for me. We dropped further back from the spies and spoke quietly.

"Someone must have been coming for that message this morning. But what I can't understand is how someone would know to come for it."

"So did I, until we were at the locker box. It will be one of the track workers. When we were ambushed the first time the only place they could have left a message was by the railroad. The rest of the time we were off the beaten track and someone would have had to trail us. That's how I worked out who one of the spies was and then it was easy to deduce the second."

We halted half a mile from the tracks. "Jacob and Wilkie, you watch the horses." Our two traitors hid their disappointment well; they had hoped that by hanging at the rear they would have been chosen as horse holders. I chose Aaron and Wilkie because they had been eliminated as suspects. As I followed them to the track I realised that they were probably not traitors. The two of them were probably patriots it was just that they were fighting for the other side. To their folks at home, they would be heroes whilst we despised them as traitors. Such are the vagaries of war.

The river was too far away to be of any use in getting rid of the rails. Harry came up with a solution. "If we carry them to the other tracks and lay them next to the existing tracks they might not be seen but they would probably still derail the train anyway."

"Good. Throw the bolts away as well. We might not have the same effect as on the Baltimore and Ohio but all we need to do is to disrupt their supplies." He threw me a look. I could see that he wanted to tell the men that the Union was rushing men down this very line to fight Jackson but he couldn't. It was eating him up. If the spies heard that and escaped they could tell their generals and we would lose the forthcoming battle.

It took an hour of sweaty labour to shift enough rails to cause some damage and then Davy rushed down from the west. "Sir, a train is heading from the west."

"Right take the tools with us and get back to the horses."

I had been watching my spies and seen the looks exchanged. They wondered why there had been no ambush. I knew that they would be wondering if their message had got through or if the ambush would come later. We had planted the seeds of doubt in their mind. Once we reached the horses we mounted and rode back a little way into the woods to see the results of the crash. We were well hidden in the trees and saw the engine lumbering around the bend. We knew when the engineer had seen the damaged track because the brakes squealed noisily. He had good reactions and might have stopped before the missing track but Harry's extra rails were not seen. Even though the engine was slowing when it hit the two extra rails it lurched to one side and crashed into the forest on the right. The tender turned over and the first carriage half twisted and ended up pointing to the skies. Suddenly hundreds of blue uniforms poured out of the carriages. It was a troop train. These troops would not get to the battle on time. What we did not know at the time was that there were pontoon bridges on the train as well and they delayed Burnside's crossing of the Rappahannock River. It was an event which had a dramatic effect on the forthcoming battle. The crash was less spectacular than the one on the Potomac but, ultimately, more useful.

Danny could see the indecision on the captain's face. We might be able to score a few hits on the disorganised troops but we could afford no further losses. He took the decision for our leader. "Wildcats, let's get the hell out of here!"

We galloped back to the camp. Although we were less than four miles from the crash scene we were far enough away to avoid anyone stumbling upon us. When we had seen to our horses Danny shouted, "See to your weapons and get some food going. We will have an officer's meeting and decide where we are going to hit the Yankees next time." There was a huge cheer from the men.

In the captain's tent, none of us felt like cheering. We were demoralised. We knew we had just avoided either death or capture by a whisker. "So Jack, this traitor…"

I held up my hand. I walked to the tent flap. "Cecil!"

The eager young man ran over. "Yes, Sarge?"

"I want no-one closer than ten feet of this tent. There are to be no exceptions," I grinned, "not even you!"

He smiled, "Consider it done." I watched him run to his tent and bring back his Henry.

They all looked at me with questions on their faces. "We eliminated him the other day and Danny said that Cecil was not with you when you went to the railroad locker which also gives him credibility."

"Your call. What do you want us to do?"

"Tonight, when we are eating I want Dago and Jed watching the horse lines. When we are around the fire we can get out the whisky bottle to celebrate our victory. I will then tell you what General Stuart has planned. If I am correct then one or both of our men will try to slip away and tell the Yankees of Stuart's plans."

Harry gave me his most laconic look. "And if they don't take the bait?"

"I have thought of that. They might volunteer to deliver a message or ask to be on point. If anyone wants to be away from the company they are the traitor. Remember sir, there are Yanks just six miles east of us and a rider could be there and back in an hour. I reckon the plan will work."

Chapter 5

We had a fine meal, having had all afternoon to prepare it. Harry had ridden to the crash scene and returned with a grin on his face. He would play his part just as we all would. We were like actors on a stage. "The footsloggers have to march down the track. There's going to be some weary boys in their camp tonight."

"Anybody searching for us?"

"I didn't see any horses and the boys made the tracks confusing anyway. They won't know which direction we have headed in. I put some trips and traps on the main trails."

Jed and Dago had given a surreptitious nod as they slipped away to their duty point. I had filled a whisky bottle with watered down coffee. I made a lot of noise as I brought it to the middle of the camp. The fire was just a glow but I noted that everyone was around the fire. The trap was ready to be baited. "Here is a present from General Stuart. He said it was just for the officers and sergeants!"

There were good-natured boos and groans but most of the men had their own bottles anyway. I poured the four of us a generous slug and we toasted each other, "The Wildcats!"

There had been enough whisky in the bottle to give off the smell but the taste was… cold coffee; cold watery coffee. We all drank it off and then poured another. Harry had already been primed. "So the general was in a good mood then? I mean he gave you this fine whisky and all."

I leaned forward and tapped my nose, "Top secret stuff! We stayed in the same fine hotel and he gave us cigars; expensive cigars." I intertwined two fingers. "We are like that!"

Confederate Ranger

Harry poured me another drink. "Come on Jack. We are all friends here." We all swallowed the drink and I shook my head as though it had been stronger than the first and I needed to clear my thoughts.

"Don't worry you'll all find out soon enough but," Harry poured me some more whisky which I drank, "the Yankees will find out sooner."

Danny joined in. "How's that Jackie Boy?"

"That train was taking Yanks to Fredericksburg. The general reckons there are five Grand Divisions going there ready to fight Lee but…" I turned and looked over my shoulder as though I might be overheard and said in a loud whisper, "Stonewall and Stuart have a Corps and they are marching towards us now. They are going to attack north as well as east. Lee will make an attack on Fredericksburg but only a feint. Jackson is going to attack the rear of the Union army while Stuart and his cavalry are going to Washington. Abe Lincoln is going to get a real shock. Stuart reckons this could end the war. They will have to sue for peace."

"And what do we do?"

"Ah, that's the good bit. We get to go to Washington first. Stuart thinks that they will think two cavalry corps will be attacking if we do our normal wild charges. He thinks a lot of us sir!" I hiccupped.

The captain slapped me on the back. "That's great news." He stood. "Looks like an early night tonight boys and tomorrow we head for Washington!"

They all cheered and went back to their tents backslapping each other as though we had won the war already. I staggered and lurched as I went to my tent. Cecil and Wilkie came over to me. "Here sarge let's help you to your tent."

I mumbled, "Thanks, boys!"

Confederate Ranger

They laid me on my blanket and then closed the flap. I heard Cecil say, "The trouble is with Lucky Jack, he might be the best soldier in the whole company but he can't hold his liquor worth a damn. Strange because like me he is Irish and we can normally hold our drink."

"Well if that is the only flaw in his character, I will live with it!"

I quickly strapped on my holster and lay in the dark. Harry, Danny and the captain could watch the tents but I had to continue to play-act the drunk. I wondered if the plan had failed as the night dragged on. Suddenly there was the crack of an Army Colt followed by two pops from two Navy Colts and then another two cracks. I jumped from my bed. There was no reason for deception any longer. The rest of the company were also out of their beds but, unlike me, they had no idea in which direction to turn. I headed for the horse lines.

I found Jed and Dago standing over the body of Colm while Geraghty lay holding his right arm. When he saw me approach he gave a sardonic grimace. "I might have known; feckin Lucky Jack had to have a hand in this. I told Colm we should have shot you when we had the chance."

Captain Boswell had heard the end of his diatribe. "You!" He glanced at me. "How did you know?"

"It was the first train wreck. There was no reason for Colm to have left his revolver there. He had a holster. When you said that these two began shouting during the ambush, it made sense. They were telling their comrades that you were there and they were Yankees. Then today I watched them as they hung back. If I hadn't been behind them they might not have even made the track."

Danny was white with anger. He was clenching and unclenching his fists. He had taken their side and asked for them in his section. I knew that he felt betrayed. It was the main reason I hadn't told the captain of their identity. He would not have believed it and might have even warned them. The rest of the company had arrived and they looked, with disbelieving eyes at the scene.

"David, see to this traitor's arm and then Harry, you tie him up and put a guard on him. We'll decide what to do with him in the morning."

Geraghty spat in my direction. It missed but Danny hit him so hard in the mouth that he fell unconscious. I remembered the last time he had done when so Black Bill had insulted the captain. "That'll keep the bastard quiet for you David!"

Dago, Jed and I went to examine the tent and belongings of the two men. The saddlebags had a hidden pocket. It would have been overlooked had Dago not slipped his hand inside the, apparently empty, leather. "What have we here?" He pulled out some folded papers. He gave them to me. "I'll check the other saddlebag."

While he found the other secret pocket I went outside to read in the glow of the firelight. "It seems they work for that Pinkerton fella; the Secret Serviceman. There is a letter here from him and countersigned by someone called Lafayette Baker. It says that they are to be afforded as much help as they need from Union troops. It looks like they are both called O'Callaghan." I looked at Danny. "They didn't appear to be brothers."

"They might be cousins. You're from Ireland Jack. You know how clannish the families are."

I proffered the letters to the captain. Dago handed him the second set. "It looks like the evidence we needed."

Confederate Ranger

The captain did not look happy. "But it has been an expensive exercise to get it. All those good men killed because of these traitors."

"What now?"

"We hold a trial. A court-martial."

"Can we do that sir? We aren't regulars."

"I hold a commission in the militia. It will have to do."

It was too late for bed and dawn was breaking as we convened the trial. David had fixed the wounded arm but the prisoner now had a broken nose too. He glared in Danny's direction. The men formed a small square around him. He stared defiantly at his former comrades. "This ain't legal you know that?"

The captain was quiet and he was calm. "Are you wearing the uniform of a Union soldier?"

"That don't make no never mind! I am a loyal American!"

"Did you swear an oath to the Confederacy and to the Wildcats?"

"I didn't mean it!"

"I will take that as a yes. Then we can proceed. Geraghty O'Callaghan. You swore an oath to this company and the Confederate States of America and you have betrayed all of the men here. You have caused the deaths of many of our comrades. Were this ancient Rome we would put you in a bag with a snake, a monkey and a dog and throw you into the river."

Danny gave a sour look at the man who had betrayed him, "I can easily find a snake, sir!"

The captain held up his hand. "What we can do is hang you like a dog. I will not waste lead on you. Has the prisoner anything to say?"

"You can never be sure now, captain, if the volunteers you get are genuine volunteers or spies." He flung his arm at the others.

Confederate Ranger

"There could be another Colm and Geraghty amongst this lot and you wouldn't have the first clue. Your days are numbered, captain, and Mr Pinkerton and others are coming for you. We nearly beat you! You damned traitor. You are all traitors!" He glared in my direction. "And you Irish boys should be ashamed of yourselves! These are no better than the English bastards who make slaves of us in Ireland!"

"Bring him with us."

Harry already had a rope and we mounted the horses, leading Geraghty by the rope which would hang him. We headed due south and headed for the railroad track. Jed had noticed a tree with a branch which overhung the lines. It was a mile or two from the place we had derailed the train and we went there. I stood on the back of my horse and looped the rope over the limb. I could see that a train would just miss him. With his hands tied behind his back, the prisoner was helpless. Danny put the rope around his neck and then said to the four men on the rope. "Right boys. Pull. But pull slowly. I wouldn't want a quick death for this traitor." When he was twelve feet from the ground they tied the rope off and we watched him squirm and twist, his face becoming bluer until suddenly he went limp. We turned and rode back to our camp. The first train through would get a real shock when they struck the swinging corpse.

Back at the camp we quickly packed away the tents. The other body was buried and we stood awaiting orders. There were now just twenty-one of us in total. We had lost half our number in a short time. I wondered if the captain's confidence was gone. Perhaps he would order us home. His face creased into a smile. "Well boys, things haven't gone so good for us lately and I know some of you are wondering if this is worthwhile. I, for one, think that it is. We may be just a handful of men but we have kept regiments busy looking for us. Every horseman chasing us is one less soldier fighting General Lee and that means we have more chance of winning. I have a mind to head on towards Washington and see what mischief we can cause. We can always swing back south and join the army if things don't go right for us. What do you say?"

They all looked at each other and then Cecil scratched his head. "I'm sorry captain. Maybe I'm just a dumb Irishman but I thought that derailing a whole trainload of Yankee soldiers was a success. And I don't know about these other guys but this is the first time in my life I have had more than twenty dollars in my pockets. As far as I am concerned we have had success and I for one don't want it to stop."

When all the other men, Dago included slapped him on the back then I knew that Irish had been accepted. He was one of the Wildcats now.

"Well there you go, captain, and, boys, I have another twenty dollars for each of you courtesy of Pinkerton's men here."

"Thank you, Danny, and thank you, men. I am touched by your loyalty. Let's head north."

We had extra horses this time and we made good time. We bypassed Manassas to the east. We could see from the roads that there had been many soldiers through the area but we saw none. Danny had the map on his saddle. "Sir, the next places are Centreville, Vienna and Falls Church. We can make any of them tonight and scout them out. The boys aren't tired and there's still daylight."

"Then let's try Centreville. Dago and Jack, take Irish and scout it out. We'll meet you north of the town. We'll be half a mile north of the last house in the town."

Confederate Ranger

Mosby was known to raid west of the town and that was likely to have an armed presence. We headed to the east and then we could sweep around and meet the captain. We could see the town to the west. The turnpike led to Washington and we halted close by that major road. We left our horses in a sunken lane which meandered towards the south-east. We went on foot to spy out this road leading from the capital. We had gone barely three hundred yards when we struck gold. There was a wagon train on the other side of the turnpike close to a gate. The threat of Mosby had meant they had put the wagons in a defensive box formation. It looked as though they were coming from Washington. We crept as close as we could get to eavesdrop on their conversation and to count the guards.

They were relatively relaxed and there were just two sentries on the perimeter of the ten wagons. The drivers and the other guards were squatting around the fire cooking their meal. One rather overweight teamster stood and noisily farted, much to the amusement of some of his friends. "Well, I don't know why we couldn't go down to the Newgate tavern. It's not like we won't need it. After this, we'll be with the army and the prices in all the inns close to the front will be doubled."

"The boss doesn't want us all drunk and we would be if we went to the tavern."

"Where is he anyway? I bet he is drinking there."

"Nah he went to arrange the escort. He wants the two companies of cavalry who have been trying to catch Mosby. He thinks we need their protection."

"Well, that's another reason. As soon as we take the road south his ghosts and the Grey Ghost himself will be over us thicker'n fleas on a dog."

Confederate Ranger

"Stop whingeing Sullivan. We are being paid double just to carry this black powder and it's gonna help beat the damned Rebs. Are you a southern supporter now?"

"Now I never said that, Billy. I am as patriotic as the next man."

"Yeah, we know. You'd join up if they could get a tent to fit you as a uniform."

"Listen, you twig, I could get into a uniform but I am the best muleskinner you know. It would be a crying shame if it was wasted in the army."

We had seen and heard enough. We headed back to the horses and made a detour around the town. It was almost dark when we found the last house and we rode north. I had an idea where they would be for I saw the woods. When I heard Jed's whistle I knew we had found them.

"We found a wagon train full of powder. It's heading to the front tomorrow with a bunch of cavalry. We either strike tonight or find another target."

"How many men and guards are there in total?"

"They had two sentries and there were about twenty men in all."

"Don't forget the boss."

"Irish is right, there was a boss. He was the one talking to the cavalry."

"And I bet he would have someone with him. Say twenty-four all told."

"T'wou'd be nice captain; a lovely explosion. Let them know that the Wildcats are in the area."

I shook my head. "They will just think it is Mosby. They are wetting themselves worrying about him."

"Then we will have to leave our own message eh?"

Confederate Ranger

We had no tents to dismantle and Dago and I knew the way. As we headed purposefully towards the wagons I realised that, for the first time since the ambush, I was not looking over my shoulder for the knife in the back. It felt good. We had had to purge the company but we were all the stronger for the experience. Dago and I led and we halted close enough to see the men around the fires. We were hidden by the brush. We tied up the horses and left David and Cecil watching them. We all hated the duty but the men knew it was an important if unglamorous task.

"There are civilians so no shooting. Jed and Dago, you two take care of the sentries. The rest of you spread out. Jack, take your men to the other side of the wagons, the side closest to the road. If any run it will be that way. I will walk into the middle with Dago and Jed."

We trotted through the dark and I spread the men out. I made sure that Davy and Jimmy were at each end of my line. They were my most experienced men. We had to wait now until the captain appeared. We watched as the men gathered around the food. The cook snapped irritably, at yet another question, "It won't be ready for five more minutes! Now skedaddle!"

Suddenly the huge fat teamster we had seen before began to walk towards us. I gestured for the men to hide. He was coming directly for me. I pressed myself into the side of the wagon and he stepped in front of me and began to undo his trousers. We were both out of sight of the camp and his comrades. I pulled my Colt and pressed the barrel into the back of his head. The sound of the hammer being cocked must have sounded like an explosion to the civilian. "Now what you can feel, my friend is the business end of an Army Colt. Don't even think about moving."

His voice sounded full of terror. "Do you mind if I pee Mr Mosby?"

Confederate Ranger

I heard a giggle from Wilkie and I shook my head. "Just don't splash me!"

By the time he had finished, I saw that the captain was stepping, unseen, into the light. The men were so intent on their food that they did not even notice their arrival. Dago and Jed pushed the two sentries. I nodded to the boys and then said to my prisoner, "Let's go and rejoin your friends."

The sudden appearance of nineteen heavily armed men who appeared like wraiths from the dark had an amazing effect. They all dropped to their knees. The fat man I was with looked nervously over his shoulder. "Just keep on moving; I'll tell you when to drop. This ain't no prayer meeting."

"Gentlemen," Captain Boswell's voice sounded cultured and refined, "we are going to do you a favour. You will not need to work in the morning. We are going to relieve you of your cargo."

There were two men who had not been there before and they were both better dressed than the others. One of them tried to struggle to his feet. "I protest sir! This is U.S. Army property and you risk severe punishment." Danny pushed him back to his knees.

"Well, sir, I am Captain James Boswell and these are Boswell's Wildcats and our avowed intent is to hurt the U.S. Army. Danny you and Harry search these two. The rest of you, tie their hands and lead them to the road. Jed and Dago put them somewhere safe."

"You heard him, boys," I spied a coil of rope in one of the wagons and I began to cut it into lengths and give it to the men. In a very short time, they were all tied with their hands behind their backs. Danny and Harry had finished their search and the two men were also tied.

Jed had found some more rope and he looped it around the men's necks. One of them began moaning. "Don't hang us, boys! I am a married man!"

Jed laughed. "You ain't gonna hang. Come on Dago. There's a tree down the lane a ways. It'll do."

I turned to Wilkie. "Go and get Cecil and the horses."

Danny was already laying a trail of powder away from the wagons. Harry was doing the same. I looked at the cauldron of food. "Seems a shame to waste this captain. We haven't eaten for a while."

He grinned, "Sure thing. Feed the boys when they get back."

"Carlton you get some food now and then go and watch the prisoners."

Carlton was always hungry and he greedily filled a bowl and began eating the pork and beans with some sourdough bread he had found. Just watching him made me hungry too but I would wait until the men had eaten first. We heard the sound of hooves as the horses arrived. "Get some food boys and then go with Carlton to watch the prisoners."

The other men were not as greedy as Carlton had been they finished at the same time. They all ran quickly down the lane to the tree where Dago and Jed waited. Danny and Harry returned. "We might as well eat. Come on, captain."

Captain Boswell was totally engrossed in the papers. He wandered over. "This is gold dust. It is a series of orders for wagons to supply the army. The boys on the general's staff should be able to work out where their supply bases are." He stuffed the papers in his pocket and then began to eat. "I think, as we have been fed, that we'll head south tonight and try to get close to our lines by morning."

Confederate Ranger

Jed and Dago brought the rest of the men up and they ate their fill. There was little left in the cauldron when we had finished. "Harry, get your men to rope the teams of horses and mules. We'll take them back. Jack, collect any weapons you can find although they won't be worth much. Right boys; mount. We'll meet you at the prisoners. Danny and I will have the pleasure of setting off this little firework display!"

The captain was right, the weapons were of poor quality but I put them on the pack horses Harry had brought. The prisoners were looking sorry for themselves as they waited, tied beneath the huge oak tree. The fat teamster looked up at Jed who was wiping the grease off his mouth. "I guess you boys enjoyed our supper."

"You can't beat food cooked on the campfire; especially if it is cooked by someone else."

Suddenly the sky lit up and then there was an enormous crump as the wagon park exploded. The shock waves almost knocked us off our feet. One of the prisoners yelled, "Jesus Christ. There goes our bonus!"

We were laughing at that when Danny and the captain ran in laughing like children. "What's up, captain?"

"We were too damned close to the explosion." He pointed to his and Danny's face. They had no eyebrows and their beards and moustaches were smoking. "That was fun though." He turned to the prisoners. "Well gentleman I can't promise you a comfortable night but I expect you will be released just as soon as the good people of the town come to see what the explosion was." He swept his hat off in a salute, vaulted on his horse and we rode east, towards Washington.

Chapter 6

We decided that we had better return to our own lines. The explosion would have been heard for miles around and it would not take them long to organise a pursuit. As soon as we were out of sight we turned south. We had to tread carefully. We knew that there were troops and munitions heading south from Alexandria towards Burnside's army. We were counting on the fact that they would not be travelling at night. We had full stomachs, rested horses and we had won. We were in fine humour. Our maps showed a trail over the hills close to Aquia Church. We left the road just before the church and Dago soon found the back trail. We felt much more secure as we clambered up hills and through forested tracks. We kept going until well beyond sunrise. We laid up for most of the afternoon. Jed and Harry had been out scouting the roads and seen them teeming with Union forces. We couldn't risk the main towns and we would have to cross the river near Falmouth again. It meant crossing through their lines and that meant we would have to wait until nightfall.

When we came in sight of Fredericksburg the captain gathered us in a circle. "I want Harry and his boys as the rearguard." He turned to Dago, Jed and me, " Jack, Danny and I will take your men with us. I want you to take Dago and Jed and scout us out a route away from Yankees. There will be vedettes out there and we can't afford a firefight. We have to sneak through their lines." He chuckled, "And you three are the sneakiest men we have. Mark the trail. Three cuts on the trees to the left should keep us straight."

"And when we are out of the trees?"

Confederate Ranger

"We will assume that we go straight on unless you put some stones in a pile. Three for left and five for right. Find us a safe place to ford."

I took out my knife in preparation. As we headed south I said, "Keep your eyes open for stones. You can collect them when I mark the trees." After half a mile I marked a tree. We were not turning but I wanted to give the reassurance that the men following were heading in the right direction. Another half mile and I marked another tree. It was all remarkably easy. Jed and Dago had a fine collection of stones and so far we had not seen any danger.

Suddenly I smelled tobacco and I held up my hand. The other two stopped. Dago went for his gun but I shook my head and mimed punching. We gave our reins to Jed and crept forwards. There were two cavalrymen at the road. It was obviously a checkpoint and I could see, in the distance, the glowing fires of a camp. We had almost stumbled upon a cavalry regiment. Dago and I had worked together enough times not to need words. I waved my hand to the right three times and I slipped left to take one sentry while Dago took the right. Despite my instructions to Dago, I took out my Colt. I wanted to frighten them. The two sentries were talking to each other and, instead of watching the road were watching each other; a cardinal error. I reached up and grabbed the back of the cavalryman's jacket. I used his straps to wrench him to the ground and pushed my Colt almost up his left nostril. "One sound and you get a ball in your head. Understand?" He nodded. "Good lad. Now stand." He was only young, no more than eighteen and he was almost shaking as he stood.

"Don't kill me, sergeant."

"If'n I wanted you dead, you would be." I looked over to where Dago had cold-cocked the other. "Stick him on his horse and then cover this one." I whistled twice and Jed rode up. We mounted our horses and then I said, "Come on sonny. Get on your horse. Dago, take them back to the captain. We'll head towards the river." I could see the moonlight glistening on the Rappahannock River just ahead. We now needed a ford.

"Come on Jed. We'll use the road. Leave five stones in the middle." I glanced over and saw that there were a pile of large rocks by the side of the road. "They'll do." We arranged them in a symmetrical pile.

I was gambling on the fact that they would only have sentries at the end of a road. We must have reached the limits of their camps. It made sense to put the cavalry on the flanks and I was grateful that their sentries had been green. "Look, Jack, there's Falmouth. The ford is just beyond it."

"You wait here for the captain and I will check it out."

I rode confidently down the road. The small burg looked to be closed up for the night. I could see neither lights nor any sign that people were awake. The main road went through the town but I could see a well-worn dirt track that seemed to go around the back of it. I took the track. It went very close to the shrubs and bushes on one side and the back of, what looked like, smallholdings and farms. There was a danger that there would be dogs if they were farms but it was a chance we might have to take. The track headed away from the river and I followed the line of buildings and was rewarded with the sight of the ford we had used to head north. I turned around and rode back. No dog had barked and I took that as a good omen.

The company were waiting for me. I made my report. "How far is it then?"

"No more than two miles. We should reach it before sunrise."

We rode in single file along the track. I thought our luck had held until we were halfway along the sheltered way when a dog began to bark. In an instant, it seemed that every dog in Falmouth had decided to join in. "Ride captain. They know we are here."

We kicked on and I raced for the ford. It was as I remembered it. It would be icy cold and this time we would be trying to get twenty horses we were not familiar with across. I rode to the island and took out my Henry. If any bluecoats came then I would have to discourage them from some distance away to give the company time to cross. Dago and Jed joined me and we peered at the northern river bank to the east of where we would be crossing. Already I could see the glow from some lights in the houses. We were so close to dawn that some of the inhabitants would have been rising anyway; the dogs merely made them curious. I saw my section leading the pack horses. I hoped that Cecil had some of the quieter ones as he was not the most confident around horses.

"Dago, you and Jed get to the other bank. When we left it was in our hands but you never know what can happen in a couple of days." I never took my eyes off the northern bank but I heard the troop splashing across.

Wilkie and Jacob brought the first horses across. "Nearly there boys. Just one more wetting!"

"I bin baptised sergeant! This is going a bit far!"

If Wilkie could joke then we were going to make it. The captain and Danny reined in. "Well done, Jack. This is a good crossing. Shame about the dogs."

"Dago and Jed are on the other bank. I haven't heard shooting so they should be safe. I'll wait here until Harry and his boys are safely over."

Just at that moment, I saw the flash and I heard the crack of a pistol across the river. "Best get them moving, Danny. I think Harry has company."

Confederate Ranger

I brought the Henry up to my shoulder. I couldn't see anyone yet but I wanted to be ready. A movement out of the corner of my eye made me drag the sight around to my left but I saw that it was Ritchie, one of Harry's new boys. He gasped, panic making him sound out of breath, "Union cavalry. Didn't stop to count."

"Well stop now, turn round your horse and take out your rifle. Just calm down son. We'll get out of this."

When he said, "Yes sarge," he sounded much calmer already.

The next two riders were older hands and they wheeled around to flank me. I saw the flash of a sabre in dawn's early light and I knew that they were cavalry. "Aim for the horses and make your shots count. Fire slowly and carefully."

I aimed at the leading rider and squeezed off a shot. A horse is a good, big target, the trick is to hit it where it will hurt. I have seen horses struggle for a mile or more with a ball in its side. I was lucky; my ball struck it in the forelock and it tumbled overthrowing the rider to the ground. The others fired and I saw at least one man fall. "Come on Harry," I murmured to myself.

As if he had heard me, my old friend reined in with the last of his men. I saw that Carlton was wounded. "Isaiah, take Carlton over the river. The rest of you join Lucky Jack here." With six of us firing at them, the Union cavalry were halting and forming a skirmish line. "I think that is us done. Cross the river!"

Harry and I fired one last shot and then we plunged into the icy waters of the Rappahannock River. A ball took my kepi off my head and sent it flying into the river. "Lucky Jack! Again!" Harry went into fits of laughter.

The captain had organised the rest of the men into a mounted skirmish line so that a volley from their guns discouraged the Union horsemen who were already demoralised. We headed south to where we could see the fires that we assumed were the

Confederate Ranger

Confederate soldiers. The first pickets we met were nervous cavalrymen from Louisiana.

"Where you boys come from? We thought we were the furthest forward."

"We've been in the north. We're Rangers!" Cecil blurted. I shook my head and he said, "Sorry captain."

"I am Captain Boswell and these are Boswell's Wildcats. Is General Stuart close by?"

"He's in the cavalry camp." He pointed to the south.

"And the quartermaster?"

"A little further south."

"Much obliged."

"Jack, you and the boys take these horses and weapons to the quartermaster. Danny and I will report to the general and then meet you."

Although the meeting with the quartermaster was productive I noticed a few strange looks from some of the officers who were standing around. There appeared to be a chilly atmosphere. Harry noticed it too but passed it off by saying that they probably hadn't heard of the train and the powder. "Besides, I don't give a bugger. "

I liked Harry. He always spoke his mind and didn't care who he offended but there was no more loyal member of the Wildcats than Harry. "How have the new boys settled in?"

Harry had been given some of those who had come from England and Scotland. As we worked in our sections I didn't get to know his men as well as mine. "Good lads, generally. A bit wet behind the ears but they will settle in. You are lucky with Davy and Jimmy. They have been around long enough to be able to give you some help. I lost Bill and Norman in the ambush. I think we are going to have to reorganise. I mean the captain and Danny have no-one left in their sections unless you count Jed and Dago."

"You are right. The ambush hurt us in many ways. But it could have been worse."

"How?"

"We could all have been captured or killed. It wasn't just Jack that was lucky, it was the Wildcats. We could so easily have missed finding those clues."

He chuckled. "You are definitely the glass is half full aren't you Jack?"

I shrugged, "I can't see the point in looking on the black side. There is always hope. I could still have been aboard that slaver but for the captain. That's hope."

We were getting worried about the two officers. They seemed to be with the general for hours. Perhaps he was showing them the same hospitality we had seen in the Newgate tavern. Their faces looked dark when they reached us.

"Where do we pitch our tents captain?"

"We don't. Let's head west. I have a fancy for a hotel." He smiled at Jed and me. "The general was telling me that you two had a fine time when he met you. Living it up like lords I think he said."

Harry and I rode with the two officers as we headed for Culpeper. They told us what had transpired. "It seems that the Rangers days are over. They are allowing Mosby to carry on as a Partisan Ranger but the rest of us are either disbanded or are to be incorporated into the Confederate Army. Apparently, Colonel Mosby has the ear of the Secretary of War. But Jeff Davis has said the rest have to be disbanded and the men can join the army."

"Which is what you want isn't it Captain? Or at least it was before we became Rangers."

Confederate Ranger

His shoulders sagged, "Before we became Rangers I would have said yes but I quite like the freedom we have enjoyed up to now."

Harry looked over his shoulder at the camp which was disappearing in the distance. "How come we aren't joining the army now?"

Danny tapped his nose. "The captain still has enemies who are opposed to him having a commission. We could all join a regiment today but I didn't think you would want to desert the captain. Am I right?" We all chorused our affirmation. "That's what I thought. Anyway, there's going to be a big battle in the next few days. When the dust has cleared there will be some new regiments formed and General Stuart wants us in one of those. We are going home for an early Christmas and then we can come back in January and the general will have a regiment for us." He looked serious for a moment. "And there is something else. The Northern Newspapers are calling the execution of Colm and Geraghty as murder. They are saying that they were Union soldiers. Boswell's Rangers are being called bandits and murderers. Some of our own side are not happy about us."

"Bullshit!"

"You are dead right, Dago, but they believe that we are murderers and there is a price on our heads. The general thought it would be easier for us if we used our skills with the army. He said he sees us as a company who scout for a regiment. He still sees us as Rangers. I quite like that idea. But, we wouldn't be Boswell's Horse anymore, nor the Wildcats."

There was a stunned silence as we took that in. We might still be Rangers but we wouldn't have our unique identity.

Confederate Ranger

The captain looked sadly at us. "I wouldn't blame you boys if you did join another regiment. I would understand. I have managed to make some really dumb decisions."

Harry reached over and put his huge arm around the captain. "Sir, there isn't one decision you made that was in any way dumb. We have had a little bit of bad luck but Lucky Jack here told me we have had more good luck than bad luck. But then again he is the half-full type."

I leaned forward and handed the promissory note to the captain, "And we have more money here from the quartermaster. I think a little break in Charleston will help us all. We can actually do something with the money we have acquired since this war started."

"There you go Jack. Half-full again!"

We reached Charleston four days later. We stabled the horses at Front Royal and took a train. Charleston looked exactly the same as it always had. It was as though the war had not happened. The rich still had their luxuries courtesy of the smugglers and the poor were just as poor as they had ever been. The house still looked as magnificent as ever. Jarvis, the captain's estate manager and former slave had kept it immaculate and it was run very much as it had been before the war. We settled back into our bunkhouse but the new men like Cecil and Wilkie had to be persuaded that this was their new home. All of us had been poor before we met the captain and for the new boys, the hospitality was a little too much. They were almost afraid of damaging the grass by walking on it.

I was feeling nostalgic and took a horse down to the docks and harbour. I looked at the paucity of ships and remembered before the war when it had been a lively and bustling port. I sat on a bollard. I could almost picture the Rose of Tralee as she had sailed away that last time. My old shipmates and my enemies were now at the bottom of the sea. I had been saved and snatched from its jaws by Captain Boswell. I shook myself free from my sad and melancholy thoughts and walked back to the rail where I had left my horse. I was about to mount when a voice called, "Mr Hogan! Jack Hogan!"

I turned and saw a small man dressed in the clothes of a clerk. I vaguely recognised him but I couldn't place him. "Yes, I am Jack Hogan."

"Its Michael sir, I work in the dock office. I used to see you when I came aboard the Rose."

Suddenly I remembered him. He too was Irish and he had seemed to like me and treated me with respect and kindness. I never knew why. "Of course, Michael, and how are you keeping?"

Fine sir, can't complain. At least we have food on the table but I have something for you, sir." He flourished an envelope. "A letter. It came last year and I knew you were in the war so I just waited until you came home on leave. I was going to call around the plantation and then I saw you stop here it is sir."

He handed me the letter. I didn't recognise the handwriting. It was addressed,

Jack Hogan
Sailor on the Rose of Tralee
Charleston USA

I shook my head. How had it reached me? I put my hand in my pocket and pulled out two Yankee silver dollars. I handed them to Michael. "Oh no, sir. I couldn't."

I closed his hands around the money. "You were kind to me when others weren't and we are both Irish. If you ever need more then just ask."

I could see the gratitude on his face. "Thank you, sir. You have become a real gentleman."

I relished the compliment as I rode back to my home. I did not want to read the letter in the street. I would find a quiet place and discover who knew that I was in America. I took the letter to the back porch of the bunkhouse and carefully slit it open with my penknife.

April 1862

Dear Jack,

I am telling the priest here, Father Nicholas, what to write as I won't be here much longer and I never learned how to write. I have no idea if you will ever read this letter so I am putting faith in God. The father here says that God works in mysterious ways.

After Black Bill died your sister, Caitlin, left for America to search for you. We heard she was going to New York or Boston. Is either of them places close to where you are? We heard from Fatty that you had left the ship in Charleston but he didn't know any more. I told you, sister, where you were and she just left.

I meant to write sooner but, well Betty was ill for the longest time and she has recently died. I am told that I haven't got long for this world and I wanted to speak to you again. I know it is a letter but I am talking to the priest as though he was you. That's how you know that this is from the heart.

I liked you Jack. I would have been proud for you to have been my kin but you weren't. I had a little money put by. Betty and me had planned on using it but we never got around to that. I want you to have it. Father Nicholas is a good man and he has given it to his bank manager for safekeeping. If you ever get back here then go to St.Patrick's church and ask for Father Nicholas. He will see you get it. It might be enough to get you a decent berth on a ship.

God Bless you Jack and I hope you find your sister,

Your friend,

Stumpy

x

Stumpy's mark.

P.S. This part is from me, Father Nicholas. You must be a special person Jack to have made such an influence on old Stumpy. I will be waiting for you should you ever make it over here.

Father Nicholas

Confederate Ranger

The ink started to smudge where my tears had splashed on the paper. I fingered the penknife which Stumpy had given to me. It was suddenly more precious than it had been. My sister was in America. She was free from Black Bill but what was her life like now? I suddenly felt responsible and guilty. I needed to marshal my thoughts and make plans. I lay on my bed for some time. Harry came in and saw the letter in my hand. He just nodded and left. He was a good friend who knew when to leave you alone. I got up and went into the house. I sought Jarvis.

"Jarvis is there any writing paper and envelopes in the house?"

"Why yes suh. There is a writing desk with all that you will need, in the library. I will post if for you when you are done."

I am no writer and I just wrote from the heart. I knew my writing could not compare to the priest's but I didn't care. I thanked the priest and told him to buy a good headstone for Stumpy and Betty. I told him to use any that was left over for the orphans and homeless children in Cork. I told him that I hoped that I would get to see him and the stone one day.

I gave the finished and addressed letter to Jarvis who smiled and nodded. "I am glad that you are with the captain sir. I feel that you are good for him. You are a good man and there's not many of those in these parts."

"Thank you, Jarvis. Tell me," I hesitated. "Do you ever resent the fact that you were a slave? I mean I know the captain freed you and your wife but don't you harbour resentment that he had you as a slave in the first place."

He smiled, "It's like this sir, I thank the lord that it was Captain Boswell who bought me. He was a kind owner. Me and my wife were born slaves. No, I don't resent it but I prefer being free and I wished I had been born free. But I wasn't I was born a slave. It makes freedom taste sweeter somehow. Perhaps one day we will all be free."

"Thank you for your honesty Jarvis and our conversation will remain private."

"That's what I mean sir. You may not have been born a gentleman but you are a gentleman now."

I borrowed a horse from the stables and went for a ride. I found I could think better from the back of a horse. This was one of the captain's finest but she was no Copper. Copper was safely in a stable in Front Royal. I needed to decide what I wanted. In a perfect world, I would get a train to New York or Boston and try to find my sister. I saw, immediately, some flaws in that plan! We were at war and I had no idea where she was. And then there was the largest hurdle, I was still a soldier. I looked up and noticed what beautiful country it was. I had been so busy working when I lived here that I had missed its beauty. I found that I had ridden across many fields and emerged looking down on Charleston and its harbour. It was beautiful and reminded me in many ways of Cork with the boats, the port and the busy life around the town. What would I do if I were in Cork and not Charleston? As with many things the idea just popped up in my head and I galloped back to the plantation. I now knew what I wanted.

I changed my clothes and had a body wash; I knew that I would reek of horses. I hoped that the captain was in for I needed his advice and guidance. "Jarvis is the captain around?"

"Yes suh, he is in the library with Mr Murphy." He paused and then said, "I don't think it is private, Mr Hogan."

He was the consummate butler and I smiled my thanks. I knocked on the door. "Come." When the captain saw me his face broke into a smile. "Ah, Jack. Your ears must have been burning. We were just talking about you." My face must have shown concern for the captain gestured towards a seat and said hurriedly, "Nothing bad I can assure you. We were just saying that there are just a handful of the original Wildcats left; just you Harry, Jed and Dago. It gives one pause for thought."

"Is it a bad thing that I hadn't thought about our dead comrades until you mentioned them?"

Danny shook his head, "No, Jack, we have to think of the living. There will be a time to remember the dead when all of this is over."

The captain saw the hesitation on my face. "You wanted to ask us something?"

"Advice and guidance sir. From both of you. You two are the men I trust most in the world and I know you will give me an honest answer to my questions."

"Of course."

"I have had a letter from Cork. My sister is living in New York or Boston. My friend was unclear which one. She came to America to look for me."

Danny grinned and slapped me on the back. "Well, that is grand news!"

The captain saw my expression, "I don't think it is as simple as that, is it Jack? New York is now in another country."

Danny's face fell. "Of course! I am sorry, Jackie."

"I know all that and I also understand that, until this war is over I can't really do anything."

"Not quite true, Jack. You can put an advert in the New York papers. She might read it."

"She couldn't read when we were in Ireland but you are right. It would be a way to keep in touch. What I wanted to ask, sir, is how much money have I got? I know that I have about four hundred dollars from our last patrol but we had money invested in other things."

"You are right Jack and the money from our dead comrades has been added so you are a wealthy man. I can find out easily enough." He leaned forward and I could see I had interested him. "What have you in mind?"

"In Ireland, my ma and da never owned their house. If you can call it a house, a hovel more like but it was a home. We knew we could be thrown off at any time. Caitlin worked for Black Bill and when he died she was thrown out. With all due respect sir but if anything happened to you then I would have no home."

He shook his head vehemently. "I would look after you and the others."

"And that is very kind of you sir but I was brought up to believe that a man looked after his own first." I took a deep breath. "Have I enough to buy a house; a nice house- here in Charleston?"

"Of course. You have enough to buy a small version of this. I can ask my friends in town and we can get one before we go back. But that wasn't your only question was it?"

"No, sir. You see I would be away with you and I would want it looked after. I would like to buy Aaron from you," I paused, "and give him his freedom. I would want him as my estate manager. Just as Jarvis is yours."

Danny and the captain exchanged a look and then the captain said softly. "You are a deep one. You can have Aaron as a gift from me and I am delighted that you will offer him his freedom but tell me, why Aaron?"

"That first patrol in the Valley; it was Aaron who was kind to me. I know he was a slave but he showed interest in me and helped me. I was new to this life and it helped. And I remembered the others who helped me like Stumpy and Fatty. They are dead now and I can do little for them but he is alive and I would like to do something for him. Don't get me wrong, you two have done more for me and I am really grateful but I don't see how I can repay you, not yet anyway."

"Jack you owe us nothing. Danny and I know that you are the heart of the Wildcats. If you were not a part of it then it would have died some time ago." He stood up. "Well, let the three of us ride into town and begin the arrangements."

I had thought that it would be a hard task and a time-consuming quest to find a suitable house but it was not so. Captain Boswell had many contacts in the business community. I suspect that not all of them were pillars of society. We discovered a number of properties which the captain assured me I could easily afford. The one we settled on had a sad story. The last owner had mortgaged the house to finance a regiment. He had been killed at the Battle of Kernstown and the bank was selling it cheaply to reclaim its losses. Money was tight in Charleston and cash was worth more than promises. I wanted to buy it unseen when I heard that the owner had died at my first battle. The captain and Danny would hear none of it and they took me out to the house. They wanted me to see what I was buying.

It was south of the city and had a slave block, a barn and a small amount of land. There were, of course, no slaves. They had been the first things the bank had sold but I could see the potential. It was larger than the squire's house back in Ireland. As soon as I stepped through the door I knew that I wanted it. It was already furnished and felt comfortable. It was less grand than the captain's but still a substantial property. Caitlin would love it. I had worried that it would be filled with the ghosts of the dead. If there were ghosts then they were the friendly type.

Confederate Ranger

We had the paperwork signed, sealed and delivered before nightfall. I was a landowner. "You still have money in the bank Jack. Not a fortune and now that we are no longer Partisan Rangers your income will drop but I am sure you could make money from the land."

"But I know nothing but growing potatoes."

"Potatoes won't grow here Jackie boy." Danny ruefully shook his head. "I found that out when I first arrived. Aaron is a good lad. He'll know what will grow."

"If he agrees to run it for me."

Jarvis brought Aaron to the drawing-room. I could see the nervousness on the young slave's face. I suspect he thought he had done wrong.

The captain smiled, "Please stay Jarvis, we would appreciate your advice. Now, Aaron, you are a good slave and you are not in trouble so for goodness sake stop frowning." The slave grinned at the words. "Now you may remember Mr Hogan here. He has just bought a house and I intend to give you to him as a house slave." He gave a wary smile and a nod at me. "Jack?"

"How do you feel about being my slave?"

"Suh?"

Jarvis smiled, "Mr Hogan the question is a difficult one to ask of a slave."

"Let me rephrase it. Would you like to work for me?"

"I'm your slave suh. I am a good worker."

He was still confused. I said quietly, "Not as my slave, as a free man." I handed Aaron the papers of manumission. "You are a free man now. Will you work for me?"

He looked at me a little suspiciously. "If I say no am I still a slave?"

Confederate Ranger

I laughed and Jarvis gave an impatient snort. "No Aaron. You are free and if you choose you can leave and find a job of your own and I will advertise for someone to be my estate manager" I peered at him. "I would prefer it to be someone I could trust, like you."

His face lit up again. "You mean I'd be like Mr Jarvis? Then yes suh and thank you, Mr Hogan. I won't let you down."

I shook his hand. "We will go over tomorrow and you can get settled in. I imagine you will have goodbyes to say tonight. But I would appreciate it if you could find time to talk to Mr Jarvis here. I want you to do as he does and that means running the estate while I am at the front. You will have to decide what to grow and your wages will be decided by how profitable the estate is."

"I get paid too? In that case suh, we will have the best run farm in Carolina."

Jarvis hurried him out but as he passed me he said, "As I said sir, a real gentleman. I will keep an eye on him but he is a good boy."

The captain poured Danny and me a drink. "That was well done. I could see that Jarvis was touched."

I was confused, "Why?"

"Well didn't you know? Aaron is his son. His name is Aaron Jarvis."

The next day we settled Aaron into the house and I gave him the small bedroom in the main house. You would have thought I had given him the keys to the kingdom. Jarvis was left with some of my money to help Aaron pay for things until he learned how to manage himself. Similarly, the slaves from Captain Boswell's plantation would work on mine until Aaron had hired men. He offered to buy slaves but I was adamant. In Ireland, we had been slaves in all but name and I would not inflict that on anyone.

Confederate Ranger

As we sat on the train, in the last days of December, heading to a Virginia where the Yankees had been soundly beaten at Fredericksburg, I wondered if the war might be over sooner rather than later. Of course, I did not have long to ruminate as my comrades decided to mock me constantly.

"So I would have thought a plantation owner would be in First Class. What are you doing with us?"

"Now Harry…"

"Ah, the thing of it is he needs all his money now to buy lace for the legs of the chairs."

"Dago…I"

"No, he will be looking in the catalogues to buy himself a bride next. Lord Hogan of Charleston. It has a nice ring to it."

When they had tired of their fun, they and some of the others asked me about my decision. I answered them with a question. "What will you do with your money?"

"Ah well when the war is over I'll go to a big city and I'll get a room in the biggest hotel….."

"And your money will be gone in a month."

"Aye Jack but I will have lived."

"True Jed, but what about the men who had as much money as you did? The ones killed in the ambush. What about them?"

"Well, they er… Well if you die who gets your house?"

I peered intently at them, "Caitlin my sister of course."

Confederate Ranger

Interlude

Caitlin cowered in the corner of the room as Mick ranted and raved. He had been throwing things around since he had arrived home on leave. The Union soldier had been this way since the letter came about his cousins. "The murdering Reb bastards. As soon as I get back to the front I am going to make it my business to find these Wildcats and I will rip the feckin hearts out of them."

"Isn't it war Mick darling? I mean soldiers get killed all the time." She could never understand men fighting. Life was hard enough without putting yourself where men could kill you. As far as she could see war brought nothing but misery, hunger and death.

He almost thrust the paper into her face. "They hanged them! You don't do that to soldiers and besides the Rangers aren't soldiers. They are bandits and murderers. I'm going to kill every single one of them."

Caitlin had to get downstairs to open the bar but she was wondering, as she went down the rickety stairs if she ought to reconsider her decision to marry Mick O'Callaghan in June. She didn't like his temper. It reminded her too much of Black Bill. And he had been less loving since he had been sharing her bed. She thought that was a little ironic but then again Black Bill had been the same. They were sweet as anything until she succumbed and then a bastard. She also felt uncomfortable about his news. Perhaps Jack was fighting too and he might find himself the victim of these murderers men like Mosby and this Boswell. She clutched her crucifix and said a silent prayer for her brother, wherever he was.

Major Beauregard had made sure he had the finest and most flamboyant uniform he could get. After all, his future father in law,

Ebenezer Winfield was paying for it. Neil's uniform was more functional. Secretary of War Seddon had not seemed as keen as Ebenezer had made out but he had given him a commission as a major in the newly formed cavalry unit, the 1st Virginia Scouts. Arthur had hoped for a colonelcy. He resented having to take orders from a damned colonial but Secretary Seddon was adamant. Money had to have changed hands for him to have been given a majority.

Arthur and his servant would have to travel to Winchester where the regiment was being created. Andrew Neil had discovered, through a conversation with some officials that the regiment would be a hotchpotch of other regiments which had too few to muster sufficient numbers and men sent from other regiments because of discipline issues. That side of it didn't worry Arthur. He would use Neil to coerce them into working for him. The rest of the men employed by Major Beauregard would continue to work in Atlanta and build up his criminal empire. He was marrying for respectability but he made his money through gambling and prostitution. The old man was being very cagey and the weeding would not be until the summer. He wanted Arthur to prove himself. The Englishman smiled. He had outwitted far cleverer men than Winfield.

"Neil, make sure that the men know they are to keep on top of the business. This is an interruption only. Once I am married I will find some excuse to leave the service of the Confederacy. Hopefully, old man, Winfield will not survive the winter."

Neil grinned, "He could have an accident, sir? Then you would be free to marry."

He shook his head, "No I am not sure of his will. I want his money and his land. It will be worth the short wait. And I want to take our own sweet time getting to this Winchester place. I do not relish the idea of sleeping in a tent. Find out, if you can, where this damned regiment is will you?"

Arthur was right in one respect; Ebenezer Winfield did not trust the slimy Englishman. His will left all of his money to a trust to keep his daughter comfortably cared for. He had hoped for a reliable man to marry her but all the decent ones were at war and she had fallen for the Englishman. He neither trusted nor liked the Englishman. He would wait to see how the wind blew once Arthur St John Beauregard fought for the south.

Chapter 7

When we arrived at Front Royal and paid our stabling bill it felt strange. From now on we would be soldiers paid to fight for the Confederacy. We would still need to provide our own horses but food and tents would be supplied. We were also acutely aware that discipline and regulations would play a much bigger part. If would have to be 'lieutenant' and not 'Danny'; 'sergeant' and not 'Jack'. The captain had told us how much we would be paid while we travelled north. "You privates will get $11 a month. Dago and Jed, $13. Harry and Jack, $17. "

The privates whistled and Dago looked ruefully at the stripes on my sleeves. "I reckon I will try for those. I could use an extra four bucks a month." Dago had expensive tastes in women and booze.

Harry and I both felt a little uncomfortable at this new arrangement. Hitherto we had shared in the dangers and shared in the profits. All of that was now changing. None of us asked how much Danny and the captain were getting, we assumed much more. But it didn't matter; we were still the men who worked for Captain Boswell and that would never change.

It was good to be back on my own horse. Copper was almost a mind reader when we rode in action. I could ask her to do anything and she would not let me down. I was also happy to have my own weapons close by. My Colts and my knives were almost part of me. The captain had said that we would be allowed to keep our own equipment but we might have to get our own ammunition or use the weapons of the rest of the regiment. None of us fancied that. The Navy Colts wouldn't be a problem but I would have to husband my dwindling supply for the Army Colts I liked. Luckily we had acquired quite a quantity when we had been freelance and Harry and I had buried little stashes of it around Winchester and Front Royal. Of course, we couldn't just disappear and collect things like that now. We were subject to regulations and we didn't want to be shot as deserters.

When we reached Winchester General Stuart was there with the Quartermaster. I was pleased that we were the first of the new men to arrive. The new colonel and the new major hadn't even made an appearance. Stuart clasped Captain Boswell warmly by the hand. "I can see that you and your men are keen. I did try to get you a majority and we nearly had one but Secretary of War Seddon intervened. It seems he owed a favour and we have an Englishman who was in the Crimea." He shrugged, "He may be satisfactory. We will have to see. Don't worry. I intend to see Colonel Cartwright when he arrives. The colonel is a very experienced commander and you will like him. He has been fighting for this country since before you were born. You and your men are to be used as scouts. I don't want your skills going to waste. You will need to train up the rest of your company when they arrive. You will need another lieutenant and you should have three or four sergeants." He leaned in to speak to the captain. "I would get your men in place now, while you can. Once I leave…." He was making it clear that the captain would be soon on his own.

"I understand. Thank you general."

"A Troop, 1st Virginia Scouts follow me."

That was the first time we actually heard our name and it made us feel good. We were now part of the army. The tents were already neatly laid out but before we could enter them the captain stopped us. "I am going to make some promotions. I know some of you will be upset but I will do the best for all of you when I can. Danny, you will be the First Lieutenant, Harry, the Second

Lieutenant. Jack, First Sergeant, Dago and Jed you will both be sergeants. Davy, David and Jimmy, you are promoted to corporal. This is enough for the time being but when we get more men then we will need to add. There are chances for all of you."

Dago was beaming. "Well, I got my pay rise!"

Harry looked embarrassed, "I think you should have got First Lieutenant, Jack."

"No Harry, sorry, sir, I think you deserve it and I am happy being First Sergeant. Still, I think we will need more corporals." I grinned, "Lieutenant, would you ask the captain if we could have three more corporals?"

Laughing, Harry said, "I agree with you but this sir and lieutenant lark will take some getting used to."

I found that, as First Sergeant, I had a tent all to myself. There were some benefits to being isolated from the rest of my friends. I organised my tent the way I liked it and then took a stroll around the camp to check up on the men, my men. What I noticed was that the tents got bigger with the rank. I had the same size tent as Dago and Jed but theirs was bigger than that shared by Jimmy and Davy and that, in turn, was bigger than the one occupied by Wilkie and Jacob. When I found Danny, Harry and the captain's tents, I found that they could stand up in theirs. This was a different army to the one I had been in before Christmas. I wandered over to the horse lines and took a handful of grain to Copper. At least my horse hadn't changed but I feared that everything else with which I was familiar would change and not always for the better.

We were one part of a huge cavalry corps. We were woken by reveille. We did not even have our own bugler! We were woken by the nearby regiments in this huge gathering of cavalrymen. No-one had organised food, for Jed was now a sergeant and the men looked around for someone to make a decision. Danny held his hands up. "I guess this is my fault boys. Until we get more men and officers, apparently I am adjutant and I should have organised this. Sergeant Smith, organise breakfast. Sergeant Spinelli, organise some sentries. "

Everyone looked around. Who were these sergeants? Dago held up his hand, "Hey morons! I am Sergeant Spinelli. Work out who Sergeant Smith is eh?"

Danny laughed, "First Sergeant and officers to the command tent!"

I followed Harry and Danny and we entered the spacious tent of the captain. He looked at us and spread his arms. "Sorry about that. We haven't made a very good start have we?"

"Jack, can you organise the men: the sentries and the food. Find someone to look after the horses and someone who can be an armourer. Danny, make a rota for officers and liaise with Jack."

"How about more corporals sir?"

"Yes Harry, er Lieutenant Grimes mentioned that. Have you anyone in mind?"

"As an armourer then Irish is your man. As for horses, it has to be Carlton. He would sleep with them if he could but I have no idea who to make cook. Jed was the best. Perhaps we ask him."

"Right Jack, you organise that and have a word with Jed." He looked solemnly at us all. "I don't want this Colonel Cartwright to find any fault with us. We already have a poor reputation and half of the staff think we are little better than bandits and murderers. We need to be better than the rest. Jack make sure the men know how and when to salute. Keep the weapons clean and make sure the sentries are on the ball."

Telling Cecil that he was promoted was one of the best moments of my life. I took Carlton and Cecil to one side. "The captain has asked me to promote you to corporal. You can choose a tent later. Cecil, you will be the armourer. That means you fix any gun the men bring to you. We want every gun to work the first time and you are the man to do that. Carlton, you will be responsible for the horses. You check them every night and every morning. I want you to assume that there may be problem. Cecil yours is the harder job I'm afraid. You might have no work and then again you might be inundated by broken pieces. But what you must both realise is that in any situation you are a leader. If any of the sergeants or officers is not there then you are in charge. In a battle or a skirmish, you may have to make decisions without a sergeant or officer nearby. You can't hesitate. Men's lives may be at stake. You can refuse the promotion." I gave them a moment. "I will not think any less of you if you refuse. This is a great responsibility."

They both shook their heads. "No, First Sergeant Hogan, I want the job. I'll check on the horses now!"

I knew that he was a good choice and I was pleased by his reaction. Cecil stood there and looked about ready to burst into tears. "I can't believe you recommended me."

"It was the captain…"

"No sarge, I know. You were the one who asked for me and I promise you I will not let you down. You have always been fair to me even when I was behaving like an idiot. I will keep my temper and be the best corporal in the regiment."

I cocked my head to one side, "I never thought, for one moment, that you would ever let me down."

It felt good to be busy again. I had many more duties than before but it filled the morning well. In the afternoon two more troops arrived but there was still neither a colonel nor a major. I think Captain Boswell liked it that way. He had independence for a little while longer. The other two troops were made up of the remnants of two small regiments. Battles, illnesses and age had meant that their numbers had dropped significantly but there were still a hundred in each troop. Our troop, Troop A was still the smallest by a long way. The numbers disparity was partly remedied when George McGill, General Stuart's aide, brought over fifty men sent from various other regiments. They were paraded in front of the officers and sergeants and I could see why many of them were here. They had the look of malcontents and trouble makers. I later found out that some had fallen foul of bullying sergeants and senior officers but more than half had been in trouble on a number of occasions.

Billy Foster, who was the First Sergeant of B Troop, wandered over to where I was standing with Dago and Jed discussing the latrine digging detail. "Anyone know where I can find your First Sergeant?"

"You've found him."

Billy was a middle-aged man with thin grey hair and he looked surprised. "Kinda young aren't you?"

I could have taken offence but I knew what he meant. I smiled. "I guess we are all a little young in this bunch." I pointed to Jed and Dago.

Billy laughed, "I see what you mean. We heard that there were some of those bandits, the Wildcats, in the regiment. Have you come across them?"

I put my arm out to restrain Dago. "Actually sarge, we are the Wildcats, or we were and I wouldn't believe all those stories you might have heard. We fought the war for the Confederacy and we did it behind the enemy lines. The Yankee papers are like all newspapers, they are filled with lies and half-truths."

Confederate Ranger

He shook his head, "Hey I'm sorry. I didn't mean to cause offence. Way we heard it you was all mean and nasty." He looked at us. "You're not what we expected."

"One of these nights we'll tell you what really happened but right now we have fifty men to allocate."

"That's why I came over. I know some of these boys. They were trouble and the old colonel got rid of them. There are some bad soldiers here. If you need any help then just ask."

"I may do. Thanks for the offer and if any of the other sergeants or men is worried about the Wildcats then send them along to see us. We don't mind telling them the way it was and not the way the Yankee press portrayed it."

"I will. I have to say that you aren't what I expected; one tip from an old First Sergeant. When you speak to them for the first time, don't let anything minor slip by. Jump on the little things. It will make it easier in the long run."

When he had gone I turned to Dago. "You can't do a Cecil on us every time someone bad mouths the Wildcats. They won't know any better until we either show them or tell them. We have a bad name and it is undeserved but we know we are good soldiers. We just have to prove it. Tell the men too." I gestured with my thumb at the men who were our replacements. They were milling around their newly allocated tents. "These are the boys we are going to have to worry about. Best get them in some sort of order. The captain will want to speak with them."

"Yes, boss!" I heard the cheek in Dago's voice but I ignored it and went for Captain Boswell.

"The new men are here. I have the sergeants getting them in some sort of order."

"Thanks, sergeant."

Confederate Ranger

"And sir? I just had the sergeant from Troop B. He reckons he knows some of these boys and they are bad 'uns."

"To be honest I expected it. We will just have to do things by the book. Oh, and I have just found out who our colonel is. He is an old-time soldier, Zebediah Cartwright. According to the general, he was a great leader and taught at West Point for a while. His two sons were killed at Antietam and he is alone now. I think he is coming here to get back at the Yanks for his sons. Tell the boys he is older than we might wish but he is a good man and a great leader. We'll do him proud."

The men were standing next to their horses. Our Wildcats were easy to spot; they had the best horses and their weapons and their uniforms looked cared for. Some of the fifty new ones looked like they had no uniform at all. The three officers and we three sergeants faced them while the corporals tried to chivvy them into some kind of order. It was not going well. As we watched the attempt at organising the men Captain Boswell turned to Danny. "Do we still have those spare kepis and slouch hats we used last year?"

"I think so. We stored them in the quartermaster's stores."

"When this is over, take a couple of men and get all the old, spare equipment we have; even the old carbines we captured and then we will see if they can look like soldiers." He smiled at us. "I am glad I have you five backing me up here. I think we will have our work cut out with some of these. Let's do it."

I strode forward. I was more nervous than the captain. I had never given an order to so many men before. I stood as tall as I could and I was thankful for my size and a voice hardened by shouting Gales in Atlantic storms. "A Troop! Attention!" Some of them obeyed and I made a mental note of those troopers; they could be the men I worked on to get them on our side. The majority just lounged next to their horse's head. Most of them had an insolent look about them and were ignoring everyone. One of them was openly grinning defiance at me. I marched over, speaking to all of them as I walked. "When I said attention I meant with a straight back and facing forwards." The grinning man laughed out loud. I saw Cecil tense and I shook my head. I reached the man. "Do you have a problem standing to attention?" He was at least as big as me and I could see from his broken nose that he was a brawler.

"You don't have to stand straight to kill Yankees." He turned and grinned at his friends. The look on my face must have had an effect for some of them faced the front and stood to attention.

"You've killed many Yankees?"

For the first time, a look of doubt came over his face. "I have been in battles before."

"Ah, so you haven't fought a man, smelled his breath and killed him? You haven't faced down four times your number at ten paces and blasted away with your pistols until there were none left to kill?" I didn't let him answer and I glowered at the rest. "Well these men you are fighting alongside, Boswell's Wildcats, have. They are the finest and deadliest killers I know." I could see that some had not heard who we were and they suddenly snapped to attention.

My grinning man was still grinning although a little less obviously. "When I have to I will kill."

I snapped my head around and roared into his face, "When I ask you a question then you can speak until then shut up!" Without looking down I reached around and pulled my nine-inch Bowie knife out and held it very close to the man's throat. "Now this knife here has killed many a man and slit many a throat. It is so sharp that you can shave with it. It looks to me as though you have come on parade without shaving. I am a kind First Sergeant; would you like me to shave you now here in front of your new comrades?"

I saw his Adam's apple move and the smile left his face. "No!"

"No what?"

"No sergeant!"

"Well, when we dismiss you shave but first let's see if you can do the same as every other man here. Parade! Attention!"

He snapped to attention and faced the front. I turned to the officers who were standing stony-faced behind me. "Parade ready for inspection sir!" I winked at Harry who let the ghost of a smile played about his lips.

Captain Boswell rode forward and looked down the line, "Thank you First Sergeant Hogan." He pointed at me. "Some of you may have heard of the First Sergeant, he is called Lucky Jack." I saw some eyes widen at the recognition of the name. "He has been behind the enemy lines so many times that Abraham Lincoln has his picture on his desk in case he comes a-calling." The Wildcats laughed and a couple of the new men joined in. "You will soon be as accomplished a scout as the sergeant here and the others who serve with me behind the enemy lines but at the moment, I am sorry to say, you are a rabble. Some of you do not look like soldiers, you look like bandits! The corporals and sergeants will work with you today to improve the way you look so that when the colonel arrives tomorrow you can, at least look like soldiers. My adjutant, Lieutenant Murphy, will allocate you to your corporals and sergeants. I will be watching this afternoon as we put you through your paces. I am not used to failure either with men or with combat!" He wheeled away, "First Sergeant!"

Confederate Ranger

I walked up to him and he leaned down. "Well done Jack but I should watch out. That thug looks like he is the type to harbour a grudge."

I smiled back at him. "I hope he does sir. When I knock him down it will bring his cronies back into line. At least we know who the bad apples are now, and we can work on them." I stood before the parade again. "Parade, dismiss!"

The malcontent was called Billy Pickles and once I discovered his name I determined to find out more about him. Danny, of course, allocated him to me in my section. I had Cecil, Davy and Jimmy as my corporals, and I knew that I was lucky. Dago and Jed had some of the newer men. Danny compensated by giving me a hard core of ten of the worst recruits.

I gathered my corporals around me. They looked worried. "We do things by the book. If they refuse to obey an order then send for me. Do not lose your temper but make sure you let nothing slip. Tonight you will need to be on your guard, literally. I have a feeling that a couple of these might try to run. We will all be tired tomorrow."

I sought David and Dago out. "I think that some of these might decide to leave us." I pointed to the horse lines. "Every man brought his own horse and I can't see them leaving without it. I will watch the horses from midnight until three and Dago you watch from three until six. Carlton, you know these horses better than anyone. You sleep nearby and I am sure you will wake if they are disturbed."

"Right you are boss."

"Yes, sarge!"

Carlton was more than happy to sleep near his precious horses and I knew that Dago wanted to have the opportunity to smack one of the bigger men and lay down a marker.

Confederate Ranger

I told the captain what we were doing. "You want one of us to be there with you?"

"If I can't handle this on my own then you need a new First Sergeant; besides you will need to be bright-eyed tomorrow for the colonel. He won't be bothered if his sergeants look tired."

Jed woke me at five to twelve. He had had the camp duty with his men until then anyway. "Quiet as the grave Jack, and that is worrying. Some of the men should be making more noise than they are. You be careful now. C Troop is providing the guards and the password is 'pistol'."

I went to the horse lines and smiled as I saw Carlton happily snoring away with his leg tethered to his horse's neck. They made a lovely couple. I stationed myself at the other end of the line and waited behind the tree to which they were roped. Copper was at the end nearest to me and I gave her an old apple I had found and stroked her mane. An hour passed and I was wondering if I had denied myself sleep to no purpose. Then I detected a movement from one of the tents at the end of the line. I saw three men emerge and begin to sneak towards the horses. They suddenly saw Carlton and headed towards me. I took out my pistol. I did not cock it. I knew the effect a cocking pistol had on a man's bowels. I would save that sound for when it would have the greatest effect. They crept quietly towards me and I had to admire their stealth. They would make good Rangers! I saw that they were going to take the last three horses. One was Copper and the other two belonged to Dago and Jed. They could not have made a worse choice. Even if I had not been there the horses would have made such a fuss that the whole camp would have heard them. I waited until they had their hands filled with their saddles and then stepped from behind the tree and crept behind them. The horses ignored me and I did not make a sound. I stood behind the man in the middle, put my Colt to the back of his head and cocked it. The click sounded like thunder in the silence.

"Now you three are deserting and you are stealing horses. One of the horses is mine and she is far moiré valuable than any of you useless apologies for men. According to any kind of law, I can you the three of you as horse thieves. And as this is an Army Colt with a ball the size of your head the burial plot will be really small for all of you." I allowed the threat to hang in the air. "Now turn around slowly. I prefer to shoot a man looking into the whites, or in your case, yellows of his eyes."

They turned around. The man in the middle found the barrel of the Colt less than two inches from his nose. "Please sarge…"

"Doesn't this barrel look big? It looks like you could crawl right inside and have a sleep doesn't it?" I stopped the bantering tone and became more threatening. "Now explain!"

"We are scared we'll get killed in battle. This is a small regiment and when we heard that we were to be scouts we knew how dangerous that could be."

"Scared of dying huh?" I swung the gun so that each of them saw the barrel pointing at them. "Now I am guessing that you three are not the sharpest knives in the drawer seeing as how you could die right now. But, even if you got away, then you would have Boswell's Wildcats after you. Now, not meaning to boast, but we have stolen colonels from the middle of armed camps. We have broken prisoners out of prisons in the middle of Pennsylvania so do you think we couldn't find you and, how shall I put it, deal with you in our own way?"

That particular thought hadn't occurred to them and they looked at each other in horror. The idea of a Ranger stalking them worried them more than the slightly better chances of death in battle.

"Now in your favour, I think that the three of you will make good scouts. You snuck out of your tent real quiet. That leads me to believe that you are not lost causes. Now you head on back to your tent and tomorrow morning, report to me. I'd like to see you in the daylight."

There was a relieved chorus of, "Yes, sarge." They scurried back to their tents.

When I woke Dago I told him what had happened. He shook his head. "These boys sure are dumb!"

When we had our first parade the next morning I noticed a difference immediately. The new pieces of uniform and equipment had made a difference to the appearance of the men. More than that they had brushed their horses and made an effort to clean leather. As I scanned the lines I suddenly stopped. There was Billy Pickles sporting a black eye and with a freshly broken nose. I walked up to him. "What happened to you, Billy?"

He glanced behind me at Dago and said, "I got up for a leak and tripped on the guy ropes."

I turned away to hide my smile and saw the bruised knuckles on both of Dago's hands. "That can happen when you get up in the middle of the night."

Captain Boswell rode down the line nodding his approval. "Boys you have made a real effort. The colonel will be inspecting you at noon so I want you to spend the rest of the morning making yourselves as smart as possible. I have five silver Yankee dollars for the best turned out trooper in each section." He allowed a pause. "The Wildcats are exempt. This is just for you new men!"

When they were dismissed they all set to with a spark which had hitherto been missing. I saw Dago. "What happened?"

"He tried to sneak out. I was hiding behind the horses at horse lines. When he tried to mount I was there. He didn't see me and I thumped him so hard it knocked him out. I dragged him back to his bed and didn't even disturb his tent mates."

"He'll think it was me who put you up to it you know?"

Dago shrugged, "He will feel a fool is what he'll be thinking. The big tough man can't even steal a horse and desert. His pals will have less respect for him now."

As he turned away three sheepish troopers approached. One of them, a tall gangly youth approached me. "First Sergeant, you said you wanted to see us."

I nodded. "Well, I am pleased you have come. It shows you are real men. You aren't afraid to take your punishment. I like that. What are your names?"

The gangly youth said, "Norman Thomas, sarge."

A slightly chubby round face young man said, "Leroy Palmer."

The older man said, "James Palmer. Leroy's big brother."

"Now listen boys, you have a future here. Believe me, you have a good chance you will survive this war. We always kill more of the enemy and we rarely lose men." I pointed to the Dago and Jed. "Those sergeants and the officers know what they are doing. We won't make stupid decisions and we won't risk men's lives. The Yankees were afraid of the Wildcats not because we were so bad but because we were so good at what we did, fighting." I saw the expressions on their faces changing. "Now the next time you feel like running, you come and talk about it to me. Right?"

Their smiles and their chorused, "Yes, First Sergeant," made me feel much better about our prospects.

Colonel Zebediah Cartwright looked every inch the southern gentleman he turned out to be. He was painfully thin with a small silver goatee and a few wisps of silver hair peeping from beneath his plumed hat. The sword which hung from his waist looked as expensive as my new house. He was not tall but he had a commanding presence. He rode in on a magnificent grey and was followed by a Sergeant Major who looked almost as old as he was. Cecil had been charged with warning us of his arrival and the regiment was in three well-dressed lines as he rode in. He rode the length of each line. When he finished he returned to the front. For a man who was in his sixties, he had a powerful voice which carried to every trooper. His voice, too, oozed Southern gentleman. I could imagine him on Captain Boswell's plantation sipping mint juleps and talking about the cotton harvest.

"Gentlemen I am Colonel Zebediah Cartwright and I am your new commander. This is a new regiment for me, a new regiment for all of you and a new and unique regiment for the Confederacy. We are scouts." He gave a wry smile to the Sergeant Major next to him. "I thought my days of scouting ended in the Mexican War but I know that many of you troopers, sergeants and officers have experience in this area and I will take your advice. We are entering a glorious phase of the war. Now that General Lee has defeated the Union at Fredericksburg the north is ripe for an attack and we will be in the fore of that attack. When we scout for the army I want you to remember that we are trying to take the fight to the Union backyard so that our people do not have to bear the brunt of the deprivation. You are fighting for your families. Remember that. I will be speaking with your officers and sergeant so you may have the next two hours off. But after that, we begin work!"

The colonel looked around for somewhere to speak with us. There was nowhere. He shook his head. "I fear, Sergeant Major Vaughan that we shall need a command tent. It is most unsatisfactory to have to speak with my officers in a field. Pray could you arrange to get one for the regiment but first I would like you to speak with the non-commissioned officers. We are of one mind gentleman Whatever Sergeant Major Vaughan says is what I would say to you."

Sergeant Major Vaughan was quietly spoken and it took all of us by surprise. He looked to be a huge blustering fort of fellow. "We will see to it colonel. Now gentlemen if you would like to follow me we will find somewhere where we can speak without little ears listening in." He led us away from both the tents and the colonel. He smiled and he looked like a kindly uncle or grandfather. "As you can see neither the colonel nor me are young men." We smiled at the humour. "When the colonel was called upon to serve again he asked for me. I served with him all those years ago. He took me away from the fishing and the telling of tall tales." He seemed to see us all for the first time. "This is a different experience for me. You are new both as an idea and as a regiment. You have come from different regiments and units. I know that some of the men may need firm handling." He chuckled. "I noticed a bruised face or two and I heard a story about a couple of sergeants watching all night for trouble." He nodded. "I like that. Those sergeants are my kind of soldiers. I am relying on you, non-commissioned officers, to handle the men you brought with you. As for the new boys, well let me know who the troublemakers are and I will deal with them." He rubbed his hands together as though relishing the prospect of building a new regiment. "As you know we are short-handed at the moment. We are awaiting major from England who is taking his own sweet time about getting here. We have no Quartermaster, no farrier, no armourer and no-one to take charge of the horses."

I put my hand up. "Actually Sergeant Major I asked one of my corporals to be an armourer and another to look after the horses. They can do the job until you find someone."

Confederate Ranger

"And you would be Lucky Jack Hogan I take it?" I was taken aback and it must have shown on my face. He laughed. "I had someone describe you and when I heard those Irish tones then I knew it must be you. Well, those two can have the job. If they are any good they will be made up to sergeant. Anyone else got a farrier or quartermaster lurking beneath a bushel?" As he looked around the room I saw that Cecil was fit to burst. He was happy.

Billy Foster drawled, "Two of my sergeants are fair hands at those jobs but I will need to promote a couple of corporals to take their place."

"Good man. Then do it." He paused and looked at all of our faces. "What you need to know about the colonel is that he is the best cavalry leader you will ever meet but his days of leading charges are, like mine, long gone. But I don't think that this regiment will be in the business of cavalry charges. We will be scouting and that means we will be looking to A Troop for advice and ideas." Everyone looked at our cluster of non-coms. "I have been following the exploits of Boswell and Mosby in the papers and while I don't believe all the stories, when Jeb Stuart tells me a couple of interesting tales then I do. A Troop may be young but the rest of you make no mistake, they aren't green. Anyway, that is the speech out of the way. We will have a briefing every morning before breakfast and last thing at night. I may not be riding as much as some of you but I will make sure all the standing orders and rotas are written up and available to you. And now I had better go and get those tents. First Sergeant Foster, where is that quartermaster of yours?"

I walked back to the camp with Dago and Jed. "I think that he is going to work out just fine."

Cecil raced up behind us. "Does that mean I am the armourer for the regiment? And if I work hard I'll be a sergeant just like Sergeant Spinelli?"

Dago looked disdainfully at Cecil, "Even if you do make sergeant, you will never be like Sergeant Spinelli." He patted Cecil on the head, "But you can dream!"

Confederate Ranger

Chapter 8

It was a few days later and our English major had still not arrived. General Stuart was keen to move his corps to the east towards the area we had recently vacated. He wanted to try out his new regiment of scouts. We could not await one man. It suited those of us who had worked with Captain Boswell before because he appeared to be the senior officer. We felt he deserved that. We all liked the colonel but we were still Boswell's Wildcats at heart.

Captain Boswell summoned his officers and non-commissioned officers. "It seems the general wants his new regiment of scouts to begin operations sooner rather than later. We only have three troops but the colonel thinks that is enough to start with. The new officer, the English major will be given the task of training and bringing along the next troop. The general has given us a couple of clerks to help him." He smiled, "I, for one, do not mind. Colonel Cartwright is a real gentleman. He reminds me of my grandfather. He speaks well and he is courteous. I don't think we could have had a better commanding officer if we had chosen one ourselves. He is such a gentleman that he even has a manservant with him. He has given us a corporal bugler. I'm afraid we will all have to learn the bugle calls. That will be new for many of us." I shrugged, I had heard enough in the campaigns so far and it would not take long to learn them. "Because twenty of us have experience of being Rangers we are the lead troop. You sergeants and corporals will have to train your new men on the job." He gave us his old look. "I am quite excited about this. I always wanted to serve the Confederacy and now I will be doing so. We won't be skulking around the back streets any more. We are part of Jeb Stuart's Corps."

Confederate Ranger

The regiment rode out in a long column which snaked down the road. We had wagons with us containing tents, spare tack and ammunition. Luckily, the rest of the corps had wagons even more wagons than we did and we would not be unduly held up; we would be able to move at the same pace. Until we reached the area of the Rappahannock we would ride with the corps but once we crossed the Blue Ridge we would be doing what we did best; sticking our noses into the Union camps.

There was a little snow on the Blue Ridge as we rode through and I was grateful for the newly issued greatcoats. The colonel had been insistent that we look like regular cavalry despite our new role. I took the opportunity of speaking with my corporals about how we would operate. "We have twenty-five men in our section and there are four of you. I need you to be responsible for looking after six men each. We are fortunate and there are four Wildcats in our section so only twenty one will need training." I smiled, "On the hoof so to speak. Some of the ones who have been in other cavalry regiments may want to use their sabres. Discourage them. Cecil, make sure that all their pistols are in good working order and try to collect as many Union guns as we can when we can."

Cecil cocked his head to one side. "I thought we weren't Rangers any more?"

"You mean you thought we wouldn't forage?" He nodded. "We still forage. We still collect Yankee horses. The difference is we don't get paid for them; we just use them." I lowered my voice. "Cecil, I have put Pickles in your section. Keep your eye on him. He has been quiet since he got hurt but I don't want him making others as unpleasant as he is. The hard time will be when you are away on your own with the new men. Just remember how we worked as the Wildcats and you should manage." Cecil gave me the serious look and nod he affected when he was showing that he meant something.

As we dropped down towards the Sperryville Pike the colonel halted the column. I saw him talking to the captain who then rode up to me with Harry alongside him. "Right, gentlemen, take your section and scout out Sperryville. We need to know how many, if any, Union troops are there." He was grinning. "I envy the two of you. This is the first action of the 1st Virginia Scouts. Enjoy!"

I turned in the saddle. "First section, Yo!"

Copper almost leapt down the road and I had to rein her in to avoid leaving Harry behind. "A little keen, sergeant." He said somewhat ironically.

I laughed, "I think it is Copper, Lieutenant Grimes, she likes the freedom."

"Don't we all," He turned in his saddle. "We might as well try out the new boys." He looked for a Wildcat, "Corporal Jones."

Davy trotted next to him. "Sir?"

"Take four men and ride around Sperryville. The road goes to Culpeper. Wait on the other side with your boys. If there are only a few Yanks in there we may flush them out and they might try to get to Fredericksburg along the east road. You can stop them."

"Sir!" He galloped away looking eager to be the first to meet with the enemy.

I was pleased to see that two of the men with Davy were Wildcats. They would be fine. They galloped hard as they would have to leave the road and go across country to reach the other side unseen. I wondered if this was the way regular cavalry operated. We were all learning from each other; the regular cavalry and the Rangers. Together we would make a potent combination.

Sperryville lay at the bottom of a valley and was surrounded by hills and crags rising to sixteen hundred feet. I knew that we could see a great deal before we ever reached the town. If this was the old days I would have made a suggestion or two to Harry but I would have to wait and see what ideas he had; he was the officer. When we were two miles from the town we halted. He turned to the men. "We will leave the road here and travel in the woods to the north. I don't want us seen until the last minute."

I heard a mumbled groan from one of the new men. "What was that Trooper Hargreaves?" I remembered First Sergeant Foster's advice.

"I just asked why we have to ride through the trees. There is snow on some of them and it will be more uncomfortable getting wet branches in the face all the time."

"Well isn't that a pity. I didn't know you were so fragile. Tell you what. Why don't you ride in front of me on point and then I can look after you."

There were sniggers from his friends as he rode in front of me. I could see the grin on Pickles' face. He had obviously been working on the young trooper. He would be even wetter now as he would be the one riding through the trees first. It was slightly harder going but we were travelling downhill which made it easier. "Right, Trooper. Halt there." I could see that we were now less than a mile away from the town. It was at the junction of three roads and I could see a Union flag flying. That meant that there were some soldiers in the town. Civilians rarely identified their leanings until they saw the colour of the army approaching them. This part of the world was constantly being retaken by one side or the other. "It looks like there are some troops there, lieutenant."

"Right boys. We'll give the corporal a few more minutes to get into position. Check that your pistols are ready. We will not be using sabres today. If there are Yankees there we will use our revolvers. I hope you know how to use them." Even though I had

Confederate Ranger

checked mine already, I pointedly took it out to go through the motions. His familiar English voice shouted, "Sergeant Hogan, lead off!"

I kicked Copper and we returned to the road. "Hargreaves, you can ride at the rear now. You have done your duty for the day." I saw the relief on his face as he wheeled to the back. My position was now the most dangerous. If there were soldiers down there and they fired a volley and fled then it would still be me who would be hit. I took out my revolver. I could fire quickly and I had learned that being the first to fire often meant being the one to survive. I could see the town clearer now. It looked to have houses and buildings on each of the three roads which suggested prosperity. Fortunately there appeared to be no barrier to halt us. I saw a handful of blue uniforms race from a building when we were less than eight hundred yards from the edge of town. Even as I wondered what type of troops they were I saw the horses being led from the barn. There was a flash from their muzzles and then the crack of carbines. I shook my head. They were too far away to be effective and they had just wasted a ball. The men were either novices or badly led. The eight men leapt on their horses and galloped along the Sperryville Pike towards Culpeper. "Corporal Mulrooney, bring your section with me." I knew that Harry would need the rest of the patrol to secure the town and Davy was up ahead with his ambush; he might need some help with eight men to contain.

The citizens had wisely decided to stay behind their doors as we galloped through the town. We were soon beyond the last house and I heard the crack of pistols and then the pop of carbines in the distance. The ambush had worked. "Ready your revolvers!"

Up ahead I saw three horses wandering around and they had no riders. I also saw some blue uniforms and splashes of blood on the frosty road. As we reined in Davy came towards me with a black look on his face. "Sorry, sir. They got away." He glared at one of the troopers who had the good grace to look shamefaced. "Trooper McIntyre decided to fire too early and they were warned. There's one dead and two wounded."

"Never mind, corporal, I am sure that a week of shovelling horse shit will help Trooper McIntyre to mend his ways. Corporal Mulrooney, get the body buried. Corporal Jones, take your prisoners back to the lieutenant. I will be along later."

While Cecil's men dug the grave I searched the body of the corporal who had been shot. They were the 1st Rhode Island Cavalry. I wondered where Rhode Island was. My knowledge of America was limited to South Carolina and Virginia. There was a picture of a stern-looking couple and I assumed they were his parents. They looked to be his only personal items apart from a pocket knife and a few dollars. He had an Army Colt and some ammunition which I took. His boots also looked in good condition. "Corporal, take his boots and see if they fit any of the boys." Some of our men had crudely made shoes and boots. Rhode Island gave its sons a decent one.

"Sir!"

I wandered over to the horse. Like most of the Union cavalry, it was a good mount. It was our first spare. His carbine was just a single shot but it was better than some of the ones my men had. The sabre was also in better condition. With the two horses of the wounded men and their guns, our troopers would be better equipped. When the body was laid in the grave and covered with soil and stones I suddenly realised that the men were looking to me to say something. I removed my hat and the men did the same. "Lord, here is a young Yankee from Rhode Island. He did his duty and I hope he gets a welcome up there. Amen."

"Amen."

I knew I had not said the right words but I hoped that the dead corporal would forgive me. I would need to find the right words to say the next time.

By the time we reached the town the people were out and greeting our men as though we were returning heroes. I was becoming more cynical in those days and I imagined that they would have given as warm a greeting to the Union soldiers who had fled. We made the most of it, however. Harry sent two sections to watch the Warrenton Road while my section was sent, with Cecil and Davy to guard the road to Culpeper. He secured permission to use a field to the west of the town for the camp which we assumed the colonel would wish to establish. This was a good base of operations. The town controlled one of the routes through the Blue Ridge and gave us good access to the Rappahannock Valley. We both hoped that the colonel would approve.

The rest of the regiment reached us a couple of hours later. I did notice the look of dismay on some of the good citizens of Sperryville as the long column and wagons pulled into their home. They should have realised that they would be a strategic town because it had fine and prosperous businesses and was one of the larger towns in this part of Virginia. That was to be expected. No one wanted two hundred soldiers camped on their doorstep. Harry smartly saluted as Colonel Cartwright halted. "Sir the town is secured. We have two prisoners. Five of their men escaped towards Culpeper. Sorry, sir."

The colonel shook his head, "That happens, son. How many casualties on our side?"

Harry looked perplexed, "Why none at all sir."

"Excellent. That is the kind of news I want. Now we shall need a camp…"

"Sir, I took the liberty of getting permission to use that field there, to the west of the town."

"Well done First Sergeant Hogan. I like resourceful men. Sergeant Major, see to the camp, will you? I will go and see the town elders and let them know that we will not be imposing military law on them. I suspect they will be worried that we will be taking their chickens and the like."

"Yes, sir! B and C Troop. First Sergeants to me." As the men galloped down the road, he nodded to me. "Well done First Sergeant Hogan."

I enjoyed the praise but I knew that my duties were not finished. "Corporal Mulrooney, when the horse lines are established, then please ensure that our designated shit shoveller gets to work as soon as possible." I saw the trooper's shoulders sag. He had thought that I had forgotten my decision. He would learn.

That evening the officers and First Sergeants were summoned to the command tent. The colonel had a bottle of whisky open on the table. "I thought just a glass each would take away the evening chill."

We raised our glasses, I wondered where they had come from, and we all said, "To the regiment" as though we had rehearsed it.

"We made a good start today. Tomorrow the real work will begin. Captain Boswell you and your men know this region. What can you tell us about it? We have the maps but you have travelled the roads and eyes on the ground are always more informative."

"Well sir, the Rappahannock is not the Potomac and you can ford it in many places. That makes it easier for groups of men to slip across the river unseen. Fredericksburg was well fortified when we were there but other smaller towns like Falmouth weren't. If the enemy is planning something then the smaller towns may give us some softer targets. The land immediately around Fredericksburg is hilly and forested. It is an easy place to sneak small groups of men in and out of." He grinned. "That was our speciality."

"And the railroad?"

"That is to the north; up towards Manassas. There are more patrols in that area than further south. It would be more difficult to hide the regiment there. The trouble is that you never know which side the people are on; a little like here. They cheer and welcome you but you don't know what is going on behind their smiles."

"Quite. Well, I plan on using this area for a little while so tomorrow the Sergeant Major and I will take some of your problematic soldiers. We need latrines digging and the like. I want the three troops to go north, east and south. Get as far as you can and bring back as complete a picture of the troops in this area as you can." He smiled and he looked, once again, like the kindly uncle. "If you could leave your armourer corporal and your medical corporal than would help us immeasurably." That would do both men good as it would show them that the colonel had selected them and would raise their self-esteem. That was really important for someone like Cecil who had had such a poor start to his military life.

It almost felt like old times as we headed towards Culpeper. We had all of the Wildcats and twenty of the more reliable men. Cecil and David had been amazed that the colonel had asked for them. I suspect it was the colonel's way of getting to know some of his men. He had been a colonel for a long time and some things didn't change. We had no idea which way the town of Culpeper would go. It was a large town with an important courthouse. They were on the border and I knew that if I lived on the border I would be loath to show my true colours. Dago led his men into the town and we were relieved when he quickly returned. "Not a Yankee in sight. The four men Davy and Jack chased warned the ones who were stationed here and they lit out for Manassas. Culpeper is free from the enemy."

We all knew that they could change their allegiance at any time. "Sergeant Smith, take your section and secure the town." Jed's eyes showed his surprise at the order and the captain gave him a reassuring pat on the shoulder. "If the Yanks come back then you skedaddle and let us know. I don't want any casualties. I just need early warning. We will head on towards Warrenton just to see if they are sending any help. Try to find some rooms. The Confederacy is paying. We'll be back before nightfall."

As we left Culpeper the captain turned to Danny. "Take Sergeant Spinelli and get as close as you can to Warrenton. We will not be far behind you."

When the two men left I rode with Harry and the captain. Captain Boswell turned to me. "Does this feel strange to you two?"

Both of us looked at each other and nodded. "Yes, captain. This feels like we are taking money for nothing. We took far greater risks when we were Partisan Rangers."

"I agree with Jack sir. I thought that being in the regulars would be different from this."

"I think you are both right. This will change and we should not become complacent but this is so easy, it is frightening."

When Dago and Danny returned from the Warrenton Road it was almost an anticlimax. The Yankees had fled. They were moving everything east. We passed through Culpeper and stopped briefly to speak with Jed. "There should be no Union soldiers within forty miles but keep a good watch."

The colonel was delighted with the news. "You have confirmed what the others have told us. The Yankees have pulled back. Tomorrow we head for Culpeper. I have sent the news back to General Stuart. I think we have the Union on the run. We appear and they decide to evacuate the vicinity." He smiled. "They must have heard of us."

The Sergeant Major stroked his chin. "I know these soldiers are not Mexicans but they are behaving like the men we fought. The thing is, colonel, we fought alongside some of their officers and they are not this bad. I think we should proceed cautiously. They may be making us think they are weaker than they are." He stared at the three First Sergeants. He was not talking to the officers; he was talking to us.

The next day I was mindful of his words. This was too easy. Why would they let us get this close to Washington? Were they laying a trap? I was not stupid. We were an under-strength regiment and our loss would not hurt the Confederacy. A horrible thought passed through my head. Were we the bait? I could not rid my mind of that thought as we collected Jed and carried on to the east. Once we cleared the town we had two choices. We could head northeast or south-east. A patrol to the south-east would take us towards Fredericksburg and northeast towards Washington. Neither was an attractive prospect as there would be huge numbers of soldiers in both vicinities. I was learning that, old though he was, the colonel was not afraid of a challenge. He took us towards the wasp's nest that was Fredericksburg.

After their defeat before Christmas, the Union had fortified the town to prevent any more advances by the Confederacy. Burnside had been sent back to Washington in disgrace and

Confederate Ranger

Hooker was in temporary command. We had learned this through the Yankee newspapers and intelligence from spies in Washington. Hooker was in no mood to be beaten by the rebs again and the town bristled with guns and defences. The colonel decided to take us, as there were no Union forces close by, to the outskirts of Fredericksburg. We would use the experience of the Wildcats. We were to lead the regiment north towards Warrenton and then head south-east so that we approached the fortified Fredericksburg from the north. General Stuart had made it quite clear that he wanted the Union forces to be nervous about where we would attack. By approaching from the north the colonel was making Hooker think that, perhaps, there was an army heading from that direction. Where General Lee would attack next was anybody's guess but we all knew that he had to keep the Union away from Richmond and that meant defeating them one more time before we could invade the north.

    The Sergeant Major had straightened out a couple of the bad eggs we had but Trooper Pickles remained a thorn in my side. He avoided all of the sergeants when he could but Dago and I knew that he was a bad influence. It was Jed who came up with the solution. "Tent him with our boys. Bill and Bert won't take any nonsense from him and they can watch him." It was a simple idea but it worked. Pickles remained truculent but he was isolated and he became more and more withdrawn. Bill and Bert were as loyal and solid a pair as you could wish to meet. It was not a perfect solution but it was a solution.

    We had no time for such distractions as we were the point of the arrow as we headed through Union territory. Fortunately there appeared to be no cavalry patrols as we headed through the empty lands of eastern Virginia. It was cold and our greatcoats were invaluable. I also wore my deer hide jacket over the top as it was waterproof. I don't think that the colonel and the Sergeant Major approved but they granted me a little leeway as I was normally the one in harm's way. Some of the things I had learned in the Wildcats were hard to shed in this new discipline, the cavalry.

We camped ten miles to the north of Falmouth in the hills. There was little cover and, if the Union had any cavalry around them we would easily be spotted. Captain Boswell had mounted vedettes a half-mile from the camp. If any cavalry came then we would soon know. We were all a little tired when we awoke but I soon became wide awake. Bill found me. "Sarge. It's Pickles. He's deserted. His horse, his gun, everything. He has fled!"

The captain was not as annoyed as I was. "Good riddance I say, Jack. We won't miss him."

"No, sir. I agree but he is a treacherous little bastard. I wouldn't put it past him to go and sell his information to the Yankees."

Unfortunately, the colonel agreed with the captain. "No, First Sergeant Hogan, we will not waste men to chase around after one deserter. I think he will sneak back home and we can catch up with him later on."

In a way the colonel was right. Most deserters had too many ties to their homes and would inevitably end up there and they would be caught. I wasn't sure about Pickles. He was one of the most unpleasant men I had ever met. There was a malevolent streak in him a mile wide and I would have preferred that snake dead.

We edged our way along the Falmouth road and then headed north to approach Fredericksburg from the direction of Stafford. We had travelled this route before and it was familiar. We saw the houses of the town in the distance and we could see that there were soldiers in evidence. Captain Boswell sought me out. "Right Jack, let's take the first two sections and see what we can discover. Sergeant Spinelli and Lieutenant Murphy you take charge of the rest."

We trotted towards the town in an open skirmish line. There were fifty of us. I think that the captain wanted to intimidate the defenders and, perhaps, encourage them to send cavalry out to capture us. With the regiment waiting just out of sight it would be a pretty little ambush. We halted about eight hundred yards from the defences of Fredericksburg. The captain had field glasses and he scanned the town. "The reports were correct. They have improved the defences. It looks like they just have infantry on this side." He grinned, "We are too far away for their little guns. I can't see any cannons. I think we can risk a closer look. I surely would like a bunch of cavalry to try to get us. Let's annoy them." We moved closer.

When we were five hundred yards from the town I heard a strange pop and a whizzing sound overhead. Suddenly I saw something climbing into the air and I couldn't work out what it was. One of the new men did and he yelled, "It's a shell! They have a mortar!"

It landed fizzed and then exploded. I saw two troopers and their horses struck by the fragments and they died instantly. The concussion from the explosion almost threw me from Copper but I held tightly on to the reins. I saw the captain and his bugler knocked from their mounts. I jumped from Copper. She would come back to me when I needed her and I raced over to help the two men who were lying on the ground. I grabbed the reins of the captain's horse as I shouted to Dago, "Sergeant, take the men out of range!" Dago began to lead the men to safety away from this dangerous and new weapon.

Confederate Ranger

The captain was dazed and he looked disorientated. "You are alright sir. Climb back on." I helped him up and then ran to get the bugler's horse. "You ride sir. I'll see to the boy." The dazed captain began to follow Dago and the others. I was just helping the wounded bugler on to his horse when I heard the whizz of the next mortar shell. I instinctively ducked down and the last thing I remembered was the crack of the explosion and then I was thrown through the air. The last thing I saw before I landed was a sky filled with smoke and flames and then it all went black.

Chapter 9

I heard the voices before I fully came too. "He is one lucky son of a bitch. They are still finding pieces of the horse and the bugler. Has he any wounds?"

"No, Sergeant McNeil, he was just knocked out and I think he will come too in a moment. Let's just try this." Suddenly there was a strong smell in my nose and I leapt up, popping my eyes open. I saw a white-coated man laughing. "Smelling salts will do it every time. He's all yours, sergeant."

To my horror, I saw the uniforms were not grey but Yankee blue. I had been captured. The sergeant was portly and had a silver beard which seemed to fill his face. "Well son, you are one lucky son of a gun!" He shook his head in amazement, "When you was brung in I thought it would have been in pieces but there is nary a mark on you." Your three comrades and their horses were not so lucky but we'll bury them." He picked up my equipment. This is a fine Bowie knife and this little bad boy is a fine weapon too." He slipped the gun and the two knives into his belt. "The fortunes of war my lad." He leaned in. "I daresay I will get a good price for the Army Colt too. One's man's loss as they say. It's the prison for you. On your feet. The major wants a word."

My hand automatically went to my Colt and the sergeant laughed. "You are now a prisoner son. Grabbing your hog leg and loosing off isn't going to happen. Major Doyle will have a word with you and then it's off to prison for you."

I then noticed the private pointing the rifle in the middle of my back. They were taking no chances. The sergeant led us out in to the street and we headed for a large building overlooking the river. There were cavalry horses outside and armed guards on the door. The sergeant paused before we went in. "Major Doyle lost a brother to you rebs in the battle here and he doesn't take kindly to grey so try not to upset him."

"Thanks for the warning sergeant."

He shrugged and pointed at my stripes. "Professional courtesy, one sergeant to another."

He knocked on the door and I was led in. The major was a thin-faced man. He looked as though he scowled more than he smiled. He looked like a picture from a magazine with his oiled hair and moustache. His uniform was well made and looked to be expensively finished. When he spoke it was with the New England twang I remembered from my days at sea.

"So Reb, you thought you and your raggedy bunch of misfits would stick your nose into my backyard did ya?" I couldn't think of a reply and I stood looking at him dumbly. "Weren't expecting our mortars were ya?" So that was what had hit me, a mortar shell. I stored that information for future use. The major looked beyond me to the sergeant. "He can speak can't he?"

"Yes, sir. Answer the officer, sergeant." As he spoke he nodded in the direction of Major Doyle and I remembered his warning. This man wanted to take out his anger on me. I sensed I was in for a humiliating time.

I looked at Sergeant Mc Neil as I answered. "I thought they were rhetorical questions sergeant but I will answer them." I turned to stare insolently at this major. "Yes, we did think we would stick our noses in your backyard because this backyard is Virginia and you are the invader. And no we weren't expecting a mortar." And then I smiled. I remembered how it had annoyed Caitlin when I had done that and there was a little devilment in me.

I heard the intake of breath from the sergeant and then the major leapt to his feet. He was not a tall man and had to look up at me still. "You impudent wretch. I am an officer and you will address me as such."

"Yes, sir." I managed to imbue the words with as much insolence as I could. If this officer wanted to be unpleasant he could do his best but I had served under Black Bill and this little dandy's rage was nothing to be feared.

"What is your regiment?"

"1st Virginia Scouts," I paused and watched as the colour rose in his face again, "sir."

"And where is your camp?"

"In the saddle… sir."

He looked nonplussed, "In the saddle? I don't understand."

"We camp wherever our horses stop and then we move on… sir." I made it sound as though I was explaining to a child. "It makes it harder for you Yankees to catch us."

"That is ridiculous. Where is the rest of your army?"

"I honestly have no idea. General Stuart didn't tell us that, sir. He just said go and find me some more Yankees to whip."

The name of Stuart made him stop. "You are with Jeb Stuart? He is in this area?"

I had no idea where the general was but as it upset the major so much I lied. "Oh yes, sir. We are with his Cavalry Corps."

He was so taken aback that he ignored my lack of a sir at the end of my statement. "The general will need to know of this. Lock this man up and keep him for questioning. We need to know exactly where the enemy is. This is vital information. We may get the jump on this upstart."

As we went out the sergeant said, "You like living on the edge don't you?"

Confederate Ranger

"You did warn me sergeant but I was still surprised at the arrogant little prick. Tell me has he fought in a battle? Apart from the one to get promoted of course."

The sergeant laughed, "I can tell that you have. No, the major has been sent from Washington. Now let me find a room with a lock on it." We went upstairs with the sergeant wheezing and puffing up the narrow stairs. He stopped at a room at the head of the stairs. The door was open and it was obvious that it had been a nursery or children's room from the toys on the shelves. It had a bolt on the outside. It did not look sturdy and I thought I would be able to break it easily enough.

"I'll get you some food and a pot to piss in." He turned to the sentry. "Stand guard here private." As the door closed I saw that the private could not be more than eighteen and he looked nervous. That worked to my advantage. If I was going to escape then it would have to be quickly. However, I would not be able to force the door with the sentry outside.

Once the door slammed shut and the bolt was drawn I examined the interior of the room. The windows had been nailed shut and there was no exit there. There was just the one door in. The bed was a small one and there was a tiny desk and chair. The shelves had dolls on them and it must have been a child's bedroom. I found a wardrobe but it was empty however there was a rail which had been used to hang clothes upon. It was held to the top by a few screws. I gave a tentative tug and it moved. I needed to take it down when there was some external noise to hide the sounds I would have to make. It would, at least, give me a weapon. I examined the walls. I would have loved to tap them but the sentry would become alerted. Then I looked at the ceiling. I could just make out the edge of what looked like a trap door. It had been painted over but it was worth investigating.

Confederate Ranger

I heard footsteps and the sergeant's muffled voice speaking to the sentry. I leapt to my feet and, as the bolt was moved wrenched one of the brackets down from the rail then, shutting the wardrobe door I sat on the pathetically small bed. The sergeant had a metal container in one hand and a bowl of something steaming in the other. The sentry held a mug in his hand and the gun in the other. I was fairly certain that I could have escaped then but I didn't know how many men were in this building and I decided to bide my time.

The sergeant was out of breath as he spoke. I didn't think he would be making too many journeys up the stairs. "Here y'are reb. It's hot at any rate. That's a mug of coffee. The major will be back in an hour so make the most of this."

When they left the bolt was put in place again. I decided to eat the stew and drink the coffee. I didn't know when I would get the chance again. My time as a Ranger had taught me to eat when I could. I didn't realise how hungry I had been until I had finished. I went to the wardrobe and found that I could slide the rail out of the other bracket. It was about four feet long and was made of hickory. It was a weapon at any rate. I then gingerly stood on the desk. It wobbled a little but held. I put my fingers up to the trapdoor and found the edge. It looked as though it had been papered over. What I needed was something to cut the paper. If I had had my knives… then I suddenly remembered, Stumpy's pocket knife was in my boot top. I slipped my hand down and found it. It had been too small to notice when they had searched me. I opened the blade and cut the paper around the outline of the trapdoor. Once I had done that I slid the blade around until I found the hinges. Once I had the hinges located I put the blade at the opposite side and began to lever the door. I had to do this silently and I could feel the sweat begin to pour off me. I hoped that the blade on the knife would not break and then, suddenly the door dropped down, smacking me on the head. I paused and listened but the sentry did not make a sound.

    I climbed off the desk and wiped away the boot marks. I grabbed my piece of hickory and clambered back on to the desk. I thrust the wooden rail into the loft and then hauled myself up. It was a tight fit but I managed to pull myself into the black hole. Once I was in I pulled the trapdoor back into the closed position. I hoped that it would stay closed. It had taken some forcing and I thought that it might. At first, it was as black as night but my eyes became accustomed to the dark and I saw chinks of light from spaces between some of the loose tiles in the roof above me. The loft was huge. I stood and saw that there were strong beams on which I could walk. I held my piece of hickory wood in my right hand and walked towards the far end. I thought, at first it was a dead end but then I found a small door with a bolt on the top. I snapped the bolt back and then slowly opened the door. There was another loft and I entered it. I began to look along the floor for another trapdoor. If I could not find one then I had exchanged one prison for another. I suddenly heard a commotion but it was muffled, as though it was in the distance. They had discovered that I had gone. I hoped that they would not find my means of escape but it added urgency to what I had to do. I peered desperately around then saw a chink of light from the floor. I found a trapdoor.

    I lay above the door and listened. I could hear no noise from below. I wondered if the door was the same as the one I had just used. I found the hinges and then slid my blade down the opposite side. This time I was able to push down and the trapdoor swung open. The sudden light almost blinded me. I still heard nothing and, holding my stick I swung myself through the narrow opening and dropped down into an empty storeroom. I closed the trapdoor again. I needed my enemies confused. There was a window and I raced across the room to it and peered outside. There was an alley running alongside the house. I could see many soldiers racing everywhere. My escape had been definitely been detected. I went to the door but it was locked. When I returned to the window I saw that it was not nailed shut and I tried to open it. I am a strong man but it took some effort and the window groaned alarmingly. I stopped and looked outside. No one was looking up. I pulled the window fully open. I took off my hat and looked along the building. There was a flat roof some twelve feet below me. I could drop down but not for a while. It was late afternoon and I would have to wait until dark. I did not want to be seen. It would be a nerve-wracking wait for dusk was still an hour away.

    Gradually the furore outside died a little. I watched the alley below empty until it became totally devoid of anyone. I opened the window and peered into the darkening dusk. My grey uniform helped me to blend into the building. I dropped my stick. It seemed to crack unnaturally loudly on to the flat roof and I froze but there was no rush of feet. I climbed out backwards and hung by my fingertips from the windowsill. The roof was a mere four feet below me. I let go and I dropped to the level surface of the flat roof. I made less noise than my stick, which I retrieved, but I still paused to listen for any noises. There were none. The flat roof was narrow and I wondered what was below it. I crawled along to the main street. I took off my hat and peeped around the edge. There were still soldiers in the street. I crawled back and then lowered myself into the alley. I had escaped my cell and I now had two objectives: avoid capture and escape the town. I took off my deer hide jacket and then removed my greatcoat. I rolled the greatcoat so that it resembled a blanket. I donned my jacket and then tied the coat around my back. I stuffed my kepi in my shell jacket. I could now pass amongst ordinary people and not arouse interest but I would need to be wary of soldiers.

I walked away from the street which had contained the soldiers and emerged at the other end. It was a quieter street. I saw lights at the end and heard the noise of clinking mugs and a hubbub of conversation. It was a tavern. I moved down towards it. It would be a good place to get my bearings and to hide in plain sight. I stood in the doorway of the building next to it. This was a time I wished that I had a pipe. It would have looked less suspicious if I had been smoking a pipe in the doorway but I had none and I waited. I saw four off duty soldiers wander down from the opposite direction. I kept in the shadows and, when they entered, I followed them into the crowded alehouse. To any in the tavern, I would look like one of the soldiers. No-one wasted a second glance on me as I made my way to the opposite end of the bar. There was a fug of smoke and the lighting was poor. It was hard to make out faces until you were close to them.

I waited for the barkeep to serve the soldiers and then caught his attention. "A beer and a whisky chaser."I tossed a Yankee silver dollar on the bar. The barman showed no interest in me now that he saw I had money. When I had my chance I leaned into the corner so that no one could approach me from my rear. I nursed both drinks. I wanted to wait a while before I tried to leave. I had my stick but a firearm would be a more comforting. There were many armed men in the bar but they were in groups and it would be difficult to acquire one easily. It was not a priority and I was still evading capture; my escape had not yet begun.

The bar began to thin out and I tossed off my whiskey and then drank half of the beer. I wanted to follow a small group out and see if any of them had horses. I had no idea where the livery stable was and I did not want to risk asking for one. I needed to find a small enough group to give me a chance of getting a horse. The less I spoke the better. I saw three men, all of them armed, leave the bar. One of them was a little unsteady on his feet. They looked to be wagon drivers from their attire. They would have a source of horses and they were not soldiers. They would have to do. I left a heartbeat after they did. They walked down the street, thankfully, away from my place of incarceration. Two of them staggered a little. When they reached the corner the one who appeared to be the least steady on his feet staggered left down an alley and his two comrades went right waving a goodbye as they did so. I followed the unsteady one. He had a gun and that was what I needed. He paused halfway down the alley and relieved himself. I waited for him to finish and then I saw that he was not moving. I wandered behind him and heard him snoring. His head was resting against the wall. He was asleep! I quickly took his pistol which I discovered was a Navy Colt. I checked that it was loaded. I was going to leave when I realised that his hat would be useful too. I snatched it from his head and retraced my steps. At the end, I crossed over. His two companions had gone in this direction and hopefully, it would bear fruit. I put the battered slouch hat upon my head.

I had not gone more than twenty yards when the unmistakable smell of horse dung hit me. There was a stable nearby. I saw a thin light emanating from within. I walked across the entrance, just glancing inside. The two men I had seen in the tavern were in there and it looked as though they were settling down for the night. I could see their wagons in the back of the building. That created a problem. To give me thinking time and to give me a better picture of the area I walked around the whole block. I saw, at the end of the second street I traversed, the building they had taken me to. I could still see the armed guards. I would avoid that road. It enabled me to get a clearer idea of where I had come from. The road out would be beyond that street. When I did manage to get a horse I would head back the way I had just travelled.

When I reached the stables I looked above the door. It said,' *Liberty Livery Stables, Jeff Davis, Proprietor*.' I decided to be bold and I walked in. The two men had not settled down for the night yet and they both looked at me suspiciously. "Which of you two men would be Jeff Davis, the owner." Now that I had a closer look at them I could see that there were definitely drivers. They dressed the same way as the men we had ambushed near Manassas. One was tall and spindly while the other looked as wide as he was tall. They were an incongruous couple.

Rather than answering me, the short dumpy one said, "Why?"

"I need to rent a horse. Mine went lame up on the Stafford road and I need to go back and collect my bags and such."

I saw the greedy look they exchanged. "It isn't cheap. Not at this time of night."

I grabbed a handful of dollars from my pocket and shook them so that they jingled. "I'm not a beggar. I'll pay a fair price for a horse. I only need it for a couple of hours anyway. I could be back by midnight."

I could almost see the wheels and cogs of their mind working. They would rent me a horse and then tell the owner that when they came in they had seen me riding out with the horse. I would be hanged as a horse thief and they would have made drinking money. "It would be five dollars and if you weren't back by midnight then it would doublc."

"Fair enough."

Confederate Ranger

"And another dollar for the rent of a saddle." I cocked my head to one side and the talkative one said, "Of course you'll get that back when you return it."

"That seems reasonable. Of course, I get to pick the horse."

The tall spindly one shook his head. "That ain't fair. We pick you one out."

I needed a good horse for I would be pursued. "Why? You aren't going to rent another one out tonight are you? It will be back before midnight." I put the coins back in my pocket. "I guess I will find another stable and another horse."

As I started to turn and leave the talkative one said, "Don't be hasty mister. You are right and you seem like a respectable sort of man. It isn't as though you came in here and held a gun to our head. You pick the horse."

"Thank you." I counted out the dollars and the dumpy man grabbed them greedily. While they were trying to divide the coins up without me seeing I looked in the stalls. Most of them were draught horses rather than riding horses and I would not have much choice. I found the Appaloosa in the last stall and she was the best one by far. I led her out.

"Hey, that one..."

The talkative one nudged the spindly one in the ribs. "Yeah, that is a fine horse." He pointed to the saddle on the sawhorse. "There's your saddle. By the way mister, what is your name?"

"Bill Bailey of Cork in Ireland."

"Well, Bill Bailey I'd watch it out on the road. Word is those Partisan Rangers are about as well as a bunch of cavalry led by Jeb Stuart himself. It's why we are watching these wagons tonight. We wouldn't want this cargo stealing. The cavalry can escort them to Warrenton tomorrow."

Confederate Ranger

I pretended I wasn't interested but, as I mounted the horse, I glanced in the back and saw boxes with 'Sharps' stencilled on them. They were rifles.

"Thank you kindly, Mr Davis. I shook the fat one's hand. They almost giggled like school girls as I rode out. I knew that I had perhaps ten minutes before they ran to tell the owner I had stolen his best horse. I trotted purposefully away from the stable. I knew the direction I wanted to go but I would have to avoid the main roads as I was sure they would have men guarding them. I went through small streets and alleys. There was an icy blast blowing in from the Atlantic and people were safe in their homes. The only ones who were out and about were soldiers and they were looking for me.

Suddenly the alley I was travelling along ended and there were fields before me. I backed the horseback into the alley, dismounted and looked out. To the left was a checkpoint with a brazier and soldiers. A mile to the right was another one. I was in the middle but the minute they heard me galloping they would be alerted. I grabbed the reins and led the Appaloosa and began to walk across the frosty ground heading for the distant hills. I realized the colouring of my horse made her difficult to see against the patches of snow and frost. Perhaps I would escape detection. I was about half a mile from the town, crossing another field when I heard a commotion. I glanced around saw some horsemen at one of the checkpoints. The missing horse had been detected. I kept walking hoping that my movements would not arouse interest and it worked until I came to the next field which rose a little and made me stand out against the moon which was just rising. I heard a yell and saw the horsemen galloping towards me. They were cavalry.

I leapt on to the back of the horse and kicked her hard. She took off and began galloping freely. I had chosen wisely. I turned her head slightly to make for the road I could see up ahead. Riding across fields was, potentially, dangerous as I didn't know what obstacles lay in my way. I had no choice for I was now being pursued. I knew that the road to my right led to Stafford and Aquia. I had told the drivers I was going there and I wanted the cavalry to think that was my destination. I remembered a road which left the main road and head west over the hills, towards Culpeper. If I could lose them then I would take that road. It was with a great sense of relief that I found the road and began to make better time. To my dismay, I saw that a second party had come directly along the road and they were less than half a mile away. I would struggle to lose them. "Come on girl. We can do this." I looked over my shoulder. There were just four of them. The other pursuers were further away but there were ten of them. I would need to deal with the four before the turn off.

The road rose up a little and then dropped down on the other side. As I reached the small rise I saw a lone oak next to it. I reined in behind it and took out the Navy Colt. It was not the time to learn the qualities of the gun but I had no choice. I lay over the neck of the Appaloosa and listened to the hoof beats. I had checked the revolver was fully loaded but this had been loaded, not by me, but a drunken driver, a civilian. I prayed that I would get at least one shot off. The riders had spread out and I allowed the first rider to close with me before I fired. The crack of the pistol told me it worked and his scream as he fell told me that I had hit him. I fired at the second man. He did not fall but clutched his arm. The third man tried to turn his horse and he gave me an easier target; I hit him in the middle of the back and he pitched from his horse. The wounded man and the survivor rode back down the road and I raced to the first dead man. He was a sergeant and I took his Army Colt and his ammunition. Leaping on to the back of the Appaloosa

Confederate Ranger

I smacked the dead man's horse so that it raced along the road. As I passed it I grabbed the reins. I want to disguise where I left the road. Glancing behind me I saw that the two parties had joined and were a mile back. The road began to curve slightly around a small hill and I urged the two horses on. I saw the track leading off into the hills some two hundred yards ahead. I stopped and tied the reins of the spare horse around the pommel of its saddle. I smacked its rump and it galloped up the road. I headed down the track. There was a hedgerow running along both sides and I kept in the shadow for a hundred yards and then I halted. Soon I heard the thunder of hooves as my pursuers hurtled past my track. As soon as the last one had gone I continued up the trail towards the hills. They would soon catch the horse and then try to find where I had left the road. I was under no illusions, they would find it but I hoped that I would lose them in the hills and forests to the west of Stafford.

    I slowed my horse down to a walk. I needed to conserve her energy. The road below was hidden from my sight. I could hear the riders on the road but could not see them. I knew that they would be looking for hoof prints. The ground was frozen but a trained man could see where a horse had stood. I figured they would have at least one such man. When I reached the top of the hill I was climbing I halted. I took out the Army Colt and loaded it with fresh ammunition from my own supply still on my belt. I tucked the Navy in my belt and holstered my new weapon. I could now defend myself. As I the road turned north I knew that I had to leave it and cross the small rise towards the lake and the old Mill Road. It meant exposing myself to view but I had no choice. I felt naked as I left the cover of the hedges and trees and rode the six hundred yards over the rise. I risked a backwards glance as I reached the top. They were now on the road which I had taken and they had seen me. I had less than a three-mile lead but I would be on the downhill section and they would have to climb the rise.

Once I was on the road I made much better time. I kept the Appaloosa going at a steady rather than a fast pace. Once I struck the Warrenton road I was back on more familiar roads. We had ridden down it a couple of days earlier. I had no idea where the regiment would be but it would be somewhere along this road. If they were close to Fredericksburg then I would have to keep going until I met Stuart and the Corps. I was aware that my horse was not moving as well as it had been. I was contemplating halting and examining it when I heard the crack of a pistol. My pursuers were less than two hundred paces behind me. I took out my Colt and waited. Their shots were ineffective; they were bouncing up and down and moving too quickly. More importantly, they were wasting balls. I aimed at the lead horse and fired. It collapsed in a heap bring down two other riders. I fired again and saw a rider flung from his saddle. My third shot missed and I whipped my mount's head around and trotted down the road. I had only bought myself a short breathing space and next time they would be warier but I had no option.

I patted the Appaloosa's head. "Come on old girl. You are doing well." She snorted and gamely carried on. I glanced over my shoulder. There were still five men pursuing me but now they were showing more caution. They were catching me but slowly now. They had also spread out so that I would not be able to bring down two riders with one shot. Dawn was just breaking behind them and I felt weary myself. The shot of whisky had long worn off. Every time I looked around they appeared to be closer. I knew that they would catch me eventually. I would have to judge the moment when I whirled around and charged them. They would not be expecting that and I would be making the decision. I would control how the fight ended. The brave Appaloosa stumbled a little and that determined my next action. I drew my gun with one hand as I whipped the game mount's head around. I kicked hard and levelled my gun at the lead rider. He panicked and fired too soon. I felt the shot as it flew over my head. I fired at the huge target of his chest and then turned the gun to the man next to him. I just kept firing. The smoke from our pistols obscured my view. I clicked on an empty chamber and I holstered my gun and drew the Navy Colt which had three rounds left.

I turned the weary horse around and then heard a familiar voice. "Good to see you are still the luckiest bugger in the land Jack Hogan."

The smoke cleared and there were four Yankees with their arms in the air and Harry and Dago with two sections of A Troop grinning at me.

Dago shook his head. "When you hear shots fired in the early hours of the morning, you know who it will be, Lucky Jack." He pointed to the hillside. "We are camped over yonder."

Harry seemed to see the horse for the first time, "Nice horse. I take it you won't need Copper any more."

"Copper? She's safe?"

"Yeah. When you were dumb enough to get blown up she had the sense to follow us. She won't let anyone ride her but Carlton's been taking real good care of her. Come on the captain will be glad to see you and Danny will want the full story!"

Chapter 10

While the men held their guns on the prisoners Harry told me what had happened. "Until I saw you just them we all thought you were dead. The captain was real upset; you saving his life and all. We saw the shell explode and pieces of horse and men flew in the air. We were sure no one could survive." He looked at me as though I might be a ghost. "How the hell did you survive?"

"Luck I guess. The shell exploded on the other side of the bugler and the horse. I was kneeling down to help him up and they must have taken the full force. The doctor who examined me said that I was lucky."

"And he was right. The colonel had us make a camp up there. He planned on heading back to the general today. He'll be happy to see you too."

"How many did we lose then?"

"Just four. It could have been worse. But what happened to you?"

I told him of my incarceration and my flight. "These boys were getting mighty close." I turned to one of them. "How come you were so all-fired anxious to catch one prisoner?"

The corporal said, "A deserter came in from your side and told us that you were the one who hung those boys up at Manassas."

I looked at Harry, "A deserter?"

"Yup. One of the 1st Virginia Scouts. That's you boys ain't it? Tell me, were you the ones who hung them, boys, up at Manassas?"

Confederate Ranger

Harry snarled, "You mean the spies sent amongst us? Yeah, we hung one. He betrayed us and a lot of good men died. What would you have done corporal?"

He nodded, "Probably the same." He pointed down the road. "And it seems to me that a lot of my friends died because of them today." He gave me a rueful smile. "Sergeant you got balls the size of mountains. We never expected you to charge all of us! Are you all crazy?"

I shrugged, "Why do you think they called us Wildcats?"

We reached the camp and as word of my return spread men rushed from their tents. Captain Boswell was in the middle of shaving and he erupted from his tent as though fired from a cannon. There was shaving foam all around his mouth and he stared at me, just laughing. "I never would have believed it! Lucky Jack back from the dead."

Dago was standing close by and he said, "Were you too ornery for the devil then?"

I dismounted and laughed as I embraced Dago. "Something like that!"

The captain wiped his face and then clasped my hand in his two. He pumped it yup and down as though he was drawing water. "Jack! You don't know how good this is! We thought you were dead!"

"Not my time sir."

The colonel came out of his tent. He had taken the time to finish dressing as had the Sergeant Major who nodded approvingly at me. "Well, First Sergeant Hogan, you are a man of surprises. Not only do you return from the dead but you bring back prisoners. Well done son."

I saluted. "Thank you sir." I waited until the prisoners had been led away by Harry and then I said. "I also have some news, sir. There is a wagon load of guns leaving Fredericksburg today with a cavalry escort. They are heading for Warrenton."

"Are they indeed? Well done. I think that we will head there on our way back to the general."

"There's one more thing colonel. The deserter, Pickles, has joined the Union side. That is why they were so keen to get me. He told them that the Wildcats are here. There is still a price on our head."

"Ah! Our sins have come back to haunt us. He will get his just desserts, trust me. For now, forget him. He has done all the damage he can." He turned to the Sergeant Major. "Strike the camp. Send a rider back to the general I will have a short report for him by the time he is mounted."

My old comrades crowded around me until Danny shouted, "Come on! You heard the colonel. We can catch up with this lucky bugger later on." He winked at me. "I knew you weren't dead! But they wouldn't believe me."

I heard a neigh and saw Carlton leading Copper over to me. She nuzzled my head and licked the back of my neck. "Yes, I missed you too old girl."

Carlton gestured to the distant horse lines. "She's a nice Appaloosa. She will make a good spare for you."

"She's a fine and game horse." I noticed a wistful look in his eye. "You can ride her you know. I am more than happy with Copper."

His face lit up. "Thanks, Ja.. er sergeant."

When the colonel emerged from his tent he handed a letter to the rider. "When you have found the general then head for Winchester and find our new major if he has arrived." Even I could hear the censure in his voice. "Sergeant Major Vaughan, officers and non-coms if you please."

Confederate Ranger

The bugler sounded the call and we formed a square around the colonel and the sergeant major. "I have just informed the general that we intend to capture this wagon train of rifles. I have also detailed the recent actions. I had previously written that First Sergeant Hogan was deceased. I had to cross that out." There was laughter from all. "I have also recommended some promotions. I am tired of waiting for my second in command and so Captain Boswell you are now promoted to Major. Lieutenant Murphy, you will become captain of A Troop and Sergeant Hogan you will become lieutenant. Corporal James and Corporal Mulrooney, you are confirmed as sergeants and Corporal Jones you will replace Sergeant Hogan." He paused to allow that to sink in. "Now Major you are now responsible for the regiment. Captain Murphy if you would like to select a First Sergeant then we can get on with this war."

There was much back-slapping. Danny said, "It's a toss-up between you Dago and you Jed. But you edged it First Sergeant Spinelli for that lovely smack you gave Pickles."

Jed was the first to congratulate his friend. "You are the better man Dago and besides I don't like the paperwork."

It took some minutes to sink in that I was now a second lieutenant. I now had more pay and more responsibility. I didn't think it would change me but I just didn't know. The men would now call me sir. Danny grinned, "I'll let you have my old uniform when we get back to Winchester."

"What do you mean? I am having one made again. You are talking to a rich man now."

"And now to our orders. Take Jed and Dago and the first two sections. Find the wagons for us."

Jed and Dago rode next to me. I explained to them what I had seen. "There were three wagons and they were heavily laden. If we assume they left at first light then we should be able to ambush them just up the road."

"I thought the captain told us to find them?"

"He did but I thought we could prepare the ambush anyway." I led them to the road I had taken earlier that morning. I felt I knew the area well enough to spot the slowly moving wagons. "Trooper Stewart, ride up to the top of that hill. You should be able to see the road from there. Give us a yell when you see them."

Dago cast his eye over the terrain. "That little hill the road rises overlooks to be perfect. The wagons will be slow up the small hill and this side will be hidden."

Jed pointed to the hedges and trees which were lined the road. "We could hide the whole regiment behind those."

"Dago, ride down the road and then come back to us. Tell us what you can see." He turned and galloped up the road. "Jed, take half the men over there to the north. "Sergeant James, take the rest to the south. Sergeant Mulrooney, you stay here with me."

I could not see my men once they had hidden themselves. I only knew where they were because I had watched them secrete themselves. Soon I heard the hoofbeats of Dago's horse as he trotted along the road. I saw his hat and then he appeared. He reined in and looked around. "Where's the boys?"

I whistled and circled my arm and they emerged from hiding and trotted over to me. "There."

He shook his head. "I couldn't see them. I saw you two when I reached the top of the road."

"Then when the major comes we will tell him that this is the place for the ambush. Did you see any sign of them?"

"No, but the road twists and turns less than a mile away. Jimmy should be able to see better from the hill." The hill was slightly higher than the road but, because it was to the north, it afforded a much better view.

Suddenly he came galloping down. "Lieutenant. Sir. The wagons are a mile and a half down the road. There look to be about fifty cavalry with them."

"Ride back to the major and tell him that and that we have an ambush position here. Tell him to approach on the northern side of the road." I turned to the rest of the men. "Right Jed back in your position. Davy and Dago go to the south. When the cavalry leave the wagons you capture them. Cecil, you go with them. Carlton, you stay here. " The newly promoted sergeant looked lost and confused. I smiled and pointed to the Appaloosa, "We are bait. The wagon drivers know I rode off on your horse and I am counting on the fact that their cavalry will want the reward more than they will want to stay with the wagons. Let's dismount and pretend to be examining the hooves of your horse."

We heard them before we saw them. The drivers were shouting and encouraging their horses and there was drumming on the road of the horses and wagons. The first wagon crested the rise and I saw one of the drivers shout something. The cavalry had been to the side of the wagons but they suddenly appeared.

"Let's go! But not too quickly eh?" We heard the bugle sound charge as we mounted and headed down the road. I glanced over my shoulder. They had left just ten men to guard the wagons. Jed and Dago could deal with them. I smiled as I saw the drawn sabres of the cavalry; our revolvers would make short work of them. I saw the road rise ahead and hoped that the regiment would be close by. The sound of our bugle almost made me jump and the major led the rest of the regiment from the north. There was a ripple of cracks and pops as they fired their pistols. It would not do much damage but it would serve as a warning to the cavalry of what we could do. They were outnumbered five to one and they were no Wildcats. They carried on south and I could see that they were heading for the Rappahannock; the wagons were forgotten. There was a chorus of whoops as the regiment hurtled after them. As we turned and rode back up the road I heard the desultory pop of a couple of guns. I was fairly certain of what I would see. As Carlton and I rode up I could see two blue-uniformed bodies lying on the ground and the rest of the escort with their hands in the air. "Well done boys." I glanced up at the tubby driver whose mouth dropped open. "I held out my hand, "I guess you guys owe me six dollars." I heard the bugle sound recall. "Secure the wagons, First Sergeant."

Major Boswell and the colonel reined in. "Good work boys. Those Yankees sure can run. Did we suffer any casualties, sergeant?"

"No, sir. When we dropped those two the rest couldn't get their hands in the air quick enough."

"Right major let's get back to the Valley. I think we have more than enough information for the general. It is forty miles or more so we'll have to find a camp. See to it, Lieutenant Grimes."

Harry turned to me with a scowl on his face. "You get to capture wagons and I get to find somewhere to sleep. How come?"

"I'm supposed to be lucky, remember?" He shook his head as I grinned at him. I was happy. I had been a prisoner but I had escaped, I was with my friends again and I had been promoted. Life was good.

The journey back was uneventful. As we passed through Culpeper I saw that the Confederate flag flew now. Who knew who would control it next week? General Stuart met us at Winchester. He was delighted with our success. He slapped the colonel on the back so hard I thought he would break the old man's back. Sergeant Major Vaughan gave the Major General a glare. He confirmed all the promotions. I was close enough to hear the conversation between the three of them.

"Your major has arrived Colonel Cartwright."

"About time."

"It is probably a good thing that you appointed James here. The last experience Major Beauregard had, was in the Crimean War and that was fighting Russians."

"Sir, have we more men then?"

"Yes major. The new man has been in charge of them but my people tell me they have done little but parade up and down on their horses. He has a really fine uniform; more gold braid than Murat!" There was an irony in the general's last comment as he was known as a peacock who dressed flamboyantly. Perhaps that explained his attitude towards the new man.

"Where do we go next then sir?"

"General Lee's nephew, General Fitzhugh-Lee is organising a brigade to head back to Stafford County. I would like your scouts to support him. You appear to know the area well already."

The colonel asked, warily, "Support him sir, or join him?"

Stuart clapped his arm around the colonel's shoulders. The colonel was one of the few men the same height as the diminutive general and I think his bonhomie made him feel taller. "All you fellas need to do is tell General Fitzhugh Lee where the Yanks are and he'll do the rest. He's a real firebrand."

As we rode to the new camp I reflected that General Stuart's nephew, Archie, whom Dago and I had rescued from behind the enemy lines, was anything but a firebrand. I hoped that this nephew of a general was a little more like Major Boswell.

I could tell that the colonel was disappointed as we entered the tented village that was our camp. There was little order in the tents and the men were just lounging around outside them. There were men playing cards and dice. No-one appeared to pay any attention to the colonel of the regiment. Sergeant Major Vaughan had always been quietly spoken but I saw a different side to him. He almost vaulted from his horse and stood in front of the men and their tents. "D Troop! Attention!" Half of the men moved the other half looked at him as though he had spoken a foreign language. "On your feet now your horrible bunch of maggots!" When he roared it sounded a bull had made the noise.

They all leapt to their feet. The colonel rode down the line. Although they were standing to attention it was not the straightest line I had ever seen. The colonel shook his head sadly and said, "Carry on Sergeant Major Vaughan!" He rode to the far end of the camp where his manservant was already beginning to erect his tent.

"I have no idea why you thought you could just lounge around and ignore your commanding officer but let me tell you it will not happen again." He glared down the line. I saw Major Boswell nod to Dago and the other sergeants and they dismounted and formed a line behind Sergeant Major Vaughan. "I want the sergeants of D Troop front and centre! Now!" Three shamefaced men shuffled to the front. "You three will see me when I dismiss this parade and we will see if you are fit to be sergeants in the 1st Virginia Scouts." He turned to the sergeants standing behind him. "When I dismiss the parade I want you, real sergeants, to inspect every tent. Any man who does not match your expectations, send them to the horse lines. We will give the real troopers a night off tonight." He glared at the Troop. All of them looked as though they wanted the earth to swallow them up. "Dismiss!"

The Major, Danny and I stayed close by in case we were needed. Vaughan spoke quietly but still with an undercurrent of anger in his voice. "Now what the hell is going on? This is a shambles. If you have served as sergeants before then you know what is expected."

The oldest looked at the ground as he said. "I am First Sergeant Hathaway, Sergeant Major and it has been like this since we arrived. I only got here three days ago and the other two a day or two earlier. This is the way the camp was run."

"Where are the officers?" They all looked up as Major Boswell spoke.

"Where they are every night sir; in the taverns in Winchester."

The major nodded, "Carry on Sergeant Major. Come along gentlemen we will report to the colonel and then deal with this problem."

The colonel was sitting in his chair outside of his tent smoking a cigar and sipping a glass of whisky. The ten of us stood there while Major Boswell reported to him. "It seems it may not be the fault of the sergeants sir. The officers arrived before the men and they established this routine. The officers, apparently, spend their evenings in the taverns."

The colonel stared into space for a moment and I wondered if he had heard the major. When he spoke it was obvious that he had. "That is a gross dereliction of duty. There should be a duty officer here at all times." He tapped the table as he formulated his thoughts. "Major Boswell, could you take a couple of officers and ask the Major and his officers to return to camp." He sipped his whisky and said, "Oh and I think that you will do well as the adjutant," he paused for emphasis, "and second in command." He smiled. "It should obviate any issue over seniority eh?"

"Yes, sir. Thank you, sir. Captain Murphy, Lieutenant Hogan, come with me."

Confederate Ranger

Carlton was still brushing down Copper when I reached the horse lines. "I've finished Apples if you want to take her."

"Apples?"

He grinned, "Yeah Apples the Appaloosa sir, and she likes apples as well as the name."

I saddled and mounted her and trotted off to find the other officers.

"This could be tricky sir."

"I know Danny. It's why I brought you two. You are both big enough and tough enough to intimidate most officers and I also trust you two to watch my back. Just play it by ear when we get there. It might all be quite innocent. Perhaps this is the way that they carry on in England. I don't know."

With so many regiments in the area, the taverns were heaving. We had neglected to find out which one they frequented but, then again, it was unlikely that the sergeants would have known that. We entered the first one and looked around for someone who looked like an overdressed general or someone that we knew.

A voice from the smoky room arrested our progress. "James Boswell."

"Ah, Sandie." The Major extended his hand. I recognised General Jackson's aide from the Battle of Kernstown. "Are you still with Stonewall Jackson then?"

"No, like you, I have moved on to other things. I am one of General Stuart's aides now."

"You might be the man to help us then."

"I owe you a favour so ask away."

"We have been away for a week or so and we are looking for the officers who were in charge of the camp. There is a Major Beauregard…"

Confederate Ranger

Sandie held his hand up. "Then say no more. They are in the next tavern, the Damson Bush." He leaned in conspiratorially. "General Stuart is less than happy about them, especially the major. It is not just the fact that they are in Winchester every night; well General Stuart likes a drink as we know. It is just that he runs card and dice games and many of the young officers in his regiments have been losing heavily. It is bad for morale and some of them have run up huge debts. It is now spreading to other regiments."

"How will I know him?"

"He dresses expensively if not well and he has a broken nose. He says he received it in the Crimea but if you ask me someone smacked him one. But just look for the biggest card game in the room."

"Thanks, Sandie and tell the general that this gambling will be curbed from now on." When we were outside the major turned to us and said, quietly, "You two stay in the background. I'll try and have a quiet word. We don't want a noisy scene here but if it starts to turn ugly…"

"Yes, sir!" We grinned and nodded. We knew exactly what he meant.

It was a dimly lit tavern with smoky candles and oil lamps. There was a heavy fug of cigar and pipe smoke filling the air. Major Boswell scanned the room. His target was obvious, even from the rear. There was so much gold braid that it seemed to light up the man's neck. "Right boys, here I go."

There was an empty seat opposite our new major and I contemplated sitting in the game so as to watch the major but then realised I needed to be on my feet. We kept a couple of paces back but we could hear everything. Major Boswell waited patiently while the hand was played. The captain to his right threw his hand down. "Damn! You are deuced lucky Beauregard. That's five hands in a row you've won. How do you do it?"

"Skill dear boy. Skill." There was something about the voice which made the hackles on my neck rise. Perhaps it was just so English and I hadn't heard an English voice since we had fled our farm.

Major Boswell leaned in. "Major Beauregard. I am the adjutant of the 1st Virginia Scouts. Colonel Cartwright sent me to speak with you."

Major Beauregard turned to speak with Major Boswell and my heart almost stopped. It was Arthur St John Beauregard the man who had murdered my father and mother! I felt my fists tightening into balls. The voice had been a warning but I saw the face again as I had when we had peered from the hut as the murder took place before us. "Can't it wait? I am playing cards."

Major Boswell gritted his teeth and gave a small cough, "Actually Major, it isn't just you, we need the other officers too, are they here?"

Major Beauregard waved an airy hand around the table. "My brother officers are here."

Major Boswell's voice changed. "Then I want the officers of the 1st Virginia Scouts to return to camp immediately. And that is an order!"

Major Beauregard laughed, "Of course that doesn't apply to me. Bye, Bye chaps. It looks like you are in trouble." He almost giggled, "More hands for me to win I suppose."

"Actually Major Beauregard it does apply to you. The colonel ordered you back to camp."

His face darkened and he stood, a little unsteadily. "How dare you! No one orders me around."

Confederate Ranger

"In that you are wrong." He glared at the four officers who were collecting their money. "And you four had better get outside before I throw you out."

"And do you think you can? Neil!"

And then Andrew Neil appeared; the other murderer. "Yes, sir?" This was less of a shock to me but it made me angry. This was the man who had started it all by killing my mother.

"This officer wants to take us back to camp. Persuade him otherwise will you?" The Englishman grinned at Major Boswell. "He is not a soldier, he is my servant so try to order him around if you can."

The bully strode over preparing his fist to strike the Major. I murmured to Danny. "This one is mine!" It was a little unfair I suppose. He was concentrating so much on the major and how he would hit him that he did not see my right hand pull back and then hit him so hard that he fell backwards over two tables. He landed in an unconscious heap with blood pouring from his broken nose.

"Thank you, lieutenant. Now Captain Murphy, will you escort these officers back to camp and I will wait while the major collects his winnings. And lieutenant you had better take the major's servant back as well."

The other officers backed away as I strode through. In their world officers did not throw punches like that and my face must have displayed my anger. I picked up the former estate manager and threw him easily over my shoulder. Major Beauregard sat stunned at the change in his fortunes. As I walked through the door I was not careful with the unconscious killer and smiled grimly as his head hit the door lintel. I suspected that it would extend his sleep somewhat.

When I got outside the other officers were on their horses looking sorry for themselves. "Which is his horse?" They pointed to a grey and I threw him over the saddle. By the time the two majors emerged we were ready to go and the tavern emptied to watch us leave.

Danny and I rode behind the four officers who themselves were behind the majors who led us. We wanted no-one to run. "You'll regret this you know? I am on first name terms with the Secretary of War."

"Well I shall bear that in mind should I ever meet him. Of course, you do realise that we operate behind the enemy lines so we have more chance of meeting the Union Secretary of War. And before you say anything else you might come up with a reason why you left a camp without a duty officer. It appears that General Stuart has noted that all of you were absent from the camp without the permission of your commanding officer."

Major Beauregard fell into Major Boswell's traps so easily it showed me who was the more intelligent. "I gave them permission as acting commanding officer."

"Ah, so it is you who will be facing a court-martial for dereliction of duty? Thank you for clearing that up. The colonel will be pleased."

Our new major sank into silence as we rode the rest of the way to the camp. The colonel was seated with Sergeant Major Vaughan and they were deep in conversation. As we rode up and dismounted the Sergeant Major rose to stand behind the colonel. The colonel did not move as the five officers stood before him. Four looked shamefaced and Major Beauregard just glowered angrily. Eventually, the Colonel spoke, "I am Colonel Cartwright, your commanding officer and none of you," he looked at each one in turn, "have made a favourable impression on me." Although he spoke quietly there was censure in his tone. "We have made a bad start so let us try to improve from here on. Pray introduce yourselves by rank and experience."

The haughty English voice sent shivers down my spine. How I hated him and everything he stood for. "I am Major Arthur St.John Beauregard formerly of Her Majesty's Foot Guards." He said it as though he expected us either to bow or to applaud. The colonel did neither. He merely looked to the next man.

"I am Doctor Harrison Marley formerly with the 5th Virginia Cavalry."

"Good we need a medical man."

"I am Captain Samuel Cooper. I was attached to the staff in Richmond."

There was the briefest of glances between the colonel and Vaughan. I knew what it meant. They had a captain with no combat experience at all. "You will have much to learn captain. This is not Richmond."

"I am First Lieutenant Robert McGee. I was with the 3rd Virginia."

The youngest looking one said, "I am Second Lieutenant Richard McGee and this is my first posting."

"Would you two be brothers by any chance?"

They both chorused, "Yes sir."

"Well, it seems there may be an excuse for two of you. If you have not served in a combat regiment before then you might not know about such things as duties and the efficient running of the camp but three of you do. As commanding officer, it is within my remit to have you all court-martialled." He allowed the words to sink in, "but in the spirit of burying the hatchet and making a new start I will merely punish you and your company by giving you the nightly picket duty for a week." I saw Major Beauregard think about snapping a comment back but then he thought better of it.

"As your duties begin in two hours then I suggest you get what rest you can."

Major Boswell stepped forward, "There is one other thing colonel. The major has a servant who was about to strike me until Lieutenant Hogan intervened and forcibly restrained him. He is slung over his horse at the moment." I saw an approving smile and nod from Sergeant Major Vaughan. "I wondered about his position."

"Ah, a servant eh?"

"Yes, colonel. It is a common practice in the British Army." Major Beauregard sounded petulant rather than forceful.

"I know. However, they also serve in the British Army too and wear a uniform." He leaned forward, "They are subject to military discipline. So if you wish to have him with us then you must enter him into the roll and supply a uniform. Of course he will still be your servant and will not receive military pay." The major gave a nod. "Good, then if there is nothing more, you are dismissed."

As I went back to my tent I decided that I would keep my thoughts on the major to myself. There was already enough bad blood between the officers and I did not want to add to it.

The next day saw us thrown into the maelstrom of preparing to campaign north of Fredericksburg. I took the opportunity of visiting Barbara Sandy; she had made uniforms for us before and I was anxious to look the part. This was even more urgent now that Major Beauregard had arrived. At first, she said that she was too busy but the jingle of coins and a hangdog look did much to expedite matters. "Come this afternoon and I will see what I will see what I can do."

"And if I could have a second…"

Confederate Ranger

"It's a good job you have a cheeky look, sir! Be off with you."

General Fitzhugh Lee arrived with his entourage to brief the colonel. Major Beauregard made a point of imposing himself on the meeting despite the fact that the colonel preferred to tell his officers of important matters himself. We waited nearby for the briefing we knew would follow. I could not hear the words but I saw the body language and the gestures. The general did not appear to appreciate the major's presence and he was soon sent packing. He stormed across to where we stood in idle chatter. He made straight for his erstwhile companions. "Well, General Lee is incompetent! That is obvious. I hope his uncle is a better general or we shall lose this war and we British do not lose wars!"

I saw Major Boswell bristle, "I believe you lost one in 1779 didn't you?"

The smiles were on all the faces but for the four officers of D Troop. Even Doctor Marley smiled and I noticed that he no long stood with the others. He had seen the writing on the wall.

When the meeting was over the general strode towards us. He held out his hand. "Major Boswell, congratulations on your promotion. I have heard much about you. We need more officers like you." He flashed an angry look at Major Beauregard who suddenly seemed to find the toe of his boot interesting. "I am confident that with you and your Wildcats scouting for me we will trounce the Yankees and lead them a merry dance eh?"

After he had left the colonel waved us in. "Well, it appears we are in for an exciting time." He grinned, "It seems Lieutenant Hogan that we are heading back to the scene of your miraculous escape." He held up a newspaper. "The general left me this. Apparently, when you escaped your cell the guards thought it was either witchcraft or magic. They do not know how you escaped from a locked room with barred windows. They are attributing the success of the former Wildcats to such witchcraft."

The ones who knew me laughed but Major Beauregard said haughtily, "Witchcraft! Stuff and nonsense!"

"Still Major Beauregard, if it makes the enemy fear us a little more, then I am in favour of it. Anyway down to business. We leave in three days. The general and the brigade will follow a day later. We have a free hand so long as we inform the general of what he can expect. We are advised to avoid battles; that will be the focus of the brigade."

"But we are cavalry! That is what we should be doing! Engaging the enemy on the battlefield and defeating him." Major Beauregard almost spat the words out.

The colonel put his fingers together, almost as though in prayer. "Rather like your Light Brigade did at the Battle of Balaclava eh? Had they had our scouts then many fine cavalrymen would still be alive. This regiment is a regiment of scouts. Our job is to find the enemy. Yes, we will hurt him if the opportunity arises but we will run when appropriate."

"A Beauregard does not run!"

"The Major Beauregard, I would look for another regiment and quickly!"

Chapter 11

As usual, A Troop led the regiment. Even the malcontents from the early days were now happy to be part of the elite troop. We rode a mile ahead of the main column and Dago led ten men in a loose skirmish line a mile ahead of that. We would not be easily ambushed. Danny rode next to me. "That was a mighty blow you struck the other night. There appeared to be a lot of venom, in that punch." Andrew Neil, or Trooper Neil as he now was known, had kept a low profile whilst in camp. The other troopers had heard of his threat to the major and there were threats against him. Although, as officers, we could not fight him, the men were under no such restrictions and Trooper Neil spent every waking minute tending to his major. "Do you want to talk about it?"

Danny of all people would understand and he would also respect my wishes. I told him what had happened all those years ago. "But don't say anything, sir. I am telling you this because you will understand and you will trust me. You come from the same neck of the woods and know how these things work."

"You aren't going to do anything stupid are you?"

"What? You mean like kill the men who murdered my parents? Not while they wear the grey but one day they will not and then all bets are off."

"Fair enough and when that day comes Jack, I'll back you. You know that?"

"Thanks, Danny." I sighed. "I feel better with that lot off my chest."

We headed down towards the Rappahannock first, because the general was keen to have a defensible base on the south side of the Rappahannock. We found a ford and a small settlement at

Confederate Ranger

Kellysville. The ford was called, appropriately, Kelly's Ford. As Danny said when we reached it, "A fine Irish name, it should do nicely. Trooper Tyree, find the general and tell him we have found a base. Sergeant Spinelli, go and find us a campsite on the other side of the river. We might as well get the prime spot." It was as perfect a spot as you could wish. The river looped around and there were two fords, one closer to the railroad line and the bridge.

The general arrived the next day and was delighted with the position. We found two high areas one which could control the ford and the other, a mile or so from the ford, would make a good camp. He spotted our hill and decided that when he had some artillery he would site a battery to control the ford. "Well done colonel. The railroad is close enough to supply us too. This will do. Now go and find us some juicy targets!"

The colonel briefed us the next day. "I shall ride with Major Beauregard so that Sergeant Major Vaughan and I can assess D Troop. We need to see for ourselves the improvements. The rest of you will cover as large an area as you can. Return in two days with your reports." The major looked as though he had swallowed a lemon whole and I saw the grim look on the Sergeant Major's face. Woe betide any trooper or sergeant in D Troop who did not perform to his best.

With four officers and confidence in all of us, the major split us into four groups. I had Cecil and Carlton as my sergeants and Davy and Jimmy as corporals. As far as I was concerned I only lacked Jed or Dago to have the perfect team. I took my men along the Warrenton Road and then up towards the hilly roads around Stafford. I wondered if we could get as far as Washington in the time available. As much as I had enjoyed riding Apple I preferred Copper. I could drop my hands and guide her with just my knees. She seemed to know where I wanted to go almost before I did. It made riding a pleasure. It was almost the same with my men. Davy took a couple of men to ride ahead of us. He was quick-witted and had a calm manner. He knew how to deal with unexpected events. Cecil was still a little hot-headed at times although he had improved immeasurably.

We skirted Stafford; that would be visited on our return journey. At the end of the day, we reached the heights above the Potomac. Davy was excited when he returned. "There's a bridge down there. It's made of wood and there are no guards. I think it would burn well."

Although we had been told to scout and then report back this was too soft a target to ignore. There were woods to the south-east of us where we could take shelter if needs be. I knew that Dumfries was such an important port that it might have troops there but I counted on the fact that, at night, they would be easy to evade. "Right boys let's do it. Jimmy, take four men and watch our backs. Davy, lead the way."

The bridge was next to an abandoned ferry and was a toll bridge. As we trotted down a man came out of the hut next to the bridge. In the dark, he must have taken us for Yankee cavalry for he waved at us in a friendly way. "A little late for you fellahs to be out. Do you want to cross the river or are you still looking for that ghost?" He laughed at his own joke.

I pulled my Army Colt out. "No sir, I am the ghost!"

My men laughed and he dropped to his knees. "Please don't kill me, boys. I have a wife and children."

I shook my head. "We don't kill civilians. Despite what you may have heard. Now is there anyone else in the toll house?"

"No sir, not this late at night."

"Good, then you may leave."

"I can go?"

Confederate Ranger

He looked surprised. "Unless you want to stay and watch your bridge burn!"

"No, sir. They don't pay me enough."

He ran to the west as though the devil was after him. "Have a look inside the hut. Cecil, see if there is anything that will burn. Carlton, take the rest of the men and find as much kindling as you can."

Cecil came out with a look of joy on his face. "He has a fire! There are red hot coals." He looked down the bridge. "If we put kindling at three places in the bridge then we can light the furthest fire and work backwards. The last fire can be the tollhouse. Four fires should ensure that the bridge is destroyed."

Cecil liked engineering puzzles and he had come up with a better plan than I could have imagined. "Get the boys on it. I'll go and see how Jimmy is doing."

"Do I wait for you to light the fire, sir?"

"You are the sergeant, just do it!"

Jimmy and his men were staring towards the Stafford road. "See anything corporal?"

"Nothing stirring sir."

"Well keep watch because in about ten minutes you should see the bridge over the Potomac burning and that means any soldiers within ten miles will be high tailing it here."

I rode back in time to see flames flickering at the far end of the bridge. I watched Cecil check that the fire had caught before he and the three troopers with shovels of coals retreated to the next fire site. By the time he had reached the toll house the far fire was shooting flames high in the sky and the other two were burning well. I heard him yell, "Get back to the lieutenant" and then he threw the last shovel of coals into the toll house. He must have found some coal oil because the whole building went up as though hit by a mortar shell. Cecil fell to the ground but, before I could race to him he stood, a little unsteadily and ran towards his waiting horse.

When they rejoined me I asked, "Are you alright? You had me worried."

"Sorry sir, I didn't run fast enough and there must have been some coal oil in there." He grinned as he dusted himself down. "Sure made a nice fire though."

We looked back and the bridge was engulfed in flame from one end to the other. "Right lads, let's head to the forest and get some rest. Tomorrow we find more targets."

I was awoken by Trooper Brown in the small hours. "Sorry to wake you, sir."

He sounded nervous. "Don't worry about it sentry. You are just doing your job. What is it?"

"I heard some cavalry moving along the road. They were heading for the bridge."

We had hidden our camp well inside the woods and well away from any tracks. "Come on then let's take a look."

I grabbed my rifle and I trotted after him through the woods. After half a mile the trees thinned and we could see the glow of the fire a mile or two in the distance. Silhouetted against the glow were horsemen. I estimated it to be company strength.

"They came from the south?"

"Yes, sir, from Stafford."

That meant there was a regiment or part of one at Stafford. "Good lad. You did well." I took out my watch. It was almost four. "Tell you what, let's brew some coffee for the boys. I am awake now and they'll appreciate it."

"Yes, sir." He gave me a strange look as though making coffee was beneath an officer.

Confederate Ranger

While he got the water I took out a handful of beans and hit them with the butt of my Colt and then ground them to make a powder for the coffee. We poured them and the water into the pot. Trooper Brown went for some dry kindling. We always carried plenty in our saddlebags. Smoke was a bad thing. It was a chilly morning and, when the fire took, it warmed us up very quickly. We put our greatcoats, framed by rifles, around the fire to shield it from view and to stop the wind fanning the flames. When I heard it bubbling I put my rifle barrel under the handle to lift it from the fire. "Get our mugs. I think we should be the first to appreciate this and then we can wake the boys."

"Yes, sir."

I used my bandana to grasp the handle and pour us the steaming black coffee. Too hot to drink it was warming to hold. As I expected the aroma of coffee woke the men. It was gentler than reveille and I had found it an effective way of doing things. By five-thirty, we were packed away and ready to go.

"Now there are a hundred cavalry around here so we will head through the woods and make our way down to Dumfries. We will have a look at the port and see what is worth having and then get to Stafford by this afternoon. We need to be careful. We have told them we are here. Let's avoid an extended stay. I for one don't like Yankee hospitality."

We crossed the creek and found a place from which to observe the port. It was no Charleston but it looked to be busy enough. There were ships waiting to enter and I took a guess that they were supplying Hooker's army. There were wagons leaving the port and heading inland. I realised that the regiment could do some serious damage to the trade if there were no cavalry nearby. From our observations, I could not see any troops but I needed to be sure. I took my deer hide jacket and threw it to Davy.

Confederate Ranger

"Get rid of your kepi and have a look-see. Don't take chances. I just need to know it there is a cavalry presence. We'll wait here and cover you in case of trouble."

"Yes, sir!" Davy was up for anything and he quickly threw on my jacket which made him look more like a civilian than a Confederate horseman.

As he disappeared from sight I turned to the others. "Ready your pistols in case anyone is pursuing him when he returns."

It was almost an anti-climax when he returned safely. "No soldiers sir but it is very busy. I managed to get down to the quayside and I was nearly knocked over by the wagons."

"Well done. Now let's head to Stafford and then home."

We followed the coast and passed Aquia. There were fewer ships there and none looked big enough to worry about. Then we found Hartwood Church. This was a small settlement of, perhaps, a dozen houses. I would have ignored it were it not for the presence of a large number of cavalry. We saw their tents and their horse lines. This time I left the men with Cecil and Carlton while Davy and I sneaked down to take a look.

There was plenty of cover for us. There were barns and hedgerows as well as small copses and outhouses. We managed to get within a hundred yards of the camp. We lay beneath a picket fence to get a full view of the camp. It looked to be big enough for at least two regiments. I wondered what was so important to keep two regiments here. We moved further south, keeping out of sight and then we found the reason. There was a freshly cleared piece of land with fences around it and in the middle were wagons. We counted twenty at least. There were armed foot soldiers all around and two secure gates. I led Davy away. When we were out of sight I said, "Well I guess our attack on the powder train had an effect eh?"

Confederate Ranger

"Yes sir but that is a good target. How many men do you estimate?"

"Two regiments? Could be over eight hundred men perhaps more."

When we reached the patrol I decided that we had enough information to take back to the colonel. "I want to avoid those cavalrymen so we will head north-west and travel over the mill road. It should be less busy."

It was now the middle of the afternoon and the men and horses were tired. We had one more obstacle to cross the Stafford Road. Perhaps it was the tiredness which made us a little lax but just after we had crossed the road there was the crack of a couple of carbines and Trooper Hart fell dead from his horse. "Troop A turn and draw." I had no idea what we would see but I knew we had a better chance of surviving if we faced our enemy. A line of forty horsemen were galloping in a loose line. They must have fired their first rounds from a stationary position for the shots were now whizzing over our heads. They were fifty yards away. "Fire and keep firing until you are empty!" I had two guns firing and the wall of lead had an effect. As the first riders fell, those on the outside moved away from the smoke filled death trap. "Now let's get the hell out of here. Carlton, lead them off!" I still had my second Colt and I kept firing blindly to the left and right. When I heard the empty chamber I prepared to wheel around. Suddenly, out of the smoke, I saw a sabre appear and it was aimed at my head. I had just enough time to jerk my head out of the way and grab the hand holding the sabre. With my right hand, I punched at the head of the trooper and clubbed him with my Colt. He fell to the ground Copper had continued her wheel and I grabbed the reins of the man's horse. "Get us out of here!" Her hooves dug into the ground and she leapt like a hare. I let go of the reins of the other horse. I would need both hands soon. We were being pursued; I could hear it. I glanced over my shoulder to confirm it and saw the Union horsemen appearing through the smoke. Ahead of me, I saw some of my troopers turning around. "Don't turn round! Ride!"

I knew that Carlton would take the men the best way to save our tired horses and I had to hope that we had better horses than the enemy. I knew we were better horsemen but this might come down to horseflesh. We hit the small road which rose into the hills. The men in front of me began to slow up and I was about to shout at them when I saw Carlton pointing. The men began galloping and as I reached the top of the small rise I saw that he was taking them over a wall. He was heading due south now, away from the mill road and towards the Warrenton Road. It was a clever move. I just prayed that his belief in the men's skill was not misplaced. I almost cheered as they all soared over it. They made it look easy and I knew it was not. Copper made light work of it and her powerful stride soon made us catch up the stragglers. I looked behind us and saw that only three of the horsemen had attempted the same jump and only two had made it. Even if they did jump the obstacle we would have a comfortably long head start.

"You can slow up now Sergeant. They are giving up."

I heard the pop of their carbines as they attempted to hit one or two of us but the range was too great. We had escaped, it was by the skin of our teeth but we had made it. It was then I noticed the riderless horse and I remembered that we had lost a man; my first as an officer. It took all the joy out of the escape. We gathered the loose horse and led it with us; a poignant reminder of our own mortality.

We were the last patrol to reach Kelly's Ford. Sergeant Major Vaughan was watching anxiously from the side of the river. I saw the relief on his face as we waded through the water. "You had me, worried sir. I didn't want the regiment to lose its lucky charm."

I pointed to the empty saddle. "Not that lucky Sergeant Major. I lost a man."

He patted Copper as we halted next to him. "And you will lose more before this war is over but the fact that you are upset shows that you are that rare breed, a good officer who has his men in his heart." He jerked a thumb behind him to the colonel whose chair was facing the ford. "Just like himself. He was the same and I can see him in you." He grinned. "I told the boys to leave you some food. So eat first and then report. I'll see the colonel and tell him you will be along shortly."

The colonel took my report and smiled. "We were all waiting for you to return lieutenant and do you know why?" I shook my head. "We knew that, somehow, you would find the best targets. I shall ride to General Fitzhugh Lee in the morning but I think he will choose this Hartwood Church for us to visit. Well done."

As I walked back to my tent, feeling the effects of almost two solid days in the saddle, I almost bumped into Andrew Neil or Trooper Neil. He saw my rank and mumbled a, "Sorry sir." Then he looked closely at me and asked, "Do I know you… sir?"

"Yes Trooper, I was the officer who stopped you from striking Major Boswell."

He stepped back as though I had punched him again. "Yes sir, I remember now but I thought I knew you from home."

"No Trooper, just the other night."

I watched him hurry back to his lord and master and wondered what he would tell him. I had too many other things to worry about. Once again it was my judgement which would be used and I was finding the pressure too much. Supposed they moved the wagons? They could increase the guards. If I was the

Confederate Ranger

Union commander I would have patrols on the back roads. I knew that I would be closely questioned by the general when he came. The whole raid would be based on what I told him.

When I reached my tent I looked at my uniform, it looked dirty. I had not had the chance to visit Mistress Sandy and pick up my second one. I put on my old sergeant's uniform and went down to the river to wash the worst of the stains from the jacket at least. As I passed the Sergeant Major he stood to walk with me. "Times were lieutenant when you would have had a servant to do that for you."

"I don't hold with servants but I surely wish I had someone to do this for me. My second uniform is being made."

"Ah! Well, there are camp women and the wives of some of the troopers. They appreciate the money you know sir."

I nodded. "I will see them next time but I need this for tomorrow. General Fitzhugh Lee."

"If you don't mind me saying so he won't care what you look like sir, so long as your report is good enough."

"Oh, the information is good enough. I found more targets than enough."

"Sergeant Mulrooney told me that you burned a bridge, sir?"

"Yes Sergeant Major. It was too easy a target to miss."

"You neglected to tell the colonel about that." My face fell and he smiled, "Don't worry lieutenant I told him. The colonel and I have been together long enough to allow such informality. Well, sir, I'll leave you to your washing."

As I walked back to my tent I realised that I now had a position to uphold. I would need to spend some of my pay getting jobs done that, hitherto, I had done myself. Worryingly as I passed Major Beauregard's tent I was aware of the two of them staring at me. Had they remembered me?

Confederate Ranger

The next day the general arrived and I was summoned to the colonel's tent. They were both seated and I stood awaiting their questions. It was General Fitzhugh Lee who asked the questions. He cut quite a dashing figure in his fine uniform and I was glad that I had made the effort to clean mine. "The colonel tells me you have found some targets for me?"

"Yes, sir. The port of Dumfries is unguarded and there are many ships there and Aquia harbour, although it has fewer ships is also unguarded." I waited for further comment but none was forthcoming and so I continued. "At Hartwood Church, there is a large wagon park but it is guarded by at least two regiments of cavalry. There is also another cavalry force close to Stafford."

"Now that is more like it. I will leave the ships for our navy. Besides horses can't walk on water can they lieutenant?"

"No, sir."

"I think that Hartwood Church will do very well. I also hear that you destroyed the bridge at Woodbridge?"

"Yes, sir. It was unguarded and too good a target to miss."

"Well done. General Stuart said you were a man to get a job done and I can see that he is right. Well, colonel, we will leave tomorrow at first light. I think that if we…" they were suddenly aware that I was still standing there. "Oh dismiss lieutenant and well done."

As I left Harry and Danny descended upon me. "Well? What is it to be?"

I had told Harry of my findings the night before. "Hartwood Church is where the general would like to go. He fancies our chances against Union cavalry."

Danny shook his head. "We have a glory hunter then. Union horsemen again! One of these days our luck will run out."

Confederate Ranger

I glanced in the direction of the Beauregard tent. I had the feeling that their eyes were upon me the whole time. Danny saw my look and said, "Is there a problem Jack?"

Harry said, when I hesitated, "If you need me to leave?"

"No Harry, we have no secrets. Major Beauregard and Trooper Neil were the ones who murdered my parents in Ireland."

"They were the ones? What do you intend to do about it?"

"I promised Danny that I would do nothing until after the war but I think that Neil recognised me and the two of them have been watching me closely ever since."

Danny shook his head and smiled. "I wouldn't worry, Jack. He can't do much about it. I seem to remember my cousins had a run in with him but they put the frighteners on him. He strikes me as all piss and wind. They both do."

"Yes sir but he is also a murderer and that has me worried."

Harry nodded, "Jack's right sir. We'll have to keep an eye on those two."

"I think the rest of the regiment is keeping an eye on those two."

The colonel held a briefing in the afternoon. "We will be leaving forty men here with the Sergeant Major and Second Lieutenant Magee. They will send out small patrols around the camp. We would like to find it here when we return." I think I saw a look of relief pass over his face. I could see why he associated with the major. "The rest of us will head for Stafford. Lieutenant Hogan discovered a wagon park and a couple of regiments of cavalry. The general would like to bloody the noses of the Union cavalry. Our job will be to provide a screen of riders to prevent them from being surprised. Any questions?"

Major Beauregard's voice seemed to jar on my ears as he drawled, "So I take it we will have no chance of glory again? We will be bystanders while General Fitzhugh Lee gathers all the glory?"

"Major we will do what we do best. We will scout but in the end, we all serve the Confederacy. Anything else?" It was appointed question aimed at the Englishman and anyone else would have recognised the tone but the major ploughed on. "Lieutenant Hogan, would I be right in thinking you come from a farm close to Cork and your family were potato farmers?" My face must have betrayed me. He gave a nasty grin, "I am amazed that a peasant from the bogs of Ireland could be promoted to lieutenant!"

I had been recognised. There seemed little point in denying it and I went on the offensive. It had worked for me as a Wildcat. "Yes sir, of course, you know that because you and Trooper Neil murdered my parents and tried to burn my sister and me alive!"

There was a shocked gasp from all but Danny and Harry. The major's voice became icy. "That sir is a lie. Were you not a junior officer I would challenge you."

Danny piped up, "I think not major. I am a Murphy from the same area and my cousins told me of an arrogant, bullying English landlord. Would that be you by any chance?"

The murderer just glowered at Danny. I could see Danny flexing his hands ready to strike the major. Major Boswell's voice cut through the icy silence. "That restriction does not apply to me sir and I will happily give you satisfaction if for other reason than the slur you cast upon one of the bravest and most truthful men I have ever known. What will it be? Pistols or swords?"

I saw the Englishman pale and knew then that he was a craven coward. "There is no quarrel between us sir and I will not fight you."

Suddenly the colonel shouted, I had never heard him shout before, "Silence! There will be no duelling in my regiment and that is an order. Is that clear Major Boswell?"

"Sir."

"Major Beauregard?"

The major looked relieved, "Of course sir. The regiment comes first."

"Then you are dismissed. Lieutenant Hogan, stay behind for a moment." When we were alone he asked. "Did he murder your parents?" I told him the details of the incident and he asked. "What do you intend to do about it?"

"As I told Captain Murphy. I will kill them both, but I will wait until the war is over."

"Do I have your word on that?"

I stiffened. "Of course sir. I may be from an Irish potato farm but I hope that I am a man of my word."

He smiled. "I have no doubt that you are a man of your word and I believe you. I also believe that the major and his man are both dead men walking for I would not like you on my trail. Dismiss and thank you for your honesty."

Chapter 12

I slept with my new Bowie knife beneath my bedroll that night. My two enemies had shown themselves to lack any kind of honour and I would not put it past them to attempt to kill me while I slept. When I awoke I found that Danny had placed a sentry outside my tent. Trooper Cole grinned at me, "Morning sir. Sleep well?"

"I certainly did and now you can get your breakfast."

"Thank you, sir!"

It was still dark as we left our camp. The general had said we would leave at first light and that meant that the scouts had to be out before first light. Harry took the point while Danny and I took the left flank. When we neared our road, my job was to direct the other regiments the right way. Troops B and C were to guard the road to Fredericksburg and Kelly's Ford. They would stop any reinforcements coming from that direction. The colonel had placed himself there as being the most strategic point in our defences. They would ambush any forces that followed us. The two majors would be left with the task of keeping the cavalry from being reinforced from the north. Major Boswell took my section as I waited with Trooper Tyree at the road junction. The colonel saluted as he took his two troops along the road to set up an ambush position. When Major Beauregard passed by me it was as though I was invisible. The other officers and sergeants all returned my salute. We waited for fifteen minutes before General Fitzhugh Lee arrived with his brigade of cavalry.

"Thank you, Lieutenant Hogan, we can take it from here. This brings us out at Hartwood Church then?"

Confederate Ranger

"Yes sir but I will leave a scout at any of the turnings which may cause confusion. You cross the main road and the wagon park and cavalry camp are there before you." I hesitated, "Don't forget general we found more cavalry to the north."

"Yes son, I remember but with two troops of scouts there I am not worried about that."

As I rode to rejoin my troop I thought that I would be happier if it was B or C Troop who were supporting us and not Major St John Beauregard's untried D Troop. Instead of working our way through D Troop which straggled untidily down the road, Tyree and I jumped the walls to ride across country. Some of D Troop saw us and whooped their appreciation. I heard orders barked and knew who had silenced them.

I reached the major and the rest of the troop who were waiting behind the trees above Stafford. "The general is on his way, sir."

"Good. We will wait for D Troop and then we can skirt north and block the road. Jack, you know this road as well as any; can we get to the north and stay hidden?"

"Pretty much sir. If I was the Yankees I would have men up here. You get a good view of the land to the sea. Still, I am glad that they don't."

Danny turned to the men. "While we are waiting make sure all your guns are loaded. I don't want to give the order to fire and hear empty clicks."

We all did as ordered. Even those, like Cecil and me who had done it back at camp. Both of us knew the value of a fully-loaded revolver or, in my case, three loaded revolvers. D Troop arrived and Major Boswell rode up to them to give them their orders. "We can approach the northern road through the trees and along this trail. That way we can escape detection."

"I, for one yearn, for detection. At least that way we can have some action."

"Don't worry major, I can guarantee you some action today." He turned to me. "Right Jack, it's your show. Lead the way."

I heard a mumbled comment from Major Beauregard and the lieutenant and captain laughed. Danny said, "Ignore them Jackie boy, we'll deal with them in our own time."

Putting the sycophantic officers from my mind I led the patrol along the narrow twisting trail. When I judged that we had passed the wagon park I led us through the trees. "Davy, go and scout the road." A few moments later there was a whistle. "Right boys, let's go." The road was clear and we headed north. I remembered a place with a deserted barn and a half-broken wall running down the Stafford road and I deemed it would make a good ambush site.

When I found it, I halted. Major Boswell rode up and nodded approvingly. "A Troop, place yourselves on the eastern side of the road. Find shelter behind the walls and buildings."

It seemed an age before D Troop meandered up. There were only forty of them as the rest were with the Sergeant Major at the camp. "Major Beauregard, place your men on the other side of the road if you please."

He seemed to notice that we were all on foot. "You mean you want my men dismounted?"

In a very patient voice the major said, "Yes Major Beauregard, it makes ambushing easier."

"Well, I will dismount half of my men. We are cavalrymen and we will use the advantage of a horse. We will wait behind those trees."

Before Major Boswell could order him to follow orders the Englishman had ridden off. "Let him go, sir. We can do this with the lads we have."

"I know Danny but…"

"Just let it go, sir. He isn't worth it and you need to be sharp today sir. If our Jack is right then there will be more cavalry coming to join them."

"You are right." He stood in the middle of the road. "This is pistol work. I want no one to fire until I say so. Sergeants, make sure your men understand!" As he turned back to us he said, "That comment was, of course, meant for the ears of D Troop, her sergeants and officers both."

"Of course sir."

Harry and I went around the men to ensure that they had their guns ready and ammunition to hand to reload. Trooper Brown asked, "Suppose they don't come, sir?"

"Then I for one will be delighted. It will mean none of our men or horses get hurt or killed but if I was a betting man, then I would bet on blue coats riding down this road sooner rather than later."

Suddenly we heard the sound of bugles mixed with the pop of carbines and pistols from down the road and the cheers of charging cavalry. I looked down at Trooper Brown. "We will soon know if this is a pointless ambush or a fight for our lives."

From up the road, we heard the Yankee bugles and they sounded close. "Wait for the major's order eh?"

The cavalry appeared in the distance and they were riding four abreast down the road. There was a slight dip half a mile north of our position and they would be hidden, albeit briefly, for a few moments. The major was at the end of our line. When they reached him he would give the command and, hopefully, they would be caught off guard. I was at the opposite end of the line. They would have the most warning at that end and we could expect them to try to give us a hard time. We were crouched behind the wall and could not see how many were still to come. Suddenly we heard, "Fire!" and we all stood and began firing our pistols. Not one of the bluecoats was further than ten feet away and we could not miss. I heard their bugle sound. We used the same calls and it was the one to reform. The bluecoats began to come back up the road. We still fired. I was on my third pistol.

Then I heard Major Beauregard yell, "D Troop charge!"

Through the thinning smoke, I saw the sabres of the twenty troopers as they launched themselves at the Union cavalry. We had hurt the cavalry but not destroyed them and the twenty men were charging a hundred men. The ones they charged had been at the back of the original column and were not disorganised in any way. They took out their pistols and fired a volley at D Troop. It was as though a scythe had swept through a wheat field. The ones who reached the Union lines were surrounded by blue uniforms and they hacked and slashed as they tried to fight their way out. We had no chance to fire as our own men would have been struck. Eventually, Major Beauregard and four men emerged from the melee and galloped down the road towards Major Boswell.

We had all reloaded and when the cavalry charged after our men we opened fire again. This time they knew where we were and they fired at the smoke. The walls we were using gave some protection but men still fell. Finally, I heard the sound of recall and this time the Union cavalry withdrew out of sight.

"Sergeant Mulrooney, check for casualties. Reload!"

Danny stormed up to me, "That damned arrogant fool. He got fifteen good men killed for no reason. I will go and take charge of the rest of D Troop. You take charge here Jack. Harry is with the major. I don't know if they will come again."

"Sergeant Spinelli, get some men and get any wounded Yanks out of the lane. Get their guns and secure any horses."

Confederate Ranger

"Yes, sir!"

Cecil ran up to me. "None of our lads are dead sir but there are a couple with light wounds. David is looking after them."

"Where's the doctor?"

"On the other side with D Troop sir."

I put that out of my mind. He should have been with the bulk of the men, A Troop. "When Dago brings the weapons you take charge of them. Any that can't be repaired get rid of and put the rest in either your saddlebags or the others."

He looked insulted, "Sir, with respect, I can repair anything!"

"Of course you can, sorry, I forgot!"

"Corporal Jones, go and see what they are up to but be careful!"

"Sir!" He leapt on to his horse and galloped off. He returned fifteen minutes later by which time the road had been cleared and the wounded made safe and secured as prisoners. "Sir, they are heading for the coast road. They are trying to get around us. "

"Ride down and tell the major." I turned to look for Carlton, "Sergeant James, get the horses, I think we may be moving." I climbed the all and stepped into the middle of the road. "Captain Murphy, they are trying to flank us. I have informed the major. I think we might be moving."

He waved his thanks and then I heard him organising D Troop. The bugle gave us the order and we all mounted. The Union prisoners, all thirty of them were put on either the captured horses or the horses of the dead troopers from D Troop. "Sergeant Smith, take six men and form a rearguard." Jed saluted. I would feel safer with him half a mile behind us watching our back; he had a nose which could smell Yankee horsemen.

Danny reined in next to me. "I know we heard recall Jack, but ride up to the Major and find out what we do next." He gestured with his thumb at D Troop. "The captain was killed and the lieutenant is with the galloping major. I can't leave these."

"Yes, sir. I'll be right back." I turned to Dago. "Take charge of my boys until I get back eh?"

I galloped down the road. The troop was well spread out and I found the major deep in conversation with the general. "A splendid victory, James, truly splendid. It is a shame so many of your men died."

Major Boswell shook his head. "We lost a handful sir."

"But I saw Major Beauregard and some wounded men galloping down the road."

"The major led an unnecessary and fruitless sabre charge at the enemy and lost fifteen men. If he had not done so then we would have lost no men."

"Oh, I see. It has still been a great victory. We have well over a hundred prisoners."

"Sir?"

"Yes, Lieutenant Hogan?"

"We have twenty prisoners too. Do you want them all together?"

"We might as well. We have wagons and we will be moving slowly." He looked at Major Boswell and I detected a sympathetic expression on the general's face. "Major your two Troops are going to have to buy us time to escape."

"We will do that. Sir, if you would tell the colonel what we are doing he can prepare another ambush." He shook his head, "Although I think that he will already have planned that anyway."

"None the less I will tell him. Good luck."

After he had galloped off the major turned to me. "Right, Jack. Who is the rearguard?"

"Jed."

Confederate Ranger

"Sound man. Take First Sergeant Spinelli and the rest of the Wildcats. I want you as rearguard. You know what to do. We need to slow them up and give the colonel time to organise. I will look for another ambush point as well. Send the prisoners up to the general. We might as well get those off our hands."

I pointed to the east. "They tried to flank us sir so I would expect them to come from that direction."

"You are right. Good luck Jack."

When I reached Harry with the prisoners I gave him the general's instructions. "You had better take them to the main column and then get back to the major he will need you."

"You know Jack the sooner you kill that bastard the better!"

I told Danny what was intended. "It makes sense but I envy you. You get the Wildcats and I get the rest. You have the luck of the devil you know!"

"They say it's the luck of the Irish so I must have your share too. Wildcats to me!" They galloped up with grins on their faces. They fought as the 1st Virginia but in their hearts, they were still Wildcats. "Right boys, we are the rearguard. First Sergeant, make sure that everyone has enough ammunition." I pointed to the dead Yankees. "Some of these will have some. I'll go and get Jed."

Jed was half a mile up the road. He looked as calm as a South Carolina sunrise. "Not a sign of them sir."

"I know. I think they are riding parallel to us. Some will be on the coast road and some will be in the hills. They will try to get us in a pincer movement. We are the rearguard and we have to slow them up. The major is laying an ambush and it is the Wildcats who are at the back."

"Then the general has no worries at all. Does he sir?"

There were just fifteen of the Wildcats left but I felt happier than I had for many a month. "Davy you and Jimmy ride up those hills to the west. Aaron and Wilkie ride to the coast. I want to know where they are and how many of them. Keep out of sight and just get a rough number."

We rode down the road at a steady pace. The fact that we had heard no firing or sounds of battle was reassuring. Then Davy and Jimmy rode in like the whole Union Army was behind them. "They got ahead of us sir. There is a regiment and they are planning on attacking the major." He pointed to a column of thin smoke a mile and a half ahead. "There is a small settlement yonder. No more'n two or three houses. The major has made a barricade. The Union cavalry is out of sight and they are forming a line. I think they intend to charge."

There was the sound of hooves and we all grabbed our guns. Aaron and Wilkie rode in. "Sir, there is a regiment of Yankee cavalry they are two miles that way and they are head west real quick sir."

I had to think quickly and the only idea which came into my head was a surprise. Do the one thing that was unexpected. "Right boys. We ride in a column of fours. When I give the word I want you all to yell orders as though you are all captains leading a troop each. We charge through the cavalry and jump the barricade."

Dago grinned, "I like it! Sir, if you don't mind me saying so, but you are mad as a fish!"

"Thank you, First Sergeant, I'll take that as a compliment. Now let's ride."

We rode swiftly down the road. I counted on the fact that the drumming of their hooves would drown out the sound of ours. I saw them half a mile ahead and then the road dipped and we lost sight of them. "Draw pistols. Ready!" As they came into view forty yards in front of us I yelled, "2nd Virginia charge! Yee Haw!"

Confederate Ranger

The others all yelled and called out different regiments. I began firing as fast as I could. I did not bother to aim. I just fired at the mass of blue before me. The Union horsemen were confused and the ones at the back had not drawn weapons. We were firing at unprepared men. I drew my second pistol and began firing into both sides as we cut a swathe through the troopers. Copper barrelled into a horse whose rider was trying to turn her and both rider and horse went down in a crumpled heap. I heard the crunch of bones breaking as Copper's hooves trampled them down. Suddenly I was through and I saw the barricade thirty yards away. "Yee-haw!" Copper leapt cleanly over the top and landed on the other side. I reined her in and sought the Major. "Sir, there is another regiment coming. They are minutes behind. Let's get the hell out of here!"

"1st Virginia Scouts mount! Bugler, sound the retreat."

Jed reined in next to me. "We lost Jack Jones."

"Everyone else?"

"They made it!"

"Good, let's escape their trap before they realise we were only a handful of men and not another regiment."

We needed no further urging. Unless they tried to jump the barricade we would have a head start and I prayed that the colonel was up ahead and had a couple of aces up his sleeve. Our problem was our tired horses and we dared not try to gallop. Dago must have had a stiff neck as he was constantly turning around to watch for pursuers.

We could see the place we had left the colonel but of him, there was no sign. However further up the road, in the distance, we could see the lumbering wagons and the cavalry. The major led us towards the road junction. Suddenly the colonel stepped out from behind the fence.

Confederate Ranger

"I am delighted that you have made it major. If you would be so good as to dismount?"

I could see that the major was perplexed. "A Troop dismount."

"I can see that you are confused. I want the enemy to think that you are too tired to fight." He turned to a sergeant standing close by. "Sergeant Wilkinson, ride up the road and watch for the enemy. When you see their scouts then return here." The sergeant sprang on to the back of his horse and galloped up the road. He had a fresh horse. "When the good sergeant returns we will make it look as though you will look as though you are walking back to Kelly's Ford. When they appear you will, of course, try to mount and flee. Do it badly, please. You will ride a little way down the road and we will ambush them." He waved his arm at the fences of the crossroads. "You did not notice that these fences were not here when we arrived. I have had the men stealing them from around here and the two companies are on both sides." The major smiled at last. "By the way you have done well and do not worry about Major Beauregard, we will deal with him later. Let us just concentrate on extraditing this regiment from, how many regiments are pursuing you?"

"About three or four."

"Well, then three or four regiments. It should make quite a tale if we succeed eh? Now tell your men what we are about. We do not want them in the dark do we?"

When the major moved off to speak with the other men I asked, "Sir, if we enfilade them from both sides of the road is there not a danger that we will hit our own men?" I suddenly realised I was telling a colonel he had made a mistake. "I am sorry sir. It is not my place."

Confederate Ranger

"No, Lieutenant Hogan, it shows a sound military mind. It would mean we would kill our own men but I will have the men echeloned so they are firing down the road. We still have crossfire but it is the enemy who will be in the maelstrom of lead. Now join your men. I want A Troop to add their fire to the ambush. The enemy must think that General Fitzhugh is attacking with his whole brigade."

I stood at the rear with Dago and Danny. "We had better ensure that the men have reloaded. This could get quite hot although how the colonel expects to turn back over a thousand men with two hundred I do not know."

"Ah well, Jack you are showing your lack of education. There are over eighty troopers you have not accounted for."

"Who is that?"

"Us."

"Sir, with due respect the men have been fighting and riding all day. Can we expect them to stand again? We are the cheese in the mousetrap."

"I am surprised at you Lucky Jacky," the major's voice came from behind me, "you of all people should know that you can defeat many times your number if you are well led and have resolve. I know that we have resolve and," he pointed to the colonel, "and we are certainly well-led."

"Sorry, sir. You are right."

His voice became softer, "It is all right, Jack. It must be hard for you to have the major so close. He is a constant reminder of what he did to your family. You are bearing it better than I would." Little did he know that the Englishman was rarely from my dark thoughts of murder and retribution.

We heard the galloping of B Troop's sergeant and the major nodded. "Right boys ready yourselves. Remember we have to look as bad as Yankees here. Make a mess of mounting and move off slowly. When I give you the word then turn and give them everything you have. We have finished running! Here we stand." I knew that we could not run any more. The best we could do would be to walk back to Kelly's Ford. This was the easiest chance the Yankees had to finish us off. I saw as the major did, the first of the Union cavalry trotting along the road. "Right boys, mount, badly!"

    I heard the bugle sound charge and, as I feigned a struggle to mount a confused Copper, I saw that they were two hundred yards from us. We began to move haphazardly down the road. Dago and I were at the back and we kept glancing over our shoulders, apparently in fear, but in reality, judging when the ambush would take place.

    Suddenly I heard, "Front rank fire!" There was a volley but even before it had finished the command, "Second rank fire!" This became almost a monotonous sequence, as it was repeated over and over. I stopped Copper for I could see the Union cavalry floundering in the face of such a fierce fire. It was almost a continuous wall of lead and I wondered how the colonel had managed this.

    The major shouted, "1st Virginia, turn and fire!"

    My pistol was already out and I fired into the smoke. Aiming shots was out of the question, we just had to add to the hail of lead pouring into the horsemen. When we heard the bugle sound retreat we knew we had won. As the smoke cleared we could see a mass of bodies, horses and men, filling the road. The whole of the regiment began to cheer.

    "Dismount! Let's save these horses for now."

    We moved down the lane putting injured horses out of their misery and moving the wounded troopers to a place of safety.

When I reached the colonel I said. "That was interesting sir. How did you manage it?"

I remembered my classes from West Point. The British used this at Waterloo to defeat the Imperial Guard. The vaunted guards of Napoleon had never retreated before but continuous volleys did the trick. Most of the men had single-shot carbines and so I placed them in two ranks. After one rank had fired they reloaded and the second rank was able to fire. Simple really. If you had breastworks you could add a third rank. And now Lieutenant Hogan I think we head back to camp. The 1st Virginia, or at least all of them here, has done their duty and the general will be pleased, I have no doubt about that."

Confederate Ranger

Chapter 13

We had lost men in the action but overall our losses had been light. If it were not for the action of the English major the losses would have been negligible, and I was interested to see how he would wheedle his way out of that. General Fitzhugh was waiting for us at the ford and he shook the colonel warmly by the hand. "We heard the firing. I was worried. The fact that you are here means that the enemy failed to penetrate your defences."

"They tried sir, but we have good cavalrymen here."

The general nodded. "You have indeed and this has been a great victory." He looked over to our camp. "It is a shame not all of your officers behaved as they should have done. Will you court-martial him?"

The colonel shook his head, "Not until I have heard all the evidence but unless there is some explanation which escapes me I think the major's days in this regiment are numbered."

"Would you mind if I sat in on this informal court of enquiry?"

"Not at all, general. It might expedite matters later on. Shall we say about seven? After the evening meal?"

"I'll be there."

I noted that the major and Trooper Neil were not to be seen and wondered about that. The colonel summoned Sergeant Major Vaughan. I was leading Copper to the horse lines and managed to catch most of the conversation. "After the men and officers have been fed I will hold an enquiry into events earlier on today. I will require Major Boswell and Major Beauregard, First Lieutenant Magee, Captain Murphy and Lieutenant Hogan. The general will be in attendance so…"

Confederate Ranger

I heard no more but I had heard enough. I wondered what the procedure would be. Before now matters like this would have been dealt with informally, as in the case of the Union spies. I would need all my wits about me. I did not enjoy the meal. We had an officer's mess now and there was no conversation. This was mainly due to the presence of Major Beauregard. None of us wished to discuss the case, or the day with him there and it made the food taste like sawdust. I began to yearn for our days as Partisan Rangers. I left to put on my best uniform; I thought I might need it.

We all gathered outside the tent. Sergeant Major Vaughan's huge bulk filled the doorway but he was pleasant enough. "Sorry to keep you fine gentlemen waiting but the general wanted to have a word with the colonel about procedure."

"Damned bad form I say. We were told to come after the evening meal and here we are. This wouldn't happen in the British Army. This is a waste of my time." Major Beauregard looked bored!

It was amazing. No-one said a word but the rest of us, apart from Lieutenant Magee, all shared a look with each other. Sergeant Major Vaughan rolled his eyes and Danny tried to suppress a grin.

The colonel's voice ended the moment, "They may enter Sergeant Major."

Opening the flap with a huge smile Sergeant Major Vaughan said, "Please come in gentlemen."

The colonel and the general were seated behind the colonel's desk and there was an empty seat next to the colonel. There were five chairs before the desk. Major Beauregard sat at one end of the five. The lieutenant sat next to him then Major Boswell, Danny and finally, me.

The colonel smiled. "This is an informal court of enquiry about the actions in the battle earlier and will focus upon Major Beauregard and his part in the action. This is not a court-martial. I want everyone to understand that. If the evidence is strong enough then a court-martial will be convened with senior officers at Culpeper Court House."

"Stuff and nonsense!"

"Major Beauregard although this is not a court-martial you will only speak when asked. Is that clear?"

The major looked beyond the colonel as he said, "Yes Colonel Cartwright."

"First of all, Major Boswell, for the benefit of the general here would you tell us what my instructions and battle orders were?"

"To block any reinforcements attacking the general's brigades during their raid on Hartwood Church and to avoid any casualties."

"Good. That confirms what I told the general." I noticed that Sergeant Major Vaughan was writing down all that was said. "And what were your orders to the troops under your direct command?"

"I ordered A and D Troops to dismount and hide behind the walls and buildings. A Troop was on the eastern side and D Troop on the west."

"And did everyone follow those orders?"

"A Troop did sir but Major Beauregard said that he was only dismounting half of his men and he rode off with the other half."

"And is this true Major Beauregard?"

"If you mean did I obey my instincts as a cavalry officer of some years and take some men to be used as they were intended then the answer is yes."

"So you disobeyed your orders?"

Confederate Ranger

The English smiled an oily smile, "But I did obey orders. There were members of D Troop dismounted and behind the wall and they were under the command of Captain Cooper."

"Who is not here to defend himself as he is dead is he not?"

"The vagaries of war."

"But you left a man who had never been in battle in command of your troop."

"He was an officer. An officer is supposed to command men in battle." The major seemed unconcerned with the man's death and gave a bored shrug.

The colonel coughed and the general began to colour. His face became redder and redder over the next few questions. At one point I thought that he would explode. "Now then Major Boswell what happened next?"

"The Union cavalry appeared and when they were level with me we opened fire. We knocked them about badly and they sounded reform and then Major Beauregard charged."

"How many men were with him?"

"Twenty."

"And how many were they facing?"

"There was a regiment but only one hundred were prepared for the charge."

"So Major Beauregard, you charged one hundred and more men with just twenty."

"In the British Army, I would have had a medal and not have to listen to this nonsense."

"Please answer the question."

"Of course I did. We are cavalry."

"And what did you do next?"

He was silent for a moment and I leaned forward slightly to get a better view of him. For the first time, he neither looked nor sounded confident. "Well I heard the bugle for recall and I left the battlefield."

"That was the Union bugle because we had beaten them."

"Was it? Noise does funny things in a battle. I remember at the Alma…"

The general finally exploded, "Major will you answer the questions damn you!" He looked at the colonel and said, "Sorry Zebediah but I have heard enough for a court-martial already!"

The colonel held an apologetic hand up. "Let us do this correctly. So major, having heard the recall why did you ride straight back to the camp?"

"I had wounded men and I assumed that we would all be retreating."

"So Major Beauregard, you admit deserting your troops whilst under fire?"

"No Colonel Cartwright. I was still with D Troop. I assumed that Captain Cooper was with the rest and I trust my officers."

The colonel pushed away the paper he had been using to make notes and leaned back in his chair. He put his hands together as though in prayer and then turned to the general. "I agree with you general. There is enough evidence to warrant a general court-martial."

Sergeant Major Vaughan coughed, "For both officers sir?"

"Well done sergeant. I had forgotten. First Lieutenant Magee. Why did you disobey Major Boswell's orders?"

"I obeyed Major Beauregard sir."

"Why did you not remain on the battlefield?"

"I obeyed Major Beauregard sir."

"So your actions were as a result of obeying the orders of your superior officer?"

Confederate Ranger

"Yes, sir." Magee was a slippery customer. He had avoided censure.

"Very well. Then the court-martial will be for Major Arthur St John Beauregard. Now then the date? What would suit you general?"

"Before I came I checked and there is already a court-martial arranged for the 17th of March. All of the necessary senior officers will be present including, I understand, Major General Stuart."

"Very well then the date is set. Until that time Major consider yourself under arrest. As a gentleman, I hope that I do not have to place a sentry at your tent?"

Major Beauregard stood and pointed an accusing finger at the two senior officers. "I see what is going on here. This man," he pointed at Major Boswell, "resents me because I am obviously a more experienced, decorated officer. Since I arrived he has had his Irish peasants making up ridiculous stories about me. Well, I have had enough. I warn you that if this proceeds it is you gentlemen who will be on trial. My sponsor is none other than Secretary of War, Seddon. You may be related to the ancient general who is mishandling the war but I have friends in high places and I am a dangerous man to cross!"

I thought that General Lee was going to leap across the table and throttle the major; so did the colonel who turned to Sergeant Major Vaughan, "Please escort this officer to his tent please."

The Sergeant Major put a huge paw on the major's elbow. "Come along sir. You heard what the colonel said."

"Get your hands off me, you lumbering oaf."

I did not see what the old soldier did, I suspect he gripped the elbow even tighter, but the major squealed like a pig and was propelled out of the tent by a Sergeant Major who looked angry for the first time since I had met him.

Confederate Ranger

Lieutenant Magee made to leave but the colonel said, "Sit down sir." Magee did as he was told and he stared at his boots not wishing to meet the gaze of the colonel. "Your behaviour has been less than satisfactory throughout this and I don't know what the general thinks but I find your story dubious, to say the least. We will be watching you from now on. You might wish to reconsider your future with this regiment. Now you may go!"

The general stood. "I do not think that Major Beauregard will be serving the Confederacy for very much longer." He turned to the three of us. "Well done gentlemen. I shall send over a couple of bottles of French Brandy I acquired. I discovered from the prisoners that the general we defeated today was an old classmate of mine General William Averell. It is an even greater victory than I had hoped. Well done!"

After he left the colonel stood and sat on the edge of his desk facing us. "I didn't like doing that and I want to thank you for your restraint; especially you Jack. Captain Murphy, I want you to take charge of D Troop. We can't trust the Magee brothers and you have shown yourself to be resourceful." Danny's face fell and I knew why. He was Major Boswell's man and always would be. "We can promote Lieutenant Grimes to be captain and Jack here can be First Lieutenant. That would mean Sergeant Spinelli to lieutenant and Sergeant Smith to First Sergeant. Any objections?"

"No sir, that seems satisfactory all round."

The first thing we did was to tell Dago and Jed of their promotions. "All these promotions. If it keeps going this way then I'll be general by next year!"

Dago was irrepressible and helped to get the bad taste that was Major Beauregard out of my mouth. Sergeant Major Vaughan was walking back and he saluted. "Some men think they are gentlemen because of the way they speak. It is nothing to do with that. It is in here what counts." He patted his heart. "Congratulations First Lieutenant Hogan. You deserve it." I stared at his back. Nothing got by the Sergeant Major. As I went into my tent I was aware of two pairs of malevolent eyes staring at me. The bowie knife was comfortably beneath my bedroll again.

Harry was a little embarrassed to be promoted. In typical Harry fashion, he bemoaned the fact that he would need to get a new uniform. "Harry, you are on more pay now. You don't even spend the money we get as lieutenants. Stop being such a miserable bugger and enjoy the moment."

He realised he was being unnecessarily morose. "So I have you two as lieutenants now eh? Well, we have a great deal to do to reorganise things. Let's get the men together."

We paraded A Troop. Major Boswell kept out of the way. Part of it was the paperwork he had to gather for the court-martial and part of it was to allow Harry the chance to tell the men himself. The major would be providing the evidence for the prosecutor. He didn't look happy. Danny had an even harder job. He had to sort out D Troop and his two lieutenants were positively antagonistic. He was lucky in that the sergeants were good sorts and he knew he had the backing of the colonel. The major had told him that if the two lieutenants didn't work out then we would promote two more of A Troop's sergeants.

All of the Wildcats who had survived, all thirteen of them, were now either sergeants or corporals. Dago was a lieutenant but it showed the rest of the troop where you would get with hard work. We divided the eighty troopers into three manageable sections each led by an officer with a sergeant. Harry had Jed and I chose Cecil. He had proved himself to be a good leader. He was far tougher than he had been when he had joined us and he had grown into someone who never lost his temper.

Confederate Ranger

We worked all day and I was tired but happy. Then Carlton found me. "Sir, there is a problem with Copper."

My heart hit my boots. I had neglected her since our return and I berated myself. "What is it?"

"One of her legs, it looks like she picked up a piece of shrapnel or bullet the other day. I am sorry sir I should have noticed."

"No sergeant. She is my horse and my responsibility. I just put her sluggishness down to her exhaustion. I never dreamed she had been wounded."

When we reached the horse lines I could see what he meant. Her head didn't even come up when I approached. He showed me the wound. It looked angry and felt hot to the touch."I know sir. That has me worried too."

"There might be something left in there."

"No sir, I had a poke around. She put up with it well, didn't you girl. Seems to me it is infected."

"Is there anything you can do?"

"This is beyond me. I sent for the veterinary officer attached to the general's brigade and he is coming over. I'll go and watch for him."

I stroked Copper's head. "I am so sorry old girl. This is my fault. I shall look after you better from now on."

When he arrived I felt a sense of relief. He was a distinguished-looking man and he had the look of someone who has been working with animals for years. He was an old fashioned horse doctor. "Now then lieutenant let's see this leg eh?"

He took out a stethoscope and listened to her chest and then he knelt down to examine the leg. When he stood his face was sombre. "I'm sorry son. The leg is infected. She'll have to be put down."

"You are joking! There must be something we could do."

"If this was a trooper I would cut off the leg. But it's a horse and we can't do that. I can make…"

"No thank you, sir. Thanks for the advice but we will try our methods."

"It will be kinder in the end."

Carlton must have seen the tears forming in my eyes and heard the emotion in my voice. "Come along sir. Let me show you the quickest way back to your camp."

When he returned I knew what to do. "Thanks for that Carlton. Do you remember when the major, he was a captain then, got wounded? Danny told us to use maggots and they ate the infection. It's worth a try."

"You are right sir and my old grandmother used to swear by a bread poultice to draw badness out of you. Let's try both."

"Good man!" As soon as we had something to do we felt better. We placed maggots in the wound and then wrapped the hot poultice around and bandaged the whole thing. "We need something to make her relax a little. If it was me I would have a shot of whisky."

"Let's try it, sir. Put a glass in with her water. I know it makes me sleepy. Sleep is always the best thing for a fever, that's what my mother always said."

"You get the water and I will get the whisky."

I went to the officer's mess. Danny shouted over, "We have the general's brandy do you want some?"

"Perfect. Give me a glassful."

Danny looked surprised. I was not known as a drinker. "Do you not want water in it?"

"No," I said as I grabbed it, "it's not for me it's for Copper." Leaving the stunned silence I ran back to Carlton who had a bucket of water. "This is the good stuff, from the general. It isn't poteen." I poured it in and she began to drink. When she had emptied it she nuzzled me and I took it as a good sign.

"Well, sir. It's in God's hands now. I'll sleep close by her tonight."

"Thanks, Carlton. I owe you."

"No, sir. I love horses and you are right, Copper is like Apples, she is special. She is worth a little love and care."

When I returned to the mess tent for dinner the rest of my brother officers were staring at me and the empty glass. "Brandy for a feckin horse? Have you gone mad Jackie Boy?"

I laughed and told them what had happened and what the officer had said. They all saw the sense in it. "Clever that." Dago was slightly drunk. It was his first time in the officer's mess and he had made the most of it.

The Magee boys suddenly realised that they were outsiders and remembered that they had duty that night. They left and the atmosphere became much more convivial. Major Boswell came in as we were all laughing at some joke Dago had just told. "Well, this is a happier mess than we are used to."

"Perhaps that is because the galloping major had his meal in his tent and his little friends have gone on duty."

"Now Danny, you especially, have to work with those two."

"The younger one is alright but the older one is sly and a miniature version of the major. He'll never cut it."

"Well, we have a couple of days to get to know our new roles and then I will be sending out patrols from every troop. The general wants to know what his old classmate is up to. We have two days to get things organised."

I went to bed that night but I was too worried about Copper to sleep. I tossed and I turned until after midnight. It was no good, I couldn't sleep. I got up. I moved quietly as I didn't want to disturb Danny who had the tent next to mine. He was a light sleeper and we had stopped the sentry watching me as his movements had woken Danny. I slipped out carrying my greatcoat. As I did I heard a thud and a groan from Danny's tent. I peered in. He had had a lot to drink and he had fallen out of bed. The cot was lying on top of him. I contemplated moving him but the thought of trying to pick up that dead weight made me think again. I got my blanket and draped it over the unconscious captain. "Sleep well, Danny!"

    I stepped over the sleeping Carlton and took out the apple I had taken from the mess tent. Copper looked better and she greedily crunched on the apple. I ran my hands over the bandage praying that this was working. I lay down in the hay next to her and covered myself with my coat. I did not think I would sleep but I felt happier just being close to her. I must have fallen asleep because the next thing I knew I was awoken by an almighty explosion. I jumped up and ran towards the main camp. I could see a fire and it appeared to be coming from my tent.

    As I approached I saw Harry and the Major pulling Danny to his feet. His tent was destroyed and he had cuts on his face but he looked alive. Cecil was there too and trying to get into my blazing tent. "The lieutenant! We have to get him out! He might be alive!"

    Dago restrained him. "No Irish, nothing could survive that, it looks like someone threw in a grenade or a bomb. Lucky Jack's luck finally ran out and he's dead."

    "Then I suppose I must be a ghost!"

Chapter 14

They stared at me. Cecil even came to touch me and then jumped back, making the sign of the cross. "How did you know it was a grenade Dago?"

The colonel and the Sergeant Major had joined us. "It was the fizzing of the fuse that woke me. I thought it was a snake and I can't abide snakes. I saw the glow from inside the tent and I threw myself to the ground."

"Then we ought to call you Lucky Dago."

Danny was shaking his head. I have no idea how I survived." He pointed to the mess that had been Captain Cooper's tent. Mine was between the two captains.

"That might have been the drink. You fell out of bed and it covered you. I put my blanket over you. They must have taken the impact."

The colonel and the inevitable Vaughan came over. "Well, lieutenant I am glad to see that you are alive although how I do not know."

"I was with my horse, she has a bad leg."

The colonel shook his head, "Lucky indeed although there are more things in heaven and earth… I digress. I think we can guess who did it although we cannot prove it."

Major Boswell looked like the general the previous day and I thought that he would explode too. "We should lock them both up now!"

"Due process major, we have no proof. I think it would be best if Lieutenant Hogan began his patrol in the morning. I assume you trust your own men?"

"Of course sir."

"And major there are four suspects I believe for the two lieutenants look to be under the spell of the major."

Danny shook his head, "No sir, not his spell. They owe him money and apparently, he has men back in Atlanta. He told the two officers that their family would be visited if they did not do all that he demanded."

"Then Captain I think that we need your troop on a long patrol. Keep them together. Major, you will remain in camp. You and I need to make sure that this case is watertight." He smiled at me. "I think the safest place for you young man is next to your horse. I believe she just saved your life."

The word spread through the camp about my miraculous escape. I saw many of the Irish boys making the sign of the cross as I passed by. They all threw black looks in the direction of the English major. He sat outside his tent smoking cigars and playing cards with Neil as though nothing had happened. Carlton told me to ride Apples and he promised me that he would watch Copper while I was away. She was already looking better and there was not as much heat from the wound. We knew we had to let nature take its course and let the poultice and the maggots work. It was probably as well that I was to be out of camp for a week or so. I would be with my horse every minute otherwise.

Danny and the major came to brief me, "Scout Falmouth and Fredericksburg; you know them both well."

"I know Stafford just as well Major."

"I know but we need to let D Troop earn their spurs and Danny here has some experience up there. There are more places to camp and hide. Your patrol area is a little tighter." He grinned. "And you have shown a propensity for getting out of tight situations." He nodded in the direction of the Englishman's tent. "The two Magees will be with Danny and there will now be a guard on the major's tent but if Neil leaves the camp he will be followed. Stay out for at least a week. The trial is set for March 17th so be back here by the 14th eh?"

"Don't worry sir. Out there it is easier. There are only Yankee soldiers trying to kill me!"

My little patrol of twenty men left the camp in mid-afternoon. There was no hurry and I wanted to travel after dark when I neared Union territory. The Major had offered me Carlton but I preferred to have him with Copper. Besides I had Jimmy and Davy as sergeants. I had three really reliable subordinates and, as Dago said, the rest of the patrol would stick close to me just to let some of the luck rub off on them.

Cecil rode next to me. "You know sir when I first joined and heard your nickname I thought it was all a big joke. But it is right, you are lucky."

"I suppose." I never questioned my luck as I did not want to jinx it but this last episode had set me thinking. Had something stopped me from sleeping? Had the grenade been thrown in when I was in then I would have been killed. The Sergeant Major had explained to me how the wicked little bombs worked.

"They haven't really changed for centuries. It is a metal ball filled with powder and a fuse. You light the fuse and you throw it. In the old days, they had tall men who threw them; they were called grenadiers. If you were a brave man then you cut the fuse short. If you cut it long then the enemy could throw it back."

They had not had to worry when they cut the fuse for me. They had thought I was asleep and they hoped to kill Danny too. A horrible thought crossed my mind. With us out of the way they just needed to kill Major Boswell and then the witnesses against Major Beauregard would all be dead. I looked over my shoulder. It was too late to do anything about that now but it was a thought worth bearing in mind; the major was probably a bigger target than me. I suspect that he saw the chance to kill two birds with one stone.

We took the trail by the river rather than the road. It was not as quick as the road but we were in no hurry. If we were surprised then we had the option of going into the river to escape. We found a loop in the land where the Rapidian River joined the Rappahannock. There was a high spot with shelter from the elements and prying eyes as well as easy access to water. It was as near perfect a site as you could get. The next day I would send out small groups to get the lie of the land. With over a week to do our job, there was little point in rushing into things. We had brought tents; mine was a new one. We had supplies but we set nets in the river and traps for game. By nightfall we were comfortable.

I briefed the men. "Tomorrow we split into four groups. I want us to cover every inch of land within ten miles of here. Take pencil and paper with you and draw what you see. When we return we will collate everything we have and then we can try to find the Yankee cavalry. Make sure that one man stays with the horses. I will not worry if you are a day or two late. If there is trouble then the one man guarding the horses can bring us word."

Davy lay back on his bedroll, "No offence to the men back at camp, Lieutenant, but I prefer it this way. We are all Wildcats and we trust each other. Every time we ride with those new boys I am looking over my shoulder."

"I know what you mean but we have to make them into Wildcats. Look at the Wildcats we have left. There are less than a quarter of the ones who joined and fought. We are a dying breed and we owe it to the Confederacy to make the rest as good as we are."

"Well I will do that sir, but I will enjoy these next seven days."

Confederate Ranger

Cecil said, "Sir, I took the liberty of making you one of these. I already have one." He took out a leather bag. He threw it to me. It felt unusually heavy. "It's what we call a cosh at home, sir. Normally it is a bag filled with sand but I put in a few bits of metal it makes it heavier. It is more reliable than a Colt when knocking someone out, and," he added, "less damaging to the Colt!" He shrugged. "I am just saving myself work in the future sir."

"Thanks, sergeant. This will come in very handy."

Some of the others looked at Cecil's original weapon and I could see that they were thinking of making their own. The Wildcats were not like the other cavalrymen. They thought of being sneaky first. They were the true Rangers.

I took Wilbur, Ritchie and Wilkie with me when I went to scout. I could have chosen any of them. They were all good men. They were troopers who would watch my back as I watched theirs. That is what makes a good soldier; it isn't a fancy uniform or even a good weapon. A good soldier can use a stick as a weapon if he has to. He can improvise and think on his feet. We rode to Fredericksburg. It was not bravado on my part; I knew the town better than anybody. I had been incarcerated and then escaped. I knew the dangers better than most and I would avoid them when we visited the Union bastion.

I headed for the hill roads intending to sweep down from the north. We had seen Union patrols on the highways and they were patrolling in company strength. We kept to the trails and hills. So far the enemy had not worked out that you could use small groups of men more effectively than a troop. We found the scene of our ambush north of Hartwood Church. There were some neat crosses marking the place they had buried their dead. We sheltered in the lee of the building as it was raining and raining hard! It was a driving rain coming in from the Atlantic. I remembered the storms well from my days on the Rose. Suddenly we heard the sound of hooves. Wilbur took off his hat and peered over the wall. "It's a Yankee trooper and he's heading for Stafford, sir."

"Wilbur, get behind him when he stops. Wilkie you and I will get ahead of him. Ritchie, watch the horses."

We ran down the side of the building. The ground was already becoming slippery. We had our Colts out and cocked. I heard the hooves and we stepped out together. "Halt! You are a prisoner of the Confederacy." I don't know if he was just scared or a hero but he tried to turn and draw his pistol at the same time. He had a good horse and it wheeled quickly. He brought his gun up and was aiming it at Wilbur. Wilbur brought his own gun up and it misfired. Wilkie and I fired at the same time. The back of the cavalryman's head was struck by both shots. Wilbur grabbed the horse to stop it bolting and we quickly took the body from the road. If he was a scout then there would be more men coming down the road. As we dragged the body away, I picked the bloody and gore covered kepi up from the road. The rain was already washing tendrils of blood away from the scene. Within minutes there would be no sign of the tragedy.

"Ritchie! Watch the road!"

Wilbur said, "Sorry sir."

"It happens. Have you found anything in the saddlebags?"

"He's a courier. It looks like orders from Hooker to a General Stoneman." He looked up. "This is gold dust, sir."

"Ritchie, any sign of others?"

"No, sir."

"Right let's take this poor boy and bury him with his comrades. Hopefully, no-one will notice an extra body and he will just have disappeared." We took everything of value from him but left his photographs and the letter from his mother. We had no time for a service so we just bowed our heads in the wet, driving rain.

"Wilbur, take the horse and the message to the colonel. Meet us back at the camp tomorrow."

"Sir."

He headed off into the murk and the gloom and he disappeared as though into a fog. "Right you two. We will head towards Fredericksburg. There is a small wood about half a mile from the outskirts. We can hide there."

When we reached the woods I dismounted. I took the slicker we had taken from the dead cavalryman. "Here Ritchie, you wear this. Get rid of your kepi." I took the hat I had taken from the drover the last time I had been in Fredericksburg and I donned my old deer hide jacket. "Wilkie I want you to wait here while Ritchie and I go to scout."

"But sir, I am more experienced than Ritchie sir."

"And he will never get more experience if he watches horses the whole time. Besides if we are not back by morning assume that we are dead or captured and you ride back to Wilbur and then report to Irish. He will need your experience."

"Yes, sir."

"I am leaving the horses here. Apples is known and any strange horses would be noticed. It is only half a mile and we will look less suspicious walking. Ritchie, put a spare revolver in the back of your belt." He looked ready and he gave a weak nod at me. "See you later and keep a watch out for us."

When we left the shelter of the trees we felt the full force of the rain. I gave a wan smile to Ritchie. "I suppose we couldn't expect anything better for March eh Ritchie?"

"No, sir."

Confederate Ranger

I looked at the tall, gangly youth. He was one of the quieter members of the Wildcats. He had moved from Harry to me and I had yet to get to know him. He was reliable but he was not one to chat unnecessarily. "Where are you from Ritchie?" I also thought it would look more natural if two men were chatting as they trudged through the mud.

"Originally Canada sir. Sidney, Nova Scotia. Ma and Pa died of fever and my two brothers left to work on a whaler but I didn't like it and I left the ship. I found myself in Charleston and that was where the captain found me." He grinned. "A bit like you sir."

"I didn't mind the sea."

"I hated it sir and I was always seasick."

"What would you have done if you hadn't joined the Wildcats?"

"Oh, I like music. I can play the guitar and sing a little. The war means there ain't much call for singers and musicians." He shrugged. "And there ain't much money to be made."

I hadn't known that about this youth. He could play the guitar. Then I remembered there wasn't much opportunity for such frivolities in war. "We'll have to get you a guitar. It might brighten up the camp a little and you needn't worry about money. You must have made a tidy sum in the Wildcats."

"Yes sir, but not like you boys who were in from the beginning. I can't afford a fancy plantation."

"You never know, Ritchie, there is plenty of time yet and we never know what is around the corner." I could see the buildings were less than thirty yards ahead and I halted. "Now I have a bold plan Ritchie and I trust you to back my play. Yonder is the headquarters building. I know it 'cos that's where they held me. It will be guarded but only by one sentry. I want you to go up to him and ask for directions to 'Lizzie's Tavern'. He'll have no idea where that is because I just made it up. You make up something about Lizzie and who told you about it and I will try out Cecil's cosh. You game for it?"

He grinned, "Yes sir. And thank you for giving me the chance. I was getting real tired of just holding horses and waiting while the rest of you did all the heroic stuff."

"There's nothing heroic about this, Ritchie. Right, let's go. Keep your holster open. If we have trouble then draw and draw quickly."

I found the alley I had used to make good my escape and we slipped down it. I led us to the livery stable. I did not intend to steal any horses but I wanted to see if it was guarded and I found that it was. The guard they had looked to be overweight and drinking so he would not be a problem but I was glad that I had checked. We walked down the main street. It was almost deserted and any people were walking as close to the buildings as possible to get some shelter. When we reached the road leading to the headquarters building I saw that they had just one sentry. He had his cape up over his head and was pressed as close into the wall as he could get.

"I will walk down the street. Give me one minute and you follow. You talk to him and I will do the rest. Make sure he faces you and comes away from the wall."

I trudged up the road. I could see there were lights within and knew that it was occupied. As I passed the sentry I said, conversationally, "What a miserable day."

"Yeah. And I have another three hours of getting wet!"

"There's no justice. You'll get your reward in heaven. See you later."

"See you."

Confederate Ranger

I slipped the cosh out and after five paces I turned. I saw Ritchie approaching the sentry. I checked that the street was empty. The dusk and the rain meant that it was hard to see more than five feet in front of you anyway. The sentry came away from the wall and I strode up my steps hidden by the driving rain and I swung the cosh. It smacked into the back of his head and he fell forward. Ritchie was quick thinking and he grabbed the sentry and his rifle stopping them both from falling to the ground.

"Can you hold him?" Ritchie nodded. " Sling him over your shoulder perhaps?"

"I think so."

I propped the gun against the wall as Ritchie hoisted the unconscious sentry over his shoulder. I eased the door open. As I recalled there was a hall and the office leading to Major Doyle's inner sanctum was at the end. There was no one there and I gestured for Ritchie to enter. We placed the soldier gently on the floor. I could hear voices from the room at the end. I took my revolver out and Ritchie copied me. I could hear the sergeant but the other was not the major. The door was slightly ajar. I held up three fingers and counted down. On three I shoved the door open and leapt into the room. The sergeant was talking with a corporal and both were seated. My Colt was pointed at Sergeant McNeil's head and Ritchie had the corporal covered. I took out my second Colt and held it to the corporal's head. "Check the back office."

As he did so I smiled at the sergeant who opened and closed his mouth like a fish. Eventually, he got the words out. "How the hell did you get by the sentry and how the hell did you escape last time?"

"Let's just call it magic eh sarge?"

Ritchie came back. "All clear sir."

The sergeant looked at me, "Sir? You got promoted?"

Confederate Ranger

"Yeah. You want to try this fighting for a change instead of sitting on your ass in an office all day. Ritchie, find something to tie them up with."

He began going through the drawers and found three sets of manacles and a key. I looked at the sergeant who shrugged. "We got them after you disappeared. We figured the next prisoner would not find it so easy to escape."

"And you won't. Ritchie, manacle them with their hands behind each other and then manacle the two of them together. Take the keys with us." As soon as he did that I put my guns away. I searched the sergeant first and found my two knives. "Well, I am glad to have these knives back sergeant. Thank you kindly. I hope you have kept them sharp." I found his wallet and there was over five hundred dollars in it. "Now I don't think you earned this legally, sergeant so we just take it. Here Ritchie, put this towards your guitar fund."

He grinned, "Thanks, sir."

"Now gag them."

"I began checking the drawers as the two men were gagged. I found official papers and a bunch of keys. I had no time to read them and so I just grabbed them. I went into the major's office and found a locked drawer. I tried each key until the drawer popped open and I found a leather satchel. I took it out and inside were more papers including some which were sealed. I put the other papers inside the satchel and then checked the other drawers. I found the Major's colt, holster and ammunition. I took them and went back into the other room. "Here you are Ritchie, have a decent gun and holster." He caught them and put them on. "You all done here?"

"Yes, sir."

Confederate Ranger

"Just check the drawers again and see if you can find anything else and I will tell these two a bedtime story." Ritchie gave me a look which suggested I had lost my mind but did as he was told. I walked behind the corporal and hit him with the cosh.

The sergeant could see what was coming and he said, "Before you hit me just answer me one thing. Are you the one they call Lucky Jack? Are you the one who was with the Wildcats?"

"Yes, but how did you hear my name?"

He gave me a curious smile. "Oh you are quite famous you know and there are some Irish lads who have put a bounty on your head and the other Wildcats. Boswell is that one of them and a Murphy. It seems those two boys you killed and hanged were their kin and they have a thousand dollars each for the three of you, dead or alive. Why our local marshal is itching to get his hands on it."

"Well sergeant, I wish them luck. They will need it." I sapped him on the back of the head and he fell unconscious.

Ritchie emerged with a sack filled with items he had found. He reached in and took out a large bag of coffee beans, "Look at this! We hit gold dust!"

"Right Ritchie, bring your treasures with you and we will examine what we have tomorrow back at the camp. Take the sergeant's slouch hat it will help us to blend in." I slung the satchel over my shoulder and we stepped out into the wet night.

We headed back the way we had come. I contemplated taking horses but it was too big a chance to risk. The three men we had hit would be out for at least an hour. We had plenty of time to make it back to Wilkie on foot. The streets were even more deserted now than they had been before. I saw the alley ahead and was anticipating slipping down it when I saw the armed man walking down the side of the building towards us. He had his head down and I saw the glint of a badge. It was the marshal. I murmured to Ritchie. "Just keep walking and keep your head down."

He was ahead of me and I stepped behind him to allow the marshal to walk by on the inside. There was a patch of mud left from someone stepping from the street and Ritchie slipped in it. He lurched towards the marshal who put his hand up to push Ritchie away and I saw his face. It was Billy Pickles, the deserter. He recognised Ritchie and was looking around to me when I hit him across the face with my Colt. He went down like a sack of potatoes. "Get him over your shoulder and down the alley, quickly."

I turned and checked that there was no-one else on the street. It was still deserted and I slipped down after him. "Wait here and watch him. If he tries anything then use your knife."

I walked back to the stables. I peered inside. The guard was still asleep. I took out the cosh and slipped behind him. I hit him hard, for he was a big man. There were only two riding horses in the stables and neither was in good condition but they would have to do. I saddled them both, grabbed a length of rope, and then led them out. I closed the doors behind me so that no-one would see the unconscious guard. Billy Pickles was still unconscious. I gestured to Ritchie. "Here get on this horse." When he was mounted I manhandled the deserter across the back of the horse and then I mounted my own horse and we headed along the muddy trail to the woods.

As we entered the woods I heard the click as the Colt was cocked. "It's us, Wilkie."

"I did wonder when I saw the three horses. Who is the man?"

I threw him to the ground as Ritchie dismounted. "This is the marshal of Fredericksburg. This is Billy Pickles!"

Confederate Ranger

Wilkie gave the unconscious form a kick in the ribs. "Treacherous bastard!"

"Here is a length of rope. Tie him to the horse and let's get to the camp."Ritchie took off the hat and the cape. "I would keep those if I were you Ritchie you never know when they will come in handy. They call me Lucky Jack but I prefer Be Ready for Anything Jack."

We headed back to the graveyard and rode down the road. I took the chance that there would be few riders out in the rain at this time of the night. We made it back to the camp just after midnight. Wilbur was alone in the camp. He audibly sighed when we rode in. "I sure am glad it is you guys. It was a little spooky on my own." He noticed the bundle over the saddle and the spare horse. "What you boys been up to then?"

I dismounted and unceremoniously threw the body of Billy Pickles to the floor. "We found us a deserter and we are going to take him back to the colonel so that we can shoot him legal! Ritchie, take the rope we found and tie him to that tree. Ties his hands behind him first and then tie his feet together."

Wilbur said, "What if he needs to take a leak?"

"He can piss in his pants if he wants but we don't take off the rope. We take it in turns to watch him tonight. Wilbur, take the first watch; you do two hours, Wilkie the second, Ritchie the third and then wake me. If he gives any trouble when he wakes up, then use my cosh. If he tries to shout, then gag him." I grabbed some of the food and hungrily devoured it. This had been a long day but a successful one. I would leave reading the reports I had stolen from the major's office until the following morning when the light would be better for reading.

Confederate Ranger

Ritchie woke me and nodded at Pickles. His eyes were open and he was glaring at me. "He's awake and not happy. I told him that I would gag him if he tried to shout. He said he needs a piss."

"You go to sleep now. Well done for today Ritchie. I want to thank you for your help. You will get some stripes soon."

As he wandered over to his bedroll Pickles spat out. "Aye across your back."

I walked over to him and kicked him hard between the legs. "You shut up, you are a deserter. You were flogged because you were a bad soldier."

"You bastard! You cut me loose and we'll settle this man to man."

"Why who is going to represent you? You aren't a man, you are an animal with neither honour nor courage. I could beat you with one hand tied behind my back but you are going back to hang or be shot. Now shut up or I won't gag you." I tapped the cosh into my open palm. "I will sap you!" That shut him up and I set too to make some coffee. I had over an hour before I needed to wake the boys. I ground the newly acquired coffee beans and I was generous. We would have a decent coffee this morning to help us to celebrate. I stirred the fire into life and took out some dried bacon. I poured the water Wilbur had collected into the pot and poured in the coffee on the top. It made the coffee taste better and less burnt. All the while I could feel the malevolent stare of Billy Pickles. It did not bother me but I was curious about the reward. I did not want to disturb the lad's sleep and I left those questions until the morning. When the water boiled I took the pot off. The coffee would brew and I could warm it up if I needed to. I put the pan on the coals and when it was good and hot threw in the bacon. It sizzled and spat. Immediately that irresistible aroma of bacon hit the chilly early morning air and mixed with the coffee. It was better than an expensive alarm clock.

"Morning sir! My but that bacon smells really good."

"Morning Wilkie." Wilbur and Ritchie opened their eyes and sniffed the air from the warmth of their bedrolls. "Give the prisoner a mug of water corporal."

Pickles moaned, "What, no coffee?"

"The coffee is for real soldiers not scum like you."

After we had eaten I went to the saddlebags to get the papers. Pickles said, "What about a leak?"

I was about to say no when Wilkie said. "There are three of us sir. His feet are tied and we can keep a gun on him."

"Ritchie, take my cosh and don't be gentle. If he so much as breathes wrong then hit him." Even as I was reading I was watching them out of the corner of my eye. Billy Pickles was a slippery customer and they were young gullible lads. My Colt rested next to me cocked and ready to fire. I noticed that Wilkie retied his hands behind him. The prisoner complained until the corporal doubled him with a punch to the solar plexus. He complained no more. By the time he had finished and they had restrained him again I had roughly read the documents.

"It seems like this General Stoneman has three thousand horsemen and six cannons. It seems to me they intend to do something about the general and not just sit in camps."

"It could be that they aren't all here yet sir."

"True Ritchie and we will wait until Irish and the others return here. If they confirm this information then we will head back to Kelly's Ford and tell the general. They are all due back here today anyway." A thought struck me. "Just search our prisoner here. We didn't have time last night."

I could see from his face that he didn't like that but he was trussed like a Thanksgiving turkey and could do little about it. He had a large bankroll as well as coins and a watch. In his jacket pocket, he had a folded handbill.

> **Wanted Dead or Alive**
> Boswell's Wildcats murdered two brave young soldiers fighting for the Union. The Irish Brigade offers a reward of $1000 for any of the members of this gang of bandits. There will be a bonus of $1000 for the capture of their leader Captain Boswell, their Lieutenant Daniel Murphy or the murderer known as Lucky Jack Hogan.
> Sergeant Mick O'Callaghan
> Irish Brigade

As we read it Billy Pickles started to laugh. "So you see Jackie Boy, no matter what happens to me, your days are numbered."

I wandered over and looked him directly in the eye. "This doesn't change anything. We never killed an innocent man and even if the whole Irish Brigade comes to take us, we will beat them, and you know why? Because we are the best soldier in the whole of the East Coast. I fear no man. But the bottom line is that you won't live to see me beat this Irish Brigade because you will be dead and the only sad thing is it won't be me that kills you."

Confederate Ranger

H thought about spitting at me but my hand was on my knife and the look in my eyes left him in o doubt about the outcome of such a foolish action.

The first of the patrols arrived by noon. I was thankful that there were no casualties. They were all surprised to see Billy Pickles as large as life and twice as ugly. We left Wilbur watching him and I took them all to one side to discuss what they had discovered.

Cecil took out his paper and used his pencil to point. "We have found at least four regiments of cavalry. They were here and here."

Davy took out his paper. "There's another regiment of cavalry and a battery of six guns and they are here; not far from where Irish saw his regiments."

"I found four regiments spread out all along the Stafford Road and we went to the bridge we destroyed. They are rebuilding it and they have a pontoon one in place."

"You three write down on a fresh piece of paper what you saw and draw your maps. I think we need to send this to the general and the colonel as soon as possible."

Just then there was a shout from the camp. I drew my gun and we raced back. Wilbur was standing with Billy Pickles' arm around his neck and what looked like Wilbur's Bowie knife aimed at his eye. "Looks like I won't be hanged then will I Lucky Jack? Things are different now. If you all drop your weapons and bring me a horse I'll be out of here."

I ignored him and walked up to within four feet of them.

"You don't come any closer or he loses the eye."

"You all right Wilbur?"

"No sir, I feel like a damned fool. He said that he was bit by a snake and he was groaning and moaning and I felt sorry for him."

Confederate Ranger

"Shut up! I'm doing the talking. Get me the horse! And get it quick or this boy loses an eye, maybe two!"

"You have one chance Pickles. You let Wilbur go unharmed and we'll take you back to camp for a fair trial and a good hanging. If you don't you die."

"I mean it. I'll take this boy's eye."

"You a righty or a lefty Wilbur?"

"What the hell has that got to do with anything?" He leaned his head to try to see me a little clearer. He obviously could believe neither my calmness nor my questions. He was confused.

"Well, you have a knife to his right eye so if he is a …" I fired and the ball went into the middle of his forehead and the knife fell from his lifeless fingers.

Wilbur fell to his knees, "I am really sorry sir."

I helped him to his feet. "I'm just sorry that you had to go through that but at least you learned a lesson. Never trust a snake, even if you think the critter is hurting. A snake is still a snake; they will always bite you so kill 'em. Anyway, we saved ourselves a trial and I got to kill him. Throw him in the Rappahannock. The good people of Fredericksburg need to know they no longer have a town marshal."

Confederate Ranger

Chapter 15

The next morning I gathered the men around me. "The general needs this information but, I think, that we still have work to do. Wilbur and Ritchie, I want you to take this information back to Kelly's Ford so that it can be acted upon. I intend to break camp and send the tents and other extra equipment back on the two spare horses" Wilbur looked crestfallen. "Wilbur, no blame is attached to you. The simple fact is that I can trust both of you to ensure that this is delivered safely and that is most important. You have both done sterling work on this patrol. Please do this vital task for me."

Ritchie spoke, "Of course sir. But you must understand that we all want to be close to you, for that is where the excitement lies. Come on Wilbur, let us ride to the general."

I gathered the remaining troopers around me. "I think we will ride to Woodbridge. We may not be able to destroy the bridge this time but we can pin down some men to guard it eh?"

Their cheers told me all that I needed to know. They were as game as ever. We rode through the night along the road. When we neared Stafford I halted the column. I suspected that there would be some patrols ahead. The sergeant and the corporal must have been released and they would be searching for us.

Davy rode back with a grin on his face. "There is a barrier across the road up ahead. There are four of them manning it."

"Then we will ride around it and deal with it on our way back. They will not expect danger from the north."

As we rode through the brush and thin woods above the road we could easily see the four men who were huddled around their fire. We rejoined the road and reached the low heights above the bridge. They had left a dozen men to guard the flimsy pontoon bridge which now spanned the river. It was secured to the bank by strong ropes on either side.

"Cecil, take half the men and go to the left. I will take the rest to the right. I will whistle. When I do we close in and secure the bridgehead. They will not be expecting trouble." I sent Jimmy with Cecil and I kept Davy. We worked well together and that was important.

We dismounted in the brush by the river. The old broken and burned bridge had been dumped there and afforded us some cover. As my men crouched in the dark I briefed them. "These men will be confident that this is an easy duty. Be confident and we can take them. Try not to use your guns; there may be more cavalry nearby."

I took out my cosh and led the way. There were four men around the fire and two on our side of the bridge. I halted the men and threw a stone in the river.

"Hey Joe, there's fish jumping." The soldier wandered to the bank and peered into the dark waters. I stood and hit him on the back of the head. He fell into the arms of Bill who hauled him off.

"Jacob? Where are you?" Joe made the classic mistake of walking towards a sentry who had disappeared. I hit him too and he joined Joe. We moved towards the men by the fire. They helped us by all staring at the fire. Their night vision would be destroyed. I waved my arms for the patrol to spread out. I hoped that Cecil had dealt with his two sentries too. If he had then we outnumbered the eight men who remained. We waited in the shadows and I saw Cecil on the other side. I gestured for the men to stand. I walked towards the fire with my Colt in my hand.

"Boys you can surrender now or die for we have you surrounded." As Cecil's men stepped out with guns drawn, they all raised their hands. "Sergeant, secure the prisoners. Corporal Jones, start a fire on the bridge and then cut the ropes. Sergeant James. Secure the weapons and find anything useful in the hut."

We were now accomplished arsonists and the fire began to blaze. As the ropes were cut it began to drift out to sea. I heard a lot of noise from the northern bank and the pontoon began to be dragged towards that side. I smiled. By the time it reached them it would be a charred ruin. We mounted and I waved a cavalier hand at the sergeant who sat forlornly amongst his section. "Goodbye boys the 1st Virginia Scouts bids you farewell."

We galloped south and headed back to Kelly's Ford. We were used to the road, even at night. Our various escapades had made us all very careful and alert. We rode through the Union checkpoint whooping and hollering. The four soldiers ran in all directions. I suspect they reported a regiment of Confederate cavalry had attacked them rather than the handful it was. What I did know was that they would waste time looking for men who were no longer in the area. We would be many miles to the west, safely in camp.

We reached the camp at dawn. We were just in time for breakfast. The first thing I did, even before I reported to the colonel, was to see how Copper was. She was totally healed. Carlton proudly showed me the scar. There was no sign of infection.

"You know sir I have a mind to take her to the horse doctor over with the brigade and show her to him."

"I am just pleased she is recovered. You get to ride Apples again."

The horse sergeant took an old gnarly apple from his pocket and gave it to the Appaloosa. "And I am glad about that too sir."

The colonel and the Sergeant Major were busy in his tent checking lists. They both smiled when they saw me. "Excellent intelligence lieutenant, although I am not certain that General

Fitzhugh is interpreting it in the same way as I am. How do you read the situation? After all, you have been closer to the enemy than any of us."

"I think they are planning an attack, sir. You don't gather that many cavalry and artillery without an attack in mind. If there were more infantry then I would have said it was a defensive move. They are going to attack."

"And the major and I are in agreement about that but the general thinks we have frightened the Union and they are getting more cavalry to stop raids."

"I would have thought, sir, that the easy way to stop raids was to hit us, here."

"And I agree. Tell me, lieutenant, if you were the Yankees what would you do?"

"That is easy sir. There are two fords, one here and another at Wheatley Post Office. Our camp is the closest to the fords but we are almost a mile away. Our main camp is more than two miles from the ford. If I was the commander of the Union horse I would force the two fords and swim some across the river. We have done that before."

"Exactly. I think, Sergeant Major we will build some defences at the mill. We could do with some artillery but there is precious little of that about. Well done lieutenant, however, I thought that you were to be away for at least a week. There are five days before the court-martial."

"I am sorry sir. I thought that an attack might be imminent and I was needed here."

"Highly commendable but… Sergeant Major?"

"Sorry lieutenant but Trooper Neil has run off. We didn't see him go and no-one was able to follow him. The major does not seem worried which makes me think he might be up to no good. He could be anywhere. So far the lads have found no trace of him."

I was not worried. I would deal with him when it became necessary.

"So lieutenant, I have another mission for you. I want you and Captain Grimes to go to Winchester. I believe you both have uniforms to collect and the Sergeant Major has a list of other items we need. Take your sergeant and some of your Wildcats. Have the night in Winchester and return here, safely." I opened my mouth and the colonel smiled, "And that is an order!"

"Yes, sir." It was not an onerous task and normally I would have relished the trip but I felt that I was running. I was not afraid of the major or his henchman. I sought out Cecil first. "Get half a dozen of the boys and a couple of pack horses then see the Sergeant Major, he will give you a list. We are heading for Winchester."

"Grand news sir. I need a few bits and bobs for my repairs." He strode off rubbing his hands.

When I told Harry he shrugged. "It's probably for the best. The rumour is that the major sent Neil to get some of his men although as they are supposed to be in Atlanta I wouldn't be that worried then again I am not one of the men they want to kill." He saw my look and shook his head. "Swallow your pride, Jack. You are not running. Besides we could both do with a nice new uniform. You have an officer's sabre and a fine one it is too. I have this one." He held up the shabby sword which would have broken had he had to use it. " I have a mind to spend some of my pay on a decent sword so let's enjoy our little trip eh?"

I went to my new tent which Ritchie and Wilbur had erected. I had told them to put it up in the same place. I was not going to be intimidated by a coward like Beauregard. I dumped my slouch hat and deerskin jacket inside. I would not need them and I picked up my sword. I would not be a scout for the next few days and I was aware that I ought to look like an officer.

As I strode to get Copper I had to pass Major Beauregard's tent. He was seated outside and I intended to pass by without comment but he made the decision to speak with me. "Shame about your tent, peasant! Still, this is a dangerous world, especially for liars with big mouths. You and your precious major will get theirs."

I turned and faced him. I clenched my fists to stop me from using them. "Listen to me, you coward. I have promised the colonel that you will live as long as you wear the grey. Unlike you, I am a man of my word. The minute you are stripped of your rank and your uniform you and that brute Neil will be mine and you will die. Make no mistake about that. Remember that you and I know that you killed my father after Neil had killed my mother. We both know that you tried to burn my sister and me alive. If you had had any honour then you would have admitted that."

"Honour is only due to those of the same rank. Gentleman! You will never be a gentleman. You will never be my equal. If this were England or Ireland then you would now be in jail."

I smiled. "I know but this is America, the land of the free. Hadn't you noticed? Make the most of the next few days. They will be your last on earth. I am not the wee bairn you tried to kill. I am a man and I am a Ranger and you are mine!" I stared at him and saw him blanch. He heard my threat and knew that I meant it. As I walked to get my horse my only nagging doubt was Neil. He could be anywhere. I could defend myself but I wanted no innocents being hurt because of me.

We decided to stop off at Front Royal for the night. It meant we did not need to push our horses too hard and would give us

Confederate Ranger

almost a whole day in Winchester. We also had good friends in Front Royal and we felt safe there. We took rooms at the tavern. Harry and I shared and the others had one bunk room in the attic. There was an easy familiarity amongst the Wildcats that was missing in ordinary cavalry regiments. We had all been equals and we retained that even though we had different ranks. I was not better than Ritchie just because I was a lieutenant. We strolled amongst the shops. We all had money to burn. Since we became regulars we had been in action and we had dollars to spend. Cecil went into a gunsmith to buy some replacement parts for the Colts and some tools. Harry went in because they had some swords for sale. I was standing with the others looking in the windows of the other shops and I saw a guitar.

"Come along Ritchie. I am buying you a present." Davy gave me a strange look. "Come on Davy. You will be interested in this."

The clerk handed the guitar to Ritchie when he asked about it. He tuned it and then began to pick out a tune. Davy's mouth dropped open. I grinned, "See. We'll take it and have you a case for this fine instrument?"

The clerk beamed. Two sales in a few moments; this was a good day. "Yes, sir." He went into the back room.

"I can't let you buy this sir."

"Of course you can! You took the same risks as I did in Fredericksburg but I get more pay. Consider this a bonus besides I look forward to hearing you play. It will liven up the camp at night." The look of joy on his face as the guitar and case were parcelled up was worth the paltry sum it had cost me.

It did not take us long to reach Winchester the next day. We all rose early normally and we were eager to get to the bustling town. Harry and I were excited to get our new uniforms. Mistress Sandy was pleased to see us. We had paid her a deposit on the uniforms but she would now be getting the balance. Cecil and Davy were there to get new jackets too. They were issued ones by the CSA but the quality was poor. As Wildcats, we had money and we liked to use it well.

We tried the uniforms on and the perfectionist that she was would not let us take them until she had finished them properly. "You gentlemen return this afternoon and they will be ready. You have both put on a little weight I think. Be off with you and enjoy the town."

We took her at her word. We took rooms at the inn opposite the imposing courthouse building. It was too early to be drinking and we wandered the city to fill the Sergeant Major's shopping list. Cecil and the boys went off to do the shopping while Harry and I sat and watched the people going about their business on this fine spring morning.

"Harry, when we started out with the captain, did you ever think we would get to be officers?"

"I didn't think we would make corporal never mind officers. We have been lucky, "he grinned, "especially you."

"I must be honest, until Major Beauregard arrived I didn't think I was worthy to be an officer. When I look at him I know that I am a better officer. Do you think he did all those things he boasts about, in the Crimea?"

He shook his head. "I know some blokes who were in the army and even the British Army wouldn't put up with him besides he is a coward."

"You are right. You can see it in his eyes. Anyway just a couple more days and he will be history. He will no longer be an officer and I can kill him."

Harry nodded. He understood revenge. He suddenly smiled. "And you know what day that will be, don't you?"

Confederate Ranger

"Of course, March 17th!"

"Yes, you daft Mick! St.Patrick's day! Appropriate eh?"

I hadn't thought of that. "Well, as the boys are here I think that is a cause for celebration. We will go and pick our new uniforms up. I think these will be good enough to get drunk in tonight and we can ride back in style tomorrow."

It was a good inn with fine food and well-brewed ale. Harry and I took it steadily as did Irish and Davy. I don't think Ritchie was much of a drinker but he was busy with his new guitar anyway. The other three had, as all young men tend to do, drunk too much. Cecil and I took Wilbur out to the back so that they could empty the fine meal into the gutter at the back of the inn. While he was heaving I happened to glance up at the next building where there was an open window. Two men was talking on the small balcony and smoking cigars. When one of them half-turned I saw that it was Andrew Neil. Although we were almost completely hidden by shadows I ducked my head back. "Cecil. Look up at that window. Who is it?"

I heard the sharp intake of breath which confirmed my suspicions. "It's the deserter, Neil!"

"Let's get this one back in and tell the others."

Harry could see something was amiss when he saw my face. "You look like you have seen a ghost. What is it, Jack?"

"Andrew Neil. He is in the next building. He is in a room on the second floor."

Harry started to rise. I shook my head. "Let's do this right. Ritchie, can you get these three to bed on your own?"

"Of course sir but I can come with you and help you."

"There are four of us and I think we can deal with the two of them."

"There are two?"

Confederate Ranger

"Yes, he was talking with someone. I heard the major had sent for some of his men from Atlanta. This may be them. Let's go." We paid our bill and left Ritchie to struggle with the three drunks.

The building next door was also an inn. There was a prosperous-looking man standing next to the bar smoking a pipe. Harry walked up to him. "Are you the owner?"

"Yes, I am Benjamin O'Connor at your service. What can I do for such fine soldiers as you?"

"Have you somewhere we can talk privately?"

"Of course," he leered at us as he led us to the small room at the back of the bar, "now you know that we are very discreet here why…"

"We believe there is a deserter staying in your hotel."

He looked shocked, "My hotel! No, that can't be true."

"Who is staying on the second floor?"

"There are four men who are travelling to join the army. It can't be them and then there is a clergyman travelling to Richmond. You must be mistaken."

"The four men who are joining the army; did they all arrive at the same time?"

He looked surprised at the question. "Why no. Mr Hogan arrived two days ago and his friends arrived this afternoon."

That confirmed it. "The cheeky bastard! He is using your name."

"Tell me Mr O'Connor would you be able to get the clergyman out of his room. We wouldn't want him getting hurt."

"He is in the bar having a meal."

"Then stop anyone going upstairs and we will deal with this."

He looked appalled. "Can't you do this quietly and without damaging my room?"

Confederate Ranger

"We would love to but I suspect that these are all dangerous men. Believe me, we will do all that we can but we can't promise anything. Which is their room?"

"The last one at the end of the passage from the stairs. It is at the far end of the hall."

We gathered at the bottom of the stairs. I took out my Colt. "Davy, you knock on the door and say the landlord sent you with a message for Mr Hogan. When they open the door we burst in. Try not to shoot, I am sure the colonel would like to speak with Mr Neil but if you have to then shoot to kill. Remember, Neil is very dangerous."

The stairs and hallway were both dark and that suited us. The floorboards creaked alarmingly but the men in the room would not suspect anything untoward. They would not know they had been seen. We stood on either side of the door, just in case they blasted first. Davy knocked on the door. He put on a wheedling voice, "Mr Neil, sir. I have a message for you. Mr O'Connor sent me."

The voices inside went silent and then I heard Neil's voice. "Just slide it under the door."

Davy shrugged and then continued, "I'm sorry sir, Mr O'Connor said I had to hand it to you especially."

I suddenly heard a pistol being cocked and I pulled Davy to the side. Four shots rang out making holes in the door. Cecil put his shoulder down and rammed the door. The door was not very solid anyway and the holes had weakened it. He crashed through and landed on a heap on the floor. I leapt into the room firing as I went. I hit one huge thug in the stomach and I fired again. He flew backwards and I stepped over him. There were six men in the room. Davy and Harry followed me and began blasting. I emptied my gun at anything not wearing grey. Suddenly a huge paw grabbed my shoulder. I whipped my Colt around and caught the man a blow to the head. I slipped my hand down to my boot and took out my Bowie knife. I lunged at the man whose hand still gripped my shoulder. I buried the knife in his throat, his blood pouring down my arm.

I slipped my gun back into my holster and transferred my knife to my right hand. There were four dead men lying on the floor and one wounded man being pinned by Cecil. "Where's Neil?"

Davy was nursing a wounded arm. "He slipped out of the window."

"Cecil, you and Davy stay here. Harry, let's get him."

The whole of the inn stared at us as we raced out. We must have looked a sight for I had a great deal of blood on my uniform. Fortunately, none of it was mine. We reached the street. Harry said. "I will check the livery stable. He might try to run."

"I'll check the alley at the back of the inn." I ran down the alley, aware that I only had a knife. Did he have a loaded gun? I would soon find out. When I reached the place he had leapt to I saw some blood. He could be wounded. As he hadn't passed us he must have gone the other way. I ran down the alley. I reached another street. This one was less busy than the main street and I saw him limping away. He was heading for the railroad. The livery stable was in the opposite direction and so I was on my own. Harry would not be able to be of assistance. I began to run and people moved out of my way. I think they were more worried by the sight of the blood on my uniform rather than the knife in my hand.

I was gaining on him and I saw his face as he kept glancing around. He knew who it was chasing him and he must have known that I was not in the business of taking prisoners. His desertion meant that he was fair game. He suddenly jinked down another alley in an attempt to throw me off the scent but he was less than twenty yards ahead of me. I raced down the alley and my eagerness for revenge was nearly my undoing. He tripped me as I ran by him, hiding in the dark, and then he leapt on my back. I jerked my elbow back and had the satisfaction of feeling it connect with something, I think it was his face. As his weight shifted, I twisted and threw him off. He slashed at me with his knife and I barely had time to parry it with my own, the sparks flying off out jarring blades. I could see the fear in his face. He was a strong man but I was stronger. I was younger. I was not wounded. This would only end one way. I pushed hard with my knife against his blade and slowly but surely I pushed his arm and knife back. At first, it was hard but the picture of this man murdering my mother gave impetus to my arm and his blade went further and further backwards. Suddenly there came a point where he could no longer hold me away and his arm almost flew back. As much as I tried to slow my knife down I could not and the razor-sharp edge sliced across his throat. He died almost instantly. I was now completely covered in blood. As I hefted his body over my shoulder and headed for the hotel I wondered if the good citizens of Winchester thought that I was a butcher with a carcass on my shoulder.

    Harry was waiting for me at the hotel and he had a worried look on his face. It turned to a look of relief when he saw the body of the deserter. The town marshal had arrived having been summoned by the innkeeper. I dropped the body to the ground as Harry explained who we were and what we were about. When we reached the room, Ritchie was there and was tending to Davy's arm. The six men were all dead. Cecil stood as we entered. "The last one died a few minutes ago. They were Beauregard's thugs. They had been sent for and were heading for the camp to kill you, the captain and the major."

    "Get rid of anyone who could testify against him eh?"

Confederate Ranger

"It looks like it sir. When they heard Davy they were suspicious and Neil fired those shots. We were lucky sir. They had poor firearms." He smiled. "They obviously don't have an armourer."

We rode into camp the next afternoon with Neil's body draped over the back of a horse. We had covered it with his greatcoat. As we rode through the camp we attracted many stares for we purposefully headed for Major Beauregard's tent. Sergeant Major Vaughan strolled over to us. I think he was worried I might take the law into my own hands. Major Beauregard stepped from his tent with a supercilious and arrogant expression on his face.

"Come visiting your betters, peasant?"

"No, I have come to bring you a present." Cecil threw the body at the major's feet. The ugly wound that had been his throat made it look as though he was grinning. The major stepped back and held his hand to his mouth as though to stop himself from vomiting. "We didn't have enough horses to bring back the other six murderers you had sent for. The major, the captain and I will still be there in two days time to testify at your court-martial."

He threw his half-smoked cigar at me with a look of pure hate and then retreated back into his tent. The Sergeant Major nodded as I stepped down from Copper. "Well done, Lieutenant. You have avenged the honour of the regiment and brought back a deserter." He saluted, "Smart uniform sir. It suits you."

Chapter 16

Harry and I went over to the colonel to report. We took Cecil with us as he had heard the dying man's confession. As we started he held up his hand, "As this appears to concern the major and the captain we had better have them present. It will save Sergeant Mulrooney having to repeat himself?"

When they arrived Danny was grinning from ear to ear. "I hear you got a second deserter? You are becoming their scourge Jackie boy." The colonel gave him a baleful stare and he murmured, "Sorry sir."

"Right sergeant, then please make your report."

"When the lieutenant and the captain took off after the deserter I tried to staunch the bleeding on the wounded man but he had been gut shot. He was a catholic sir, and he saw the crucifix around my neck and he said he didn't want to meet his maker without confessing his sins." The colonel cocked his head to one side. "I know sir, I'm not a priest but he wanted it off his chest so to speak. Anyway, he said that the major, Major Beauregard, had sent a message to his men telling them to get to Winchester and meet Trooper Neil, except that he called him Mr Neil. When they met him he told them they had to kill Major Boswell, Captain Murphy and Lieutenant Hogan. He said they had tried a grenade but the lucky bastard, sorry sir but that was what he said, had escaped. Then he died. I made the sign of the cross after he passed away." He shrugged, "It was all I could think of to do sir."

The colonel smiled. "You did well sergeant and you are a credit to the regiment. Anyone have any more questions for him?" We all shook our heads, "Then you are dismissed, sergeant. Well done."

Confederate Ranger

After he had left the colonel reached into the desk and took out two letters. "In light of what the sergeant said these letters are most interesting. The general brought them over last night." He held the first one up and it had the seal of the Secretary of War. "This is from Mr Seddon. He was most concerned about the treatment of Major Beauregard. In the letter, he stresses that we must have irrefutable evidence of the major's guilt."

Major Boswell frowned. "Is he telling us to drop the case then sir?"

"No, he is quite clear on that. Let us say it is a warning that we must do things correctly. I think he wants evidence that the major is guilty."

"And the other letter sir?"

"Yes, Lieutenant Hogan. This too is most interesting. It is from a well-respected citizen of Atlanta, A Mr Ebenezer Winfield. It seems his daughter has recently agreed to marry the major and Mr Winfield wants to know why these charges have been brought. I suspect that the Secretary of War and Mr Winfield are friends. Like Mr Seddon, he makes it quite clear that he wants the truth to emerge but if we are trumping up charges then we will suffer."

"But we aren't sir!"

"I know lieutenant, but I think that the version they have had has come from the major who has made him sound like the innocent party. Major Boswell, you must have everything written in detail, get Sergeant Mulrooney to write his statement and sign it. That is damning evidence." He pushed his chair back. "In light of the intelligence recently gathered we could do without this distraction. I want to make the ford as defensible as possible." He smacked the desk with both palms as though he had made a decision. "Major Boswell, you keep working on the court-martial material." The major sighed, "I know, I know. Sergeant Major

Vaughan will aid you. Captain Murphy, take D Troop and make a new camp at the ford close to Wheatley Post office. Make a defence there in case the enemy tries to force the crossing. Lieutenant Hogan, ask Captain Grimes to do the same with A Troop at Kelly's Mill. We can leave the horses here, B and C Troop can guard them. This will keep at least two of the major's targets out of harm's way."

Major Boswell shook his head, "Keeping them safe by placing them closer to the enemy?"

"It is a sad fact that they are in more danger from a Confederate source than a Union one. Still, I am sure that both men would prefer that eh?"

Danny and I grinned, snapped a salute and said, "Yes sir!"

As we left I heard the colonel say, "It is just two days until the court-martial James, and after that, this will all be just a bad dream and we can go back to making this regiment the best in the corps."

Harry was in the officer's mess telling Dago what had transpired. They both looked at me expectantly when I walked in. "Well?"

"It seems our major has friends in high places and Major Boswell has to be scrupulous about his facts. By the way, what did we do with the body?"

"Sergeant Major Vaughn had some men from D Troop bury it. Well, we can get back to the normal duties of a cavalry troop now."

"Not quite Harry. The colonel wants us to fortify the ford. We are going to be sharpshooters and defend the crossing."

"All of us?" I knew that Dago preferred to be scouting than digging.

"I think we need to leave those with other responsibilities like David, Carlton and Cecil up here but the rest can be given work."

"How many men will we have Harry?"

"I reckon about sixty. There are some still in sickbay and others recovering from their wounds. We don't want any down there who are not fully fit. I take it we build a camp there?"

"It makes sense and it looks like it is my fault. The colonel wants me safe. If it is ay consolation Danny is doing the same at the northern ford."

Harry suddenly looked happy and he rubbed his hands together. "Well let's get on with it. I hate being idle and the good news is that we make these decisions not anyone else. Let's make it too hard for them to cross eh?"

The first thing we did was to move the tents. Luckily it was spring and the mosquitoes and bugs had yet to infest the river bank. However, the ground was hard and made digging difficult. While the men erected the tents the four of us walked the area. On our northern flank, we had the building that was Kelly's Mill. It was a solid end to our line and could be easily defended. The river went along a low bank and curved back on itself. We decided to use the natural features to our advantage. We collected as much discarded lumber from the mill and made breastworks along the ridge. Behind them, we dug trenches to give us even more shelter. Jed and I paced out the distances from the water so that we could sight our rifles as accurately as possible.

When we reported to Harry he said, "We could do with a couple of guns you know."

I shrugged, "I think that the colonel has asked for some." I pointed to the hill behind us. "If he gets them then up there is the best place for them. They can fire over us at anyone attacking."

Dago shook his head, "I am not sure I want our artillery firing over my head."

Jed laughed, "Just put yourself next to Lucky Jack and you'll be safe."

The men toiled away all afternoon. By nightfall, we were not finished but it looked better than it had done. We found plenty of lumber to build breastworks behind which we could hide and take shelter. We dug pits by the river and used them to cook fish we caught in the river. As we ate by the bubbling Rappahannock I pointed to the men. "When this is over we ought to promote a couple of these boys to sergeant. David, Cecil and Carlton have specialist jobs. I think Davy and Jimmy have earned the extra stripe."

"I agree, Jack. When we report to the major tomorrow I will ask him." A thought seemed to suddenly strike him, "Have we enough ammunition? We are a good way from the camp here."

Dago stood, "Come on Jed, let's check and we can get some more tonight if we have not."

When they had gone we both walked the river. Our men would be thinly spread out and I could see that Harry was as worried as I was. "Look, Harry, if we put those with repeaters by the ford itself then they can slow the enemy down. The single shots can be down here." I pointed to the river which was still quite shallow but moved swiftly and had many rocks. "Anyone coming here would have to come much slower and the single shots could cope."

"When they get close enough, their pistols will be just as effective as carbines anyway."

"You are right. I am just glad we still have fourteen Wildcats. They are all good shots and as reliable as sharpshooters."

Confederate Ranger

We walked back along the breastworks. We had a good field of fire. The range was about a hundred and fifty yards which meant we would hold the advantage. The nagging fear I had was concerning the sheer numbers of men who might come this way. Harry and I had counted the numbers from our own intelligence reports and there could be three thousand cavalrymen coming towards our eight hundred and odd men. That was a lot of men for one under-strength troop to deal with.

I managed to get the first duty with ten of the men as sentries. With four of us for watchkeeping duties, it just meant losing two hours sleep. I walked amongst the troopers who peered across the black waters of the Rappahannock River. Some of them were only young boys but I sensed that they had learned much from Wildcats like Wilbur and Ritchie. As we had walked the trenches we had heard our old comrades telling the others some of the stories of our raids behind enemy lines. They had heard of them as legends and now they knew them as fact. Every one of them wanted to emulate the Rangers who were now just ordinary cavalrymen.

The next day we completed our defences. We left Jed and Dago while Harry and I sought out the major and the colonel. "How are the defences looking, Captain Grimes?"

"Sound enough sir but we need some artillery or they will walk right over us. We have enough ammunition and we have logs for defence but there are only sixty of us."

"Well, we now have two guns which have been sent by the general. I am going to place them on the heights above your position with B Troop there. C Troop will be our reserve." The colonel gave a disarming smile, "It may be that we are wrong and they do not come. In that case, the only interest this week will be the two court-martials tomorrow. I believe General Stuart is coming over to see that it is well done."

Confederate Ranger

"Well, he will find no holes in my argument." Major Boswell looked red-eyed. He had been burning the midnight oil, quite literally.

"James, you have done sterling work and tomorrow you will be vindicated and then when the Union arrive the day after we will trounce them and celebrate a good week of work!"

The colonel had a way of making you feel better just by his tone and his peaceful demeanour. He could and did fight like a hellcat when necessary but he could also be a calming influence and we all felt better.

I thought this the best chance to make my request. "One more thing Major Boswell, I would like to promote Corporal Jones and Corporal Stewart to sergeant. With the armourer, the medical sergeant and the horse sergeant we are a little short of leaders on the ground."

The major looked at the colonel who nodded, "Very well. Tell them today and I will get it confirmed in the morning."

The two corporals were delighted with the promotion and, to be fair to the other corporals, there was acceptance that these two were the besting the troop and well deserved their promotion. It made our dispositions easier. Harry was in the middle of the defensive position and he had First Sergeant Smith with him. From there they could see both wings. Dago took the right flank with Davy as his sergeant. I had Jimmy with me on the left flank, next to the mill and the ford itself. We were spread out so that each man had to cover about ten yards of the river bank. As I took my first watch, just before midnight, I prayed that the general was right and no one would be coming to test our flimsy defences. I spent the two hours working what I would say the following day at the court-martial. It prayed more on my mind because within hours of the decision I would avenge my mother and father.

Confederate Ranger

Awoke before dawn, as was my practice and I went to the horse lines to see to Copper. The horses were all getting a much-needed rest while we were defending the camp. C Troop was taking all the patrols and scouting missions north of the river. After I had checked Copper's leg I went to the officer's mess. I found Major Boswell up already. He poured me a cup of coffee. "Well, I will be glad when today is over Jack. This trial has been a most unwelcome distraction. We can all get back to the proper work of this regiment."

"Yes sir but it is just one day isn't it? I mean the regiment has come on a great deal since the day we rode in with the colonel." I pointed at my collar. "We have all been promoted and we have better-trained men than we ever did before."

He laughed, "You are right, Jack. You are definitely a half-full man."

"What time do we need to be at Culpeper sir?"

"Not until noon. We are the second trial and they don't expect we will be needed until after one."

"Good. Then I can help Harry improve the defences a little although some of the men don't think the enemy will try anything at all."

"The colonel seems confident and don't forget you gathered the intelligence and it seems complete."

"But they could attack anywhere sir. We know that cavalry can cover huge distances."

"Yes Jack, and that is why they have to get rid of us first or we could find wherever they went and our cavalry is definitely better than theirs. Anyway, it won't be today so you will have time to tinker with your defences."

"I'll see you later then sir." The major's arguments had made sense and I felt happier as I returned o the men.

Confederate Ranger

I felt even better with a cup of coffee inside me and I headed back to the river. Harry had the men at their breakfast even though it was still dark. Suddenly Wilbur shouted, "Yank cavalry!"

I peered across the river and saw that there were half a dozen scouts approaching the ford. Harry turned to me. "Get your men to their positions. Bill, go and tell the colonel that there are scouts at the river. Keep your men hidden and we will give them a surprise."

I ran to the mill where Jimmy was waiting with the rest of the men. "Keep hidden men and don't fire until you get the order. We don't want to give away our position."

I checked that my rifle was loaded and slid it between two logs. In the dark, the enemy would see nothing. The logs had been placed to look as though they were sawmill cast-offs. I looked along the barrel and saw the scouts two hundred yards away. Wilbur had good eyes to have spotted them so early. I took my watch out and angled it so that I could read the time. It was barely six o'clock. I wondered if these scouts presaged an attack or they were doing what we would have done and evaluated a crossing. When they began to come across I knew that this was an attack. The question that crossed my mind was; was this the main attack or just a feint to draw us out?

I heard Harry yell, "Fire!"

"Only fire if the target is close to you. Don't waste ammunition."

I saw one scout fall and the others raced back across the river. When I heard the bugles on the opposite bank I knew this was an attack. Their first attack came in the form of a hundred men trying to force their way across the ford. They could not see us and as only a few men had fired they could not know how many defenders opposed them. "Fire only when you have a clear target. Do not waste balls."

Confederate Ranger

I aimed at the officer leading his men with his sabre held high, urging his men on. His horse reared as I fired and I merely wounded him. Their attack failed and they retreated back across the river. Ritchie turned and asked, "Is that it, sir? Is it over?"

"I don't think they will give up that easily. Just watch your front."

After a short time, another attack materialised, this time all along the river. I could see that they had the weight of numbers to enable them to try a large attack. There was a volley from them and then the river was filled with smoke and milling horses. It was impossible to see the targets and we fired blindly into the smoke. I heard Harry shout, "Cease fire!"

The smoke began to thin and I saw that they had retreated again. The problem was we were spread too thinly. We could not fire a wall of lead and a moving individual horseman was always difficult to hit. Then we heard the crack of artillery to the north. Danny and D Troop were there. They had more men but we had the easier position to defend. I glanced behind me at our two guns and wondered why they had not fired. The third attack was launched across the river and this was much as the others. They charged into the icy water and fired their revolvers, more in hope than expectation. We fired at them until the smoke hid them from view. When the cease-fire was sounded and the air cleared we could see their wounded limping away from the water.

Suddenly Jimmy pointed behind us. "Sir, they are moving the guns."

As dawn broke I could see that the guns had not fired because they were being limbered and moved. I did not have the view of the whole battlefield but I hoped that no-one had panicked and moved the guns out of fear. That would be a disaster. There was a

Confederate Ranger

lull which allowed us to check for casualties. There were a few cuts from wood splinters but nothing serious.

I checked my watch again and saw that it was almost seven-thirty and we had been at this for almost ninety minutes. We had managed to hold them off for a long period. I wondered if this was a feint and then I saw the two guns being unlimbered on the opposite side of the river. "Well boys, we are in for a little shelling. Keep low!"

The next charge coincided with the first shots from the two guns. The major leading their attack urged his men on. I saw the officer hit by a ball but he carried on urging his men and suddenly they were across. Harry shouted, "A Troop! Retreat!"

"Right boys, keep low and keep together. We will head up the rise to where the artillery was. Jimmy, you take the rear."

The cavalry might have made the southern bank of the Rappahannock but the trees we had felled made a barrier which would take some moving. We had bought some time. We scrambled up the bank. My men had the shortest journey and we reached the heights successfully and well ahead of our pursuers. We were out of breath but we had made it without further loss. The gunners had built breastworks and we threw ourselves behind them. I levelled my rifle and looked at the Union cavalry milling around the river bank. To my right, I saw Dago and his men scrambling up the bank. They looked to have wounded with them. "Support Lieutenant Spinelli. Discourage those Yankee boys who are following him." Our fifteen rifles bucked as we sent a wave of lead balls down the slope. We had to aim slightly higher than we would have to avoid hitting our own men but it had the desired effect and the cavalry retreated to shelter.

Wilbur said, "This is as good a spot as any sir. We can hold them here."

Confederate Ranger

I shook my head and pointed to the south. There was another lower hill and behind that the road to Brandy Station. "They can outflank us. When the captain gets here I think we will be heading back towards our camp." The rest of A Troop's troopers were hurling themselves over the breastworks and I could see hundreds of horsemen crossing the river and beginning the ascent of the hill.

Dago helped his men over the top. "Thanks, Jack. We found ourselves outflanked. Those Rhode Island boys swam the river. I think they must have been studying us."

"There are too many of them anyway. Sixty men can't hold this position for long. I just hope that we gave the general enough time to organise the rest of the men. I looked at the land around us. The trouble is this isn't cavalry country. I think we will all be fighting on foot today and that suits the Yankees. They have more men and more cannons."

As soon as Harry clambered across the logs I could see that his men had some casualties too. He shook his head. "We can't hold them here. We will head back to the camp. Jack, your men are in the best condition. You will be the rearguard."

"Yes, sir."

"Let's get moving. The sooner we reach camp the sooner we will have some support."

They began to move out and I spread my men into a semicircle facing the river. "Pair up so that you can support each other. One man fires at the enemy while the other retreats. Keep leapfrogging each other. Ritchie, you are with me." I knelt and aimed. There was no one coming up the hill yet but I was ready. "Right, run!" As he ran I saw a blue kepi appear over the breastwork. I fired and heard a scream. That would slow them down.

"Run sir!"

Confederate Ranger

I turned and ran. Ritchie was about a hundred yards behind me and I could see that I was the last man. As I reached him he fired. "Go!" I turned and saw that the Yankees had dismounted and Ritchie had wounded one. The rest were lying down. I knelt and fired three spaced shots. I was just trying to slow them down to allow the rest of the troop to make camp. I hadn't run this much in my life and I could feel the strain on my legs. The camp was still half a mile away. As I stopped and turned I noticed that the enemy advance had slowed. Our fire had made them wary and they were waiting for greater numbers.

Suddenly Major Boswell was next to me in his horse. "Come on Jack, the rest have made the camp. You and Ritchie are the last." He held his pistol and emptied it at the distant cavalrymen. "That will keep their heads down. Now go and I will cover you."

When I reached the camp the colonel and the Sergeant Major were marshalling the men. Danny came over to me. "Glad you made it, Jackie boy. They forced us from the post office. The general wants us over there to the west. He is forming a defensive line."

I looked for the horses. "Where are the horses?"

"The colonel sent Carlton and some of B Troop towards Culpeper. He did not want to risk losing them."

As soon as he said Culpeper I remembered the trial. I glanced over to the major's tent. "Danny! The guard!" I ran towards the major's tent. The trooper who had been guarding him lay dead outside. I drew my Colt as I ran. Danny thundered behind me. I crouched outside the tent and, when Danny reached me, threw myself to the floor of the tent. It was empty. When we checked the guard we could see that his pistol and rifle were gone. We ran back to the colonel and Major Boswell.

Confederate Ranger

"Sir, Major Beauregard has killed his guard and escaped. He is armed."

"Damn! Well, we can't do much about that now. Gentlemen take your troopers and head north. We are going to hold the road to the north of the Brandy Station road. Good luck. Come along Sergeant Major Vaughan, we at least can ride there." The major escorted the two older soldiers and they disappeared towards the woods.

"Column of fours and let's try quick march eh?"

We slung our rifles and looked like infantry as we hurried after the major. We could hear the pop of rifles and pistols away to our left and I hoped that we would make it on time. If the general couldn't hold them then the Union cavalry could ride through Virginia doing what we had been doing to them!

As we reached the line I saw General Stuart. He looked pleased to see us. "Well colonel, I came for a court-martial and I have arrived for a battle eh. Your men can defend this wall. Major Pelham and I will go and join the 5th Virginia. They are facing the artillery and Major Pelham is an expert in that field."

Major Boswell strode down the line. "Get behind the wall boys. We aren't as exposed as the lads were by the river. When they come this time they will face all two hundred of us." The men all cheered. I noticed then that the colonel was sitting down and Sergeant Major Vaughan was looking concerned. A battlefield was no place for an old warrior like the colonel. I hoped that the Sergeant Major would keep him safe.

There was a rolling volley as the enemy artillery opened up. They were using shells which exploded in the air. I shuddered as I remembered what they had done to our bugler and his horse. I snuggled down a little more behind the wall. I was glad I had the security of stone in front of me.

Dago's voice sounded, "Here they come!"

The Union cavalrymen were also dismounted and they made their way across the field. Major Boswell roared, "Fire!"

I aimed at a sergeant. The smoke from our guns hid the results of my shot. I aimed at a point I thought they would be and fired again. They were returning fire and pieces of stone flew off all around us. They were as deadly as the lead balls. Wilbur suddenly fell to the ground and I went to him. A fragment of stone had ripped open his cheek. "David!"

The sergeant lowered his gun and ran over with a dressing already in his hand. He smiled at Wilbur. "You'll live although another inch and you would have lost your eye."

I returned to the wall and loosed more shots at the hidden enemy. The shells were still exploding to our right. If the centre fell then we would be isolated. Major Boswell appeared at my side. "Jack, take your men and work your way around their right flank. See if you can make them think we have a whole regiment attacking. All your men have the best guns. You need to make as much noise as you can."

"Yes, sir. How will we know when to attack?"

"As soon as you get in position, you begin to fire and keep firing. If they attack you then retreat towards the railroad." He leaned in closer. "Today we need all of your luck, Jack!"

"Wilbur, you stay with Lieutenant Spinelli. Wildcats, on me."

They gave a 'yee-haw' and then trotted behind me as we ran along the wall. We kept as low as we could and we trailed our rifles. Suddenly the wall ended and we found the road. I peered down it and could see no one. To our left, the road headed towards the railroad bridge over the Rappahannock. We had our escape route if we needed it. "Right boys, we can make good time down this road. Keep your weapons cocked but don't fire until I tell you." I felt better about this type of fighting; it suited me and my men better than standing in a fixed line waiting for an attack. This way our destiny was in our own hands and we relied on each other. That was the Wildcat way.

I caught a glimpse of blue ahead and I waved the men into cover to the left of the road. "Let's see how far we can get through these trees." The Union cavalry had their attention to their fore where they thought the whole Confederate force was. They were behind a wall and firing at our men ahead of them. I halted the men. "We need to make them think there are more of us than there are. I am not concerned with aiming, I want as much noise and as many shots as we can manage. As soon as your carbine is empty then empty your Colt." I knew that they would all have, as I had, an extra gun in the back of their belt. "Into a line and wait for my order. When we fire make as much noise as you can."

I lead them through the woods until we were forty yards from the right flank of the cavalry. I noticed from their standard that they were from Pennsylvania. I raised my carbine and shouted, "Fire!"

Every man yelled and cheered as we poured shot after shot into their flank. Soon we were wreathed in smoke. As soon as I was empty I took out my Colt and began to fire. When that was empty I reloaded my carbine and we fired until the barrels were too hot to touch.

Jimmy shouted, "Almost out of ammunition sir!"

I heard the chorus of the others as they confirmed their situation. We had done enough and if not we could do no more. "Right lads, let's get back up the road. Jimmy, you lead them." I took out my spare Colt and waited for the men to get some way away. Three cavalrymen raced down the road with their carbines raised I fired four quick shots. Two of the men fell and the third took cover. As I ducked behind the tree a fusillade of lead crashed through the trees; thankfully well above my head. I dodged and ran through the trees, leading them away from the road. After thirty paces I turned and headed north again. I could see the trees thinning to my left and I ran that way hoping that the road was close. To my relief, I found the rest of my men and they were waiting for me. "Keep going!"

Jimmy shook his head. "We don't need to sir. They aren't following."

I now had a decision to make. Did I go back to the Major? We were all out of ammunition and we could do no good there. Then I remembered that Carlton and the men had taken the horses to the railroad and that was less than a mile away. "We will run to the railroad and get more ammunition then we can rejoin our friends. There's no point going now, we would be as well throwing rocks at them." I quickly checked the thirteen men with me. None looked injured but I knew that they could be hiding one. "Any wounds?"

Isaiah said, "I burned my hand on my barrel but it doesn't slow me down."

"Let's go then." We trotted down the road. Jimmy took the rear and I led. I still had two rounds in my Colt and that was more than most had. The railroad loomed into view and I saw the Confederate flag still flying. Even more importantly I saw the horses and the rest of our men.

Carlton looked relieved to see me. "We wondered what was going on sir. Are we winning?"

"It's hard to say. How many men do you have here?"

"Twenty all told. Right, Isaiah, you stay here with five of the sergeant's men. Carlton, bring the rest with us and we are going mounted this time."

"That is a relief."

"Is there any spare ammunition here?"

"Yes, sir. The wagon over there."

"Get your ammunition from the wagon. Mount your horses and then reload. We are going to become a regiment again! We'll take the spare ammunition to the regiment. They will probably need it."

Chapter 17

I now had thirty-three men under my command and we were all fully armed. It felt good to be back on Copper. I always felt more comfortable when mounted. The battle was raging to our right. I decided to take us back the way we had just come. I knew that was where their flank was and we could worry them by appearing on horses.

"Column of fours. Yo!"

We rode back down the road and I held my Colt in my hand. The Pennsylvania cavalry had turned their line to face the new threat. They had gone into the woods to seek this phantom regiment which had suddenly appeared. "On my command fire your pistols in fours and then retreat to the rear." The colonel's Waterloo tactic might work again. "Forwards." I lead them to within forty yards of the cavalry and then shouted. "Fire!" As soon as I had emptied my gun I yelled, "Fall back!" I took out my second Colt and then shouted, "Fire!" By the time we had done this four times, the Pennsylvanians were moving backwards in the face of this wall of balls. We were also taking casualties I had heard the shouts as men were struck. After the last four had fired I shouted, "Fall back!"

We regrouped by the railroad line. As far as I knew the battle still hung in the balance. Carlton, rode next to me, "Well sir, what now?"

"We have done what the Major wanted. I think now is the time to rejoin him. Besides we have wounded men who need attention." We rode down the railroad track. We knew that we held the other side of the track and we could join our own men a little easier. The Union artillery was still giving our lines a good pasting.

Confederate Ranger

Our two cannons still popped away but they were struggling to hold their own against superior numbers. I halted the men and led then down the slope from the railroad track towards our lines. When I reached the Sergeant Major I knew that Major Boswell would not be far away.

The troopers all turned around when we thundered back to the wall we had left a short while earlier. Major Boswell looked grim. "Good to see you, Jack. The colonel isn't so good. I think this has taken it out of him and I have taken charge."

"I have brought some ammunition, sir. We ran out and assumed some of you would have too."

"Good. Get it distributed."

"Sergeant, see that the troopers get their ammunition replenished. How is it going here, sir?"

"Not so good. The general tried an attack with the five regiments he had. The 2nd Virginia was knocked about a bit and ran. The attack failed and they began to attack and something stopped them. They turned to face their right flank."

"That would have been us, sir. When we got the horses from the railroad we charged their flank to make them think we were a regiment. It must have worked."

The major suddenly slammed his right fist into his left palm. "That is it! We will use the horses you brought to charge this flank. We have thirty-four horses and we know our boys can ride. It might just make some of those boys you scared, run. No one likes to face a charging horse."

I wasn't sure he was right but it looked to me like we were losing this battle. "Very well sir. I'll get the men to load their pistols. How long before you need them?"

"I'll ride over and tell the general what we intend. Let's say in an hour. Tell Danny he is in command until then."

Confederate Ranger

As I walked down the line I could see that there were wounded men. I could see no bodies and I thanked the lord for that. When I reached Danny I gave him his orders and explained what we were going to do.

He shook his head, "It seems to me that there are five cavalry regiments who are trained to do that sort of thing. We are scouts."

"I think he means to use a pistol charge. When the general attacked with his men they were using single-shot rifles. We have thirty-three men with two pistols. That is one hell of a lot of lead!"

Major Boswell came back with a smile on his face. "It seems the general likes the idea. He is worried they might break through to the railroad. Jack, you take the right and I will take the left. I think that will suit me. If we ride hard and fast and then halt thirty paces from them we should be able to do some damage." He suddenly looked a little apprehensive. "Do you think our men can stop that quickly and fire?"

"If they can't then no one can."

"You go and get the men ready. I want to have a word with Danny."

When I reached the men I noticed that Jed was mounted on one of the horses. He gestured with his thumb at a trooper who was vomiting over the rear wall. "He was one of the boys with Carlton. It seems the cook at the railroad ain't as good a cook as me."

I suddenly felt better. "Good, then you can ride on the right. We are going to charge. Halt at thirty yards, empty our pistols and then skedaddle."

He gave me a wry smile. "Well that doesn't seem hard does it sir?" He looked around at the men. "You heard the lieutenant. You all stop on command, empty your pistol and get back here. Any man who gets himself killed will be on a charge and shovelling horse shit for a week!"

Confederate Ranger

The major arrived. "As First Sergeant is here I thought that I would ride in the middle. It gives us more command sir."

He nodded his approval. "Let's get this done."

We returned to the wall. I saw what he and Danny had arranged. Troops A and D were ready to run out into the open ground between our two forces and fire. They would retreat and hopefully draw some eager Yankees on. Major Boswell nodded.

"A and D Troop, charge!"

The one hundred men leapt over the wall cheering and roaring. After twenty paces they threw themselves on the ground and began firing at the distant woods. They were just throwing a wall of lead at the enemy to keep their heads down. I kept my eye on the woods to our left in case any of them tried to sneak there and flank us.

"Retreat! Look like you are running scared boys! Pretend you are Yankees!"

They raced back and hurled themselves over the wall and lay prone beneath its rocky protection. I could see that many blue uniforms had raced across the open ground to pursue the retreating troopers. I saw officers with swords trying to force them back.

"Wildcats! Charge!"

We all galloped forward and leapt the wall. The blue soldiers before us looked in horror as this mass of horseflesh hurtled towards them. It was the nightmare of every soldier who fought on foot; to be caught in the open by charging cavalry. They emptied their guns in our direction and ran. The major shouted the order to enable us to take advantage of the situation. "Fire!"

It is not easy to fire a Colt from the back of a charging horse but we had all mastered the technique and I saw Yankee cavalrymen falling to the lead of the 1st Virginia. As we neared the tree line I saw that the boys from Pennsylvania were fleeing. The major turned and shouted to the dismounted regiment, "Danny! They are retreating! Charge!"

It was our moment of triumph. The whole of the right flank of the Union line was going to crumble. Just then, I caught a movement out of the corner of my eye. I saw a grey coated officer, wearing no hat, appear from the trees to the left of the major. He raised his pistol and shot the major in the back. It was Major Beauregard. He dragged the wounded major from the saddle and leapt onto Major Boswell's horse.

"Jed, stay with the men and see to the major. I am off after Beauregard." I holstered my revolver as I would need both hands to control Copper.

I had no idea if he had heard me but I had no time to waste. The Englishman had a fifty-yard head start and was riding a mount as good as Copper but I could not let him escape me. I urged Copper on as my enemy dived into the woods. He was a good horseman, there was no doubt about that. My only advantage was that I knew the land around here better than he did. He was heading north and the railroad tracks. I was trying to second guess him. Where would he go? He had three enemies he needed to be rid of, the major, Danny and me. He thought he had eliminated the major but so long as Danny and I lived then he would be tried. He could now be found guilty of attempted murder. He must have been desperate. Perhaps the death of Andrew Neil had unhinged him but it allowed me the freedom to do as I chose. All I had to do was to catch him and he was extending his lead which was making that unlikely. As he scrambled up the bank to the railroad tracks I saw that I had a chance. The major's horse was struggling to carry the much heavier Englishman. If he made the mistake of trying to climb hills and banks then Copper would catch him. He rode down the railroad tracks and headed west. Once again he began to extend his lead. He glanced over his shoulder and slapped his horse's rump. He began to move away again.

"Steady girl, just keep this pace. You can catch him." I leaned forward and stroked her mane. He must have been confident that he could outrun me. Suddenly a train appeared a hundred yards ahead of him and sounded his whistle. The major jerked his horse to the right. It was a bank! Instead of heading hard right I just took Cooper on an oblique route to take the slope at a gentler pace. The major had panicked and was trying to climb the steep bank. He was moving slower than I was. The train hurtled along the tracks and the hiss of steam made the major's horse skitter and he slid a little way down the bank. The was now just forty yards ahead of me and he began to take the same tack as I was on, still climbing but gentler. He had taken too much out of his horse and, like a fisherman with a big fish, I was reeling him in, inexorably. I could have drawn my Colt and shot him but I risked hurting Major Boswell's horse. I now knew that I could and would catch him. He made for a break in the trees and briefly disappeared from sight. I slowed down. I had ambushed too many men to walk into an obvious trap. I headed to the right of the gap and I saw that he had halted and had his captured gun aimed at the gap through which he expected me to charge. I kicked hard and Copper leapt forwards. He tried to bring the gun to bear on the sudden apparition but we crashed into him and I leapt from my horse and knocked him to the ground. The two horses ran down the slope. He still held his Colt and I reached for mine but it had fallen from my holster. I slipped my hand down to my boot and grabbed my knife. He was a bigger man than me and he pushed hard against me as we rolled down the bank. I held his right hand in my left and tried to bring the Bowie knife up and into his stomach. He grabbed my right hand but I was the stronger and the blade inched its way up as we rolled down the bank. We struck the rails and our downward journey was halted. Our faces were inches apart.

"You and your sister should have died with the scum that were your parents. You do not deserve to live!"

I was not angry. My anger had been burned away years ago. I was ready for revenge and I did not need to talk him to death; I would just kill him. The knife was moving closer to him and I saw the panic in his eyes. My left hand had his right pushed back almost on the ground. He pulled the trigger and the recoil jerked our hands up but the gun came no closer to me than before.

I felt the knife catch on his belt and I pushed a little harder. Hauling sails in a force nine gale gives you a solid strength and the blade slid over the belt and began to cut into his jacket.

His eyes showed his fear. "Please! Let me live. I'll give you money. I am a rich man!"

I said nothing but focussed on pushing the point of the knife into him. Suddenly he could resist no longer and the blade suddenly slipped into his gut. I felt the warm blood dripping down my arm. He cried out and dropped the gun. I rose to my feet and twisted the blade free. The movement of the twisting blade had the effect of pulling his intestines and the terrified major tried to push them back in. I stood and watched him as he cried and moaned. "Help me! Please help me!"

Finally, I spoke. "You have killed my parents. You have tried to kill me and my friends. You have led brave men to an unnecessary death and you want me to help you." I shook my head. "I am going to watch you die. And you will die. But you will not die quickly. You will have the chance to reflect on what you have done before you die and then rot in hell. The last thing you will see will be my face and the memory that a potato farmer's son killed you."

Confederate Ranger

His face became whiter and the blood pooled beneath his body as he died. It took twenty minutes for all life to leave him and I waited for another ten to allow all the blood to pour onto the ground. I did not want to distress Major Boswell's horse with his blood. I went down to the railroad tracks and collected the two horses. They had had time to calm down and they followed me docilely to the dead body. I heave the carcass on to the back of the major's horse. I crossed the tracks and headed for the sound of the distant pop and crack of desultory gunfire. There was still fighting but I felt at peace. I had avenged my parents.

General Fitzhugh and Jeb Stuart saw me and my trophy. General Fitzhugh lifted the major's deadhead. "So we did not need a trial."

"No sir, he ran and shot the major in the back!"

"Is he alive?" I could see the shock on both their faces. Leaders like Major Boswell were few and far between.

"I don't know sir. I went after the killer. I didn't want him escaping."

"Send a messenger to me when you know the condition of the major. His charge and the actions of his regiment saved the day. The Yankees have withdrawn back over the river."

"I will tell the colonel the news sir."

I wondered what I would find when I reached the regiment. Both the colonel and the major had been in dire straits when I had left. Would they still be alive?

Dago shouted my welcome, "Yee-haw! He's alive. Lucky Jack sir, and I think he has got another deserter." He patted Copper as I passed. "Glad to see you, Jack."

"How is the major?"

He shook his head. "Not so good. The doctor and David are with him. I'll take care of this piece of meat."

Confederate Ranger

I dismounted and led Copper towards the huddle of men around the doctor. Danny came over and clasped my arm. "I am glad you are safe and glad you got the murdering bastard." He gestured at the doctor. "The ball is lodged in his back. It is close to his spine. If they make a mistake he may never walk even if he does survive."

Suddenly I heard the doctor shout as he stood up. "I can't do this! If he dies you will all kill me!" Before we could do anything he had turned and fled.

Danny and I went over to David. "You are his only hope, David."

"I am not a doctor."

I put my hand on his shoulder, "But you know what to do don't you? You have a steady hand and the sawbones left his tools. We'll help you won't we sir?"

Taking off his jacket Danny said. "Of course and with Lucky Jack helping then he is sure to survive."

I took off my jacket and we looked at David. He sighed, "Take an arm and a leg each. Do not let him move. We have given him something to knock him out but any movement could be a disaster."

I put all of my weight on the arm and the leg on my side and I watched Danny do the same on the other. Danny laughed as David poured alcohol over the scalpel he had selected. "Well, it looks like two Irishmen who are a little on the large side do have a use after all.

"Well let's add an old fat Sergeant Major to that. I'll hold his head." Sergeant Major Vaughan joined us on the ground.

"How is the colonel?"

"He's just tired. He'll live but I think it is time for him to go back home. Fighting is a young man's game."

Confederate Ranger

David took a deep breath, "Right here we go." H gently probed the back of the wound. As the scalpel touched the skin I felt an involuntary movement from the major but my grip was so tight that he did not move. "That's it sir; just lean on him as hard as you can. I have found the ball." He took some forceps and eased them into the wound. A soft moan came from the major. David said, "He can't feel anything. This will be like a dream to him." I could see the sweat on his forehead as he eased the forceps out. Suddenly there was a clunk as he dropped the ball into the metal bowl. Danny cheered but David said. "We have to clean out the wound and make sure there's nothing left in. Remember when his wound was infected before? I am not risking that." He took some gauze and began to mop around the wound. He suddenly dropped the scalpel and pick up the forceps. There was a little chink as the tiny fragment of ball was dropped in to the bowl. "And now we can stitch him up."

The next ten minutes seemed to last forever but when he was bandaged we rolled him gently on to his back. The four of us just dropped, exhausted to the ground. We all jumped when we heard his sleepy voice say, "Did we win then?"

Epilogue

March 18th 1863

The 1st Virginia Scouts rode back to Front Royal without either a colonel or a major. Colonel Cartwright was persuaded by the redoubtable Sergeant Major to retire. Captain Murphy and Lieutenant Hogan were summoned to General Stuart's Headquarters.

The two generals, Fitzhugh and Stuart were smiling from ear to ear. Captain Murphy thought that it was inappropriate given the serious injury to his beloved major but he was used to obeying orders. The two of them stood to attention listening to the fulsome praise being heaped upon the whole regiment but the two of them in particular.

"Now we don't want to bring an outsider in to what is a very efficient regiment. The loss of Colonel Cartwright does leave a gap which needs filling. We have discussed the matter and we believe that the best man for the job will be Major Boswell when he is recovered. He will need rest for a month but by April he should be back at the reins, so to speak. In the meantime, while Colonel Boswell recovers, we would like you, Major Murphy, to run the regiment. You have moulded D Troop into an efficient fighting machine. And, in addition, we would like to promote Lieutenant Hogan to Captain Hogan."

Danny couldn't hide his smile. Jack had the same look he always had when he received praise- it was a look of absolute shock as though he was the last person deserving of any notice.

"Well gentlemen, what do you say?"

Major Murphy saluted and said, "On behalf of all three of us I would like to accept."

Jack mumbled a, "Yes sir, thank you, sir."

"Now we will be in action within a few weeks and, hopefully, Colonel Boswell will be fit enough to assume command. Until then you need to establish the chains of command in the regiment. Appoint a new Sergeant Major...."

"And, sir, if you don't mind, a doctor."

"Quite. Any other requests while we are both here."

"The Magee brothers sir, I think it would be better for all if they were transferred to another regiment. I don't doubt their loyalty but their close relationship with Major Beauregard..."

"I see your point. Very well. If that is all then you are dismissed."

As the two officers left the building neither could quite believe the change in their fortunes. Jack turned to Danny, "I wouldn't have accepted it if they had any other colonel in command."

"Me neither but you realise that we are Confederate soldiers now and we don't have much say in it. At least the major, er the colonel will be well looked after. Jarvis will see that he gets the best of everything."

"It would have been nice to go back with him."

"Aye Jackie Boy, but we have a deal of work to do. The Yankee cavalry is getting better and they will need our skills well enough. And now we had better break the good news to the lads."

Jack shook his head, "I dread to think what Dago will say. He will be bound to have some sarcastic comment."

"Well, we will just have to deal with it. At least we still have the heart of the Wildcats beating in the regiment."

Jack didn't know it but Danny was talking about him. Lucky Jack Hogan was the heart of the regiment. He always had been and the last few months had just proved it to Danny and James. They had seen the effect of his leadership and his courage. Amidst all that was his luck- he had it in abundance.

Atlanta
Ebenezer Winfield was sniffing the smuggled brandy he had just acquired. He was feeling pleased with himself. It had all worked out rather well. His daughter had had her fling and she would now accept a husband of her father's choice. He had not known that Beauregard would have been quite as black a character as he had turned out but the old man had a nose for villains, after all, he was one himself, and he was glad he had set the man the challenge he had. He was also celebrating for he had become much richer. His own investigations had discovered the criminal empire being run form Beauregard's home and he had gained control of it as soon as the leading members of the gang had left for Winchester. Yes, it was a satisfactory outcome to something which could have turned out much worse.

Boston
Caitlin read the advertisement again.

> Jack Hogan of Cork is seeking his sister Caitlin whom he believes is living in New York or Boston. If anyone knows of her whereabouts please contact Aloysius J Murgatroyd Attorney at Law Charleston, South Carolina. There is a $100 reward for information about the young lady.

Jack was alive and in the south. She knew that it might as well be the other side of the world but the important thing was he was alive. She was glad that she had postponed her marriage. That, if it ever happened, could wait until after she was reunited with her brother.

In the bar downstairs Mick O'Callaghan was sitting with his cronies. He had a leg wound which had earned him three week's sick leave and he would use it well.

"We have found out the names of some of those bastards who killed Geraghty and Colm: Boswell, Murphy and Hogan. The fact that two of them are Irishmen makes it worse. As soon as I get down to the front again me and the lads'll be looking for them. They are in the 1st Virginia. When I have killed them then our family honour will be avenged." He glanced upstairs. "And I want you lads to watch Caitlin. She has some funny ideas lately, like postponing the wedding. When the three killers are dead then we'll be married or else."

"Or else what Mick?"

"Or else I'll be left the bar in her will because one way or another this bar will be mine."

The End

Maps

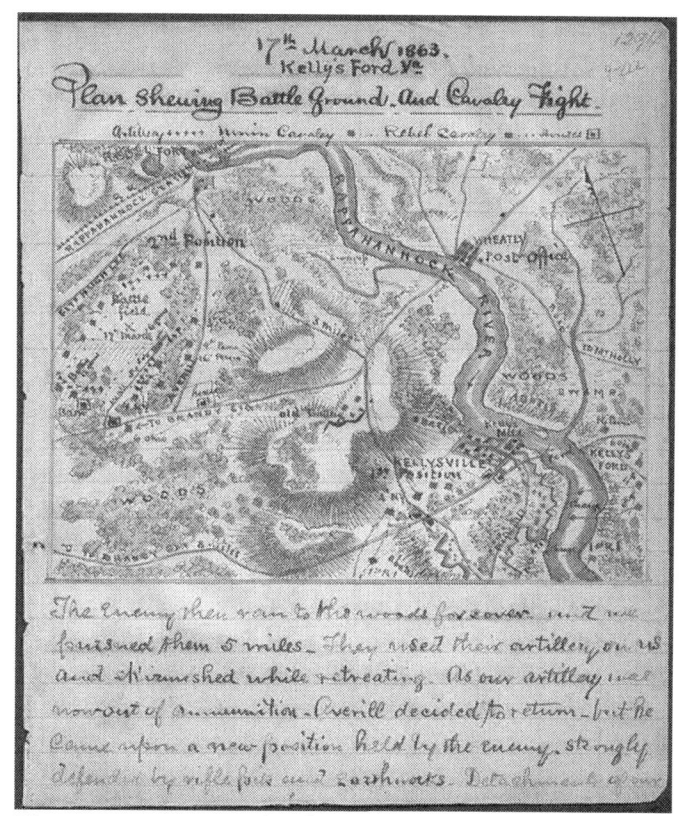

*This image is a work of a U.S. Army soldier or employee, taken or made as part of that person's official duties. As a work of the U.S. federal government, the image is in the **public domain.***

Confederate Ranger

Confederate Ranger

Historical note

My heartfelt thanks to the re-enactors at Gettysburg in July 2013 for all their help and advice. Any historical errors in the book are mine and not theirs. I realise that there were few Springfield carbines in the war but the nature of the business of James Booth Boswell meant that he would be rich and, like the chaps in Silicon Valley, would have ensured that he used the most up to date technology. The irregulars I described are loosely based on Mosby's Rangers and I used William S. Connery's excellent **"Mosby's Raids in Civil War Northern Virginia"**, extensively. Mosby was called the Grey Ghost and I used that appellation as the inspiration for my title. Boswell is not Mosby and this is a work of fiction; however, the incidents such as the charges using pistols, the wrecking of the trains, being mistaken for Union horsemen are all true. Mosby and his men carried three or four revolvers and I have used that idea for Boswell and his men. They used captured guns which explains why they were formidably armed. I also used **"The American Civil War Source Book"** by Philip Katcher and that proved a godsend for finding who fought where, when and with what.

Sandie Pendleton was an aide to Jackson in the Valley and it was he who alerted Stonewall to the dangers from their left flank.

The Confederate cavalry preferred raiding to charging infantry and rarely used their sabres. They preferred to use pistols or carbines. This proved useful most of the time but, as Gettysburg showed, Stuart and his cavalry could let down his general at crucial times. It was said that the biggest supplier for the Confederate Army, and especially the cavalry, was the U.S. as they captured so many of the Union supplies.

Confederate Ranger

The raid on Hartwood Church in Stafford County did result in Hooker ordering General Stoneman together a large force of cavalry and stop the frequent Confederate cavalry raids. The Battle of Kelly's Ford took place largely as described and marked the point at which the Union cavalry became more confident. Stuart was at the Courthouse in Culpeper for a court-martial and he rode with his friend Major Pelham to watch the battle. The Confederate cavalry fought on foot. Sixty sharpshooters held up the Union advance at the ford for over two hours. This action enabled Fitzhugh Lee to reorganise his forces and, ultimately, defeat a force much larger than his own. The Union cavalry were about to defeat the Confederates when Averill decided to retreat. He cited the sound of railroad cars and train whistles indicating that the Confederates were being reinforced. I have used that and adapted the idea to allow Jack to earn the general's praises.

Thanks to Wikipedia for these public domain maps made by Hal Jespersen. I used *"Civil War: The Maps of Jedediah Hotchkiss"* by Chester G. Hearn and Mike Marino for the detailed maps of the valley. (Thanks to Rich for loaning me his copy!)

The events such as the capture of a colonel, the routing of larger numbers were all well documented and Mosby's Rangers had an effect which was disproportionate to their unit size. They did profit from their raids and others, further west such as Quantrell could be considered as bandits. The Rangers did wear uniform but they were adept at deception. Having seen the Blues and the Greys on a battlefield and at dusk, I can tell you that there is sometimes little to be seen to differentiate them. The main indicator was that the Union had identical uniforms whereas the Confederacy tended to be a little more idiosyncratic. I do not know if there was a prison for officers in Gettysburg but, as officers were frequently exchanged then I assume that there must have been somewhere for that purpose. Bearing in mind its later significance I chose Gettysburg. I apologise to the purists especially as this is a Brit trying to write about American history!

I used the terms darkie, negro and nigra rather than the more offensive words which would have been used at the time. The words I have used would have been the words used to describe the Afro-Americans in the period and I hope that none of my readers are offended. I used darkie rather the others more often because, if you listen to the songs such as Swannee River you will see that they were used by the song writers at the time. We may question their use but this is a novel of the time and I have tried to make it as accurate as I can. Any mistakes I have made are honest ones.

Griff Hosker August 2013

Confederate Ranger

Other books by Griff Hosker

If you enjoyed reading this book, then why not read another one by the author?

Ancient History

The Sword of Cartimandua Series
(Germania and Britannia 50 A.D. – 128 A.D.)
Ulpius Felix- Roman Warrior (prequel)
The Sword of Cartimandua
The Horse Warriors
Invasion Caledonia
Roman Retreat
Revolt of the Red Witch
Druid's Gold
Trajan's Hunters
The Last Frontier
Hero of Rome
Roman Hawk
Roman Treachery
Roman Wall
Roman Courage

The Wolf Warrior series
(Britain in the late 6th Century)
Saxon Dawn

Confederate Ranger

Saxon Revenge
Saxon England
Saxon Blood
Saxon Slayer
Saxon Slaughter
Saxon Bane
Saxon Fall: Rise of the Warlord
Saxon Throne
Saxon Sword

Medieval History

The Dragon Heart Series
Viking Slave
Viking Warrior
Viking Jarl
Viking Kingdom
Viking Wolf
Viking War
Viking Sword
Viking Wrath
Viking Raid
Viking Legend
Viking Vengeance
Viking Dragon
Viking Treasure
Viking Enemy
Viking Witch
Viking Blood
Viking Weregeld

Confederate Ranger

Viking Storm
Viking Warband
Viking Shadow
Viking Legacy
Viking Clan
Viking Bravery

The Norman Genesis Series
Hrolf the Viking
Horseman
The Battle for a Home
Revenge of the Franks
The Land of the Northmen
Ragnvald Hrolfsson
Brothers in Blood
Lord of Rouen
Drekar in the Seine
Duke of Normandy
The Duke and the King

New World Series
Blood on the Blade
Across the Seas
The Savage Wilderness

The Reconquista Chronicles
Castilian Knight

The Aelfraed Series
(Britain and Byzantium 1050 A.D. - 1085 A.D.)
Housecarl

Confederate Ranger

Outlaw
Varangian

The Anarchy Series England 1120-1180
English Knight
Knight of the Empress
Northern Knight
Baron of the North
Earl
King Henry's Champion
The King is Dead
Warlord of the North
Enemy at the Gate
The Fallen Crown
Warlord's War
Kingmaker
Henry II
Crusader
The Welsh Marches
Irish War
Poisonous Plots
The Princes' Revolt
Earl Marshal

Border Knight 1182-1300
Sword for Hire
Return of the Knight
Baron's War
Magna Carta

Confederate Ranger

Welsh Wars
Henry III
The Bloody Border
Baron's Crusade
Sentinel of the North

Lord Edward's Archer
Lord Edward's Archer
King in Waiting

Struggle for a Crown
1360- 1485
Blood on the Crown
To Murder A King
The Throne
King Henry IV
The Road to Agincourt

Modern History

The Napoleonic Horseman Series
Chasseur a Cheval
Napoleon's Guard
British Light Dragoon
Soldier Spy
1808: The Road to Coruña
Talavera
The Lines of Torres Vedras

The Lucky Jack American Civil War series
Rebel Raiders

Confederate Ranger

Confederate Rangers
The Road to Gettysburg

The British Ace Series
1914
1915 Fokker Scourge
1916 Angels over the Somme
1917 Eagles Fall
1918 We will remember them
From Arctic Snow to Desert Sand
Wings over Persia

Combined Operations series
1940-1945
Commando
Raider
Behind Enemy Lines
Dieppe
Toehold in Europe
Sword Beach
Breakout
The Battle for Antwerp
King Tiger
Beyond the Rhine
Korea
Korean Winter

Other Books
Great Granny's Ghost (Aimed at 9-14-year-old young people)

Confederate Ranger

For more information on all of the books then please visit the author's web site at www.griffhosker.com where there is a link to contact him.

Printed in Great Britain
by Amazon